MIKE

Mike Grist is the British/American author of the Chris Wren & Girl 0 thrillers. He has lived and worked in the UK, USA, Japan and Korea as a teacher, photographer and writer.

HAVE YOU READ EVERY GIRL 0 THRILLER?

Girl Zero

They stole her little sister. Now they'll pay.

Zero Day

The criminal world is out for revenge. So is she.

Learn more at www.shotgunbooks.com

HAVE YOU READ EVERY CHRIS WREN THRILLER?

Saint Justice

They stole his truck. Big mistake.

No Mercy

Hackers came for his kids. There can be no mercy.

Make Them Pay

The latest reality TV show: execute the rich.

False Flag

They framed him for murder. He'll kill to clear his name.

Firestorm

Wren's father is back. The storm is coming.

Enemy of the People

Lies are drowning America. Can the country survive?

Backlash

He just wanted to go home. They got in the way...

Never Forgive

His home in ashes. Vengeance never forgives.

War of Choice

They came for his team. This time it's war.

Learn more at www.shotgunbooks.com

GIRL ZERO

A GIRL 0 THRILLER
BOOK 1

MIKE GRIST

SHOTGUN
BOOKS

SHOTGUN BOOKS

www.shotgunbooks.com

Paperback ISBN - 978-1-7398496-4-1

For Su

1

GIRL ZERO

Sixteen-year-old Girl Zero sat on her too-small bed, surrounded by the faded, Pinocchio-print wallpaper on the walls of her tiny underground cell, wondering if she was going to die tonight.

The dinner her mother had brought down an hour ago lay untouched on its tray on the threadbare covers. She clutched her hands to stop them shaking, looking around the space that was all she'd known since she was seven years old. The TV was off. The heating was dialed down. The small fridge hummed low and the taps were closed so tightly they barely even dripped.

Every time it began like this.

Her father had rules. There were rules for everything. The first rule was to eat what she was given. The second was to do as she was told. The third was to say thank you when it was all over.

Tonight she hadn't eaten.

Tonight she was already cold on the inside and out, dressed in her thin cotton pajamas.

Tonight had to be different.

A sharp sound came from beyond the door and Zero

flinched; the rasp of a deadbolt being pulled loose. There were two, and they always shrieked like smothered piglets, rusted stiff from the damp soaking down from the pig farm above. The second bolt followed, ratcheting home as loud as a discharged bullet, then footsteps clacked closer along the concrete flooring.

Girl Zero looked up at her mother, standing beyond the metal-barred door. She was old and twisted like a dying white pine, dressed in a cream gown spotted with faded brown bloodstains, with those wide white eyes staring down.

"You didn't eat, Girl."

She looked down at her hands twined in her lap. If she stared back, it only grew worse. "I feel sick," she said quietly.

"You should eat."

"I can't."

The cell door opened and her mother stepped in. The first slap was a rising blow that rang off Zero's forehead, forcing her head up. The second caught her flush across the cheek; her mother's rings cutting into her soft skin, her mother's farm-weathered skin and hard bones driving her head to the side and forcing tears from her eyes.

She gasped from the shock and the pain.

"You'll eat," her mother said.

"I'll be sick," she said softly. "I'm sorry. I can't."

For long moments nothing happened.

"Don't think this is an excuse. Your father's ready. Everyone's ready."

It took everything she had not to sob.

Her father didn't come for her every night. Sometimes as much as a week went by, when every meal brought down was wholesome and good, with none of the knockout drugs that stank like chemicals and made her woozy and forgetful. Days and nights could go by, where she'd re-read the few old books and re-watch the few old TV shows they allowed her, but all along the terror would grow as the next time drew nearer.

There were other girls, in those times. She could hear them; their long and muffled cries sounding down the passageway. Some lasted for weeks, but Zero never saw any of them, never spoke to them. They were all other numbers, each eventually extinguished and gone. She only saw their bloodstains adding to her mother's gown, and listened to the silence when they were gone.

"Very well," her mother said. "You will regret it. Now stand up."

Zero stood up. Her mother grasped her by the hair. They were the same height now, the same build, but her mother immediately forced her head down and dragged her forward into the passageway. She tried not to whimper as her scalp lit up with pain.

Seven steps passed along the passageway with cold concrete beneath her bare feet, then they emerged through into her father's hall.

Her mother roughly raised her head and bright white pierced her eyes. Through the glare of the lamps she saw seven blinking red lights; her father's cameras in position on tripods, already livestreaming her arrival to his 'friends', capturing her from every angle. Next she saw her father, standing in the center of the ten-yard-square hall, flanked on all sides by leather-padded walls.

He wore the Pinocchio mask he'd carved himself, through which she could just pick out his eyes. His white gown was spotted with old bloodstains just like her mother's, but beneath it his frame was broad and powerful. A lifetime spent wrestling pigs into submission in the mud had made him strong. Just catching his eyes terrified her, and she swiftly looked down.

"She wouldn't eat," her mother said. "Says she's sick."

She thrust Zero forward by the hair. She staggered and dropped to her knees before her father.

For a long moment there was silence. Then he took a step toward her. Her pulse boomed in her ears and the shuddering grew out of control. He reached down and lifted her chin with his rough, thick fingers, forcing her to look up at his mask. It wasn't the Pinocchio figure from the happy books, all pink and round, but something older and cruder; a wooden carving he'd whittled himself, seamed with dark lines and boasting an obscenely long hooked nose.

"Are you too sick, Girl," he asked in the soft, low tones that woke her from nightmares most nights. "Too sick for the work?"

"No father," she whispered.

He stared into her eyes. Already she could hear the chimes ringing in on his Internet display; all his hundreds of friends making their comments and asking their requests. He called them his 'Pinocchios'.

"Good," he said. "I think tonight will be very special. I know you'll make me proud. Now stand."

She stood.

He pointed at the metal frame beside him. Zero didn't know what it was, but she had her suspicions. This was the final toy, the same one all the other girls had died on. There was a bench, and shackles, and a large rotating drum at the top.

He'd never put Zero on it before.

"Do you like it?" he asked. "I built it for you. For your enrichment."

Tears ran down her cheeks. Enrichment. Long were the nights that he'd lain alongside her, his big chest sucking in and spewing out the foul air from the pigs above, teaching her about enrichment.

"It's the same for the pigs," he'd whisper in her ear.

"Sealed in their enclosures, they become manic. They bite themselves. They bite each other, sometimes to death. So I give them treats to eat, just like I give you books to read and shows to watch. It's called environmental enrichment. They love me for it, just like you love me. The secret is giving just the right amount. To keep my pigs, and my girls, happy and working hard."

"Yes, father," she'd whisper.

"Everybody has their work to do," he'd whisper, on the edge of sleep. "My pigs' grow fat, make babies then die to feed us. Your work is so much grander."

Her mother's hand rang across her face abruptly, slapping Zero back to the present. "Your father asked you a question. Do you like it?"

Tears welled in Girl Zero's eyes, but she willed them back. Rule three: always say thank you.

"Yes, father. Thank you, father."

"That's my good girl," he said, and pulled her into a tight embrace.

His body was hard with muscle. His thighs, his stomach, his chest; he squeezed hard enough to stop the breath in her lungs. It always began this way. An embrace, as if he truly loved her. An invitation would follow, as if she was there by choice. When she'd eaten her meal, she barely felt the things he did. On the few occasions she hadn't eaten, whether because she was sick or was being punished, it was horrible.

Sometimes it went on for hours, until the chiming of the many Pinocchios on her father's screen finally fell silent.

Now was the time.

As his arms fell from around her, Zero lifted her left arm and shoved her thumb as hard as she could toward his right eye.

It was a one in a thousand chance. Easy to miss. Easy to be punished for months to come. But she'd practiced this moment for years; hour after hour spent stabbing her thumb into her bed or her pillow or against the walls, until she could strike a pinpoint spot without fear or hesitation, until her thumb was rock-rigid and scaled with calluses.

It was this or die, so she flung the strike with everything she had. Barely half a second passed but it felt like forever.

The strike landed. Her thumb punched clean into her father's eye and gouged deep.

He roared at once and shoved her away. She fell back, stumbled and hit the ground, but there was no going back now.

She found her feet and came up with one of the camera tripods gripped like a staff in both hands. Her father was staggering backward, both hands clamped to his ruined eye while blood gushed down his cheek. Her mother stood to the side, mouth wide in disbelief.

Girl Zero swung. Her father raised his left arm and she brought the camera down with everything she had. The tripod glanced off his elbow but the heavy camera atop it continued, sweeping down to crunch into his head like a hammer blow.

The camera shattered and her father dropped where he stood.

Girl Zero's chest heaved and her vision spun with the sudden exertion, then her mother hit her from the side.

They went down together. In seconds her mother was straddling her chest, screaming and slashing at Girl Zero's face; wild blows that disoriented and shook her, but she had known pain all her life and was ready.

She snuck her right hand free and shot it upward.

Another lucky chance. One in a thousand or more, but God or fate or maybe the devil was watching over her, and again the strike landed. Her fingers plunged into her mother's gaping mouth, where they dug deep, grasped hold of her tongue and yanked.

Her mother's roars of fury became shrieks of pain. Her blows became efforts to push Zero away, but she'd practiced this too; lifting her bed with her fingers pinched; squeezing the metal bars together until her whole forearm throbbed; working her grip until these tiny muscles were the strongest in her body.

She pulled and pulled until her mother's screams strangled in her throat and she gurgled and tried to get her feet under her. Girl Zero rose with her, following as she backpedaled wildly across the hall until she slammed into the wall, squeezing and pulling harder with every second.

Her mother's blows became frantic, but Girl Zero couldn't stop now.

They'd never stopped hurting her. They'd tortured her every night of her life. This was nothing next to that.

2

SILENCE

In the silence that followed, Girl Zero lay curled up and shuddering in her threadbare Pinocchio blankets, on her faded old bed, alone in her tiny cell once more.

It was so quiet. She wasn't sure how long had passed, maybe just minutes, maybe hours. She distantly remembered banging her mother's head against the floor, and hoisting her father limb-by-limb into the frame he'd built for her.

Now her head throbbed, her left thumb ached where she'd stabbed it into her father's eye and there was a ring around the knuckles of her right hand, where her mother had kept trying to bite down.

There was a plan, though, and she had to stick to it.

She stood, and pushed open the barred door to gaze down the passageway beyond. Now she could hear her parents breathing. Her mother was a gurgling suck. Her father was a high wheeze. She padded down the passage toward them, back into the bright lights.

Her father's head rotated to face her. He lay on his back, shackled into his own machine at wrist and ankle, a gag tight in his mouth. Her mother sat by the side, cuffed into a metal chair bolted to the floor, in the perfect position to watch her husband.

The room stank. Zero's heart pounded. She sidestepped bloodstains, vomit and the few camera tripods still standing until she stood over her father.

He glared furiously up at her with his one good eye. This was the man who'd tormented her for so long. Who'd taken everything from her. Just looking at him made her shudder with all that remembered terror, and she had to bite back the instinct to unlock him, apologize and beg for forgiveness.

He deserved this. They both did. They'd had it coming for nine years' time. She mustered her courage and spoke.

"Where's Hope?"

For a long moment the words didn't seem to register on her father's face. Zero thought maybe she hadn't said it correctly, so she coughed to clear her throat and tried again.

"Where's my little sister. Where's Hope?"

Slowly recognition dawned in his eye.

Hope. Zero's little sister. For nine long years she'd waited to ask this question, ever since her father had brought her down here at seven years old, leaving her mischievous, flaxen-haired five-year-old sister behind. Back then Zero had had a name too, one that was so long ago it felt like a fairy tale.

Mona.

Hope and Mona.

And Mona had never seen Hope again.

Her father started making a rough, guttural noise. At first Zero thought he was trying to say something, but the sound became too repetitive, too regular, and even from behind the gag she recognized what it was.

Laughter.

It almost drove her running back to her cell. She wanted nothing more than to pull the covers over her head and hide, like she'd hidden for so many nights. But there was no hiding from this. Whatever she'd been through, Hope had had it worse. Hope needed her still, so she had to be strong. She had to do what was necessary.

"You'll tell me," she said, but her voice came out shaky and weak, and her father only laughed harder. Now her mother joined in.

"You'll tell me," she repeated, louder this time, and went to the controls for the machine. There was a piston attached to an engine, primed to pummel her father's body, always in a different position, at the same time as the barrel at the head of the rack turned, tightening her father until his joints popped.

Breaking him.

"Where is my little sister?"

He kept on laughing. His face went red. His eye bugged.

Zero flipped the switch, the engine fired up and the piston began its first pass, thumping against her father's body.

His laughter turned to grunts of pain. Her mother began to shriek through her gag. The piston sped up and his grunting grew louder, until after maybe thirty seconds he fell completely silent.

For a terrifying moment Zero thought he had died. But his eye was still open and fixed on her. She couldn't look away. To look away for even a second felt like a defeat. All she could do was ramp up the machine, though it made her sick to do so.

The machine moved in a blur. The hammering sound was all-consuming, but now her father stayed silent throughout. Her mother moaned. Seconds stretched on into minutes, and still he was silent.

Zero went to her mother. This was the woman who should have protected her. Instead she'd simply watched throughout.

"Where is she, mother?" Zero asked.

Her mother barely even looked at her. She only had eyes for her husband.

"Where is she?" Zero shouted, but it was no good. There'd never been room for her as a person between her mother and father. Only as a thing.

She stepped back. The room spun around her. Blood and pain and cameras were everywhere, and she knew what had to come next. Carefully she picked her way around the hall, lifting the camera tripods she'd knocked over. Many of them still had red lights blinking, which meant the signal was still going out.

Her father's Pinocchios were watching still.

One-by-one, she pointed each camera at her mother and father. She didn't say anything. She didn't need to. The message was clear.

When all the cameras were pointing at them, and all the feeds were live, she cranked the piston up to max and left the hall by the exit she'd only ever used once in her life: the passageway leading back above ground.

3

HOPE

Concrete stairs led up through a trapdoor in the living room, into the farmhouse.

It was silent but for the distant hammering of the piston and the grunting of pigs. Zero went to the window and looked out into the night, where myriad stars blazed across the heavens.

Tears ran down her cheeks.

The farmhouse was the same as she remembered it: the same furniture, the same smells of old hickory, cinnamon spice and pig-filth. The same stairs creaked leading up to the bedroom landing, where her old room was the same it had always been, minus most of the bedding and the books and toys now kept in her cell below.

Across the hall, she tentatively laid her hand on the handle to Hope's door. She had no idea what to expect. Her hand shook and her pulse raced. She took a deep breath then pushed the door open.

The room was empty.

Zero stared. She tracked the wooden boards of the narrow room.

She remembered there'd been a tiny bed just there, and an

old cot, and some toys and a cupboard. But the room was completely empty. Just a void in space. Zero walked in and stood at the center for some time, on the bare floorboards, trying to picture exactly how everything had looked. It was almost as if she'd never had a sister at all.

But she had. She was sure of it.

From her old room she gathered a few blankets and a pillow, then lay down in the middle of Hope's empty room and cried herself to sleep.

She woke with sunlight on her cheeks for the first time in years. She looked out over the pig farm and saw the enclosures stretching away as far as she could see, an uninterrupted grid filled with thick, ghost-pale bodies. The sky was a pale pink and so beautiful it hurt her eyes. She opened the window and the foul air of the pigs poured in, and she welcomed it. It smelled different. It smelled like life.

She didn't go back to the dungeon for a day and a night.

For all that time, she lived in the farmhouse. She ate her parents' food and watched their television, no longer limited to old cartoons and ancient sitcoms. The range of choices was overwhelming. there was so much to learn, and found herself watching for hours straight,.

Sometimes she went outside and fed the pigs, thinking about the limited 'enrichment' her father had provided. It had always been just enough to stop her mind turning to jelly, but not enough to drive her mad with all the things she couldn't have.

It was strange already, thinking back on the last nine years; like some feverish dream she had finally woken up from.

She looked out at the pig enclosures, and remembered the ramshackle fallout shelter somewhere in the middle. It had been a simple dugout, preparation for a war that never happened, with a corroded tin roof and a dirt floor lined with hay, surrounded by the pigs. Hope and Mona had used to curl up together hand in hand down there, hiding and whispering about all the things they were going to do when they escaped Idaho and left the pigs and their parents behind.

She couldn't see the shelter now for all the pigs in the way. Maybe it had finally collapsed in on itself.

On the second day she opened the trap door in the living room again, and stood at the end of the passageway to her father's hall, and listened to the moans of her parents through their gags. They sounded like pigs crying out in the night, just audible through the hammering of the torture machine.

She advanced toward them.

The air in the hall was vile. Her father looked pale and sick on his rack, with the piston still hammering and his body at full stretch. He'd fouled himself; his white gown was stained with waste. Her mother looked faint and feeble, weaving in her chair with blood basted down her chin and neck from her ruined tongue, her eyes round with exhaustion and fear.

For long moments Zero simply stood there, cameras still blinking red all around. She tried to imagine how they ever could have enjoyed this. There was no pleasure in it, only a certain sense of justice.

She went to the machine and switched it off. The hammering sound diminished and her father let out a long, aching sigh. Her mother sobbed but no tears came. Soon there was silence, and Zero studied the man on the rack. He met her gaze, then his eye swiftly flickered away. A day and night on the rack had changed him.

"Where's Hope?" she asked.

He babbled something into his filthy gag. She pulled it away.

"We sold her!" he croaked. "She's gone. Please, Mona, this is inhuman. But we can help you find her. I swear."

The begging didn't touch her. They'd done worse to her every day of her life. At seven years old they'd plucked her from her sister on that lonely, haunted pig farm and brought her down here to this damp and cold hell, promising an adventure.

"What about Hope?" she'd asked back then, all bright-eyed and eager at the thought of the fun to come.

"This is your special adventure," her father had said with a rare smile. "Hope's going to stay upstairs and have her own, but you'll see her again very soon, as long as you're a good little girl. We're building a foundation, here, Mona, and you will be ground zero for it all."

He'd said that again and again to her, over the years.

"I want to see her now," she'd said. "I want to share the same adventure."

He'd smiled then, something he rarely did. "One day, if you're good, my darling, you will."

So she'd been good. For half of her young life, she'd been good, despite all the horrors they'd done.

Now Zero stared at her parents in disgust. Now they looked on the outside exactly how they'd always been on the inside; sick and twisted. This was an eye for an eye.

"You're inhuman," she said, finding strength in her voice. "You deserve this."

"Perhaps we do," her father said, nodding eagerly. "Or I do! But your mother. Let her go."

Zero looked over at her mother; weak and half-dead. She looked back down at her father. He was willing to die for his wife, and that broke Zero's heart. He had love inside him after all. Just not for her. The lie came easily to her lips, just as easily as it had come to his all those many times before.

"I will. I'll let her go, if you help me."

"Anything," he blurted. Perhaps he even knew she was

lying, but he wasn't the strong man he'd once been. He was nothing, now. "I'll do anything."

"Hope first. Tell me everything."

He did.

He explained how he'd built up his organization, called the 'Blue Fairy', using the backdoor to a secret 'dark Internet' he'd created years ago. He explained how he'd sought out and recruited men to join his group, calling them 'Pinocchios'. The words didn't mean much to Zero then, but in the days and weeks to come they would. From there he'd created a very special part of the Blue Fairy, called the 'Exchanges', where fellow Pinocchios could buy, sell and trade photographs of their 'adventures', and stream video, and make requests of each other followed by payments. After some time, the trades became larger .

Children were bought and sold.

"You were the first in the Blue Fairy," he said, voice reduced to a bare croak. "Girl Zero. But Hope was the first to be sold. The payment we received for her financed everything to come. The things we've built, Mona, you should see-"

She slapped his face hard. "Don't say that name."

"I won't," he said quickly, "but Hope, you see-"

She slapped him again. "Don't say her name."

He gulped and nodded. "OK. Yes. But we need water. We need to eat. We need to rest. I want to help you. I want to help you find H-, I mean, your sister. But we're going to die like this."

Zero looked over at her mother. "I think she's got a few more hours. Talk."

He kept talking. He spilled everything he knew, about the dark Internet and the Blue Fairy Exchange and other strange things, until gradually she began to understand that no immediate answer was possible.

His 'Blue Fairy' network was completely anonymous, it

seemed, designed to protect the identity of all his Pinocchios. As a result, he didn't even know who he'd sold Hope to nine years ago. He didn't know where she was, or how to find her, though he promised to teach Zero how to look.

He told her all his passwords, so she could begin the search for other Pinocchios who might know more. Zero wrote everything down carefully. He told her about the skills she'd have to learn to use his darknet, coding and hacking and data analysis, along with an endless stream of strange words like C++ and Python and Tor. For hours he talked, helping to lay the foundation of the new person she would become, and when he was done, he begged for water again.

Zero didn't give him any. Instead she walked over to her mother. She kneeled down before her and lifted away the gag. Her mother's eyelids fluttered weakly and she sucked at the air.

"Mother," Zero said.

Her dim eyes focused. She was too far gone to show any fear. Perhaps, though, there was recognition.

"You're good at watching, aren't you? I want you to watch this."

"No!" her father shouted hoarsely. "You promised."

"So did you," Zero answered, then went back to the machine and hit the button. The engine wound up. The rack tightened on his body and the thumping began again. Now her father sobbed.

Zero took a breath, steeled herself, then turned to face the cameras.

For so many years she'd feared and despised her father's 'friends'. The Pinocchios. She'd known all along that hundreds of them were watching every moment of her pain and humiliation. The chimes of their vile requests and messages coming into her father's computer had carried into her nightmares and dreams alike.

Now she had a message for them. This time her voice came out strong and hard, no longer shaking and uncertain.

"You call me Zero. You think it makes me nothing, a foundation for you to build on. But you're wrong." She paused. Not a single chime rang out. "It's a promise. Because I'm going to find you. Every one of you. And I'll ask you three questions. If you give me the answers I need, you will live. I guarantee it. But if you don't, then I will erase you completely." She gestured to her father, sobbing and gasping on his frame. "So be ready. I'll see you very soon."

She walked away then, through a mirrored door in the torture hall and down a passage on the left, toward a room she'd never been in before; her father's 'office'. The rack and the piston continued hammering in back, watched by her mother and all the cameras. Zero saw no reason to turn it off, now or ever. It was a lesson for them all.

Let the hunt begin.

4

SEVEN YEARS LATER

Krakow, Poland. Zero stood on an elevated gantry in GOMA-49, an abandoned rubber factory now repurposed as an illegal nightclub, scanning for her target. She called him Perp 35. He liked to drug young girls, take them home and murder them with a hammer and nails.

He'd killed at least seven so far, but there could be more.

Zero surveyed the converted dance floor fifteen feet below, where drug-addled bodies gyrated and churned. They were crammed in between a half-dozen old chemical anodizing vats which bloomed through the concrete floor like huge copper mushrooms. Lights swept over the ravers' twining limbs and smoke pumped in hissing clouds from a maze-like network of rusted pipes overhead. The air stank of spilled beer, sweat and urine, but over and above everything was the sound.

GOMA-49 roared with a feverish bass beat, like the pulse of some dark and ancient god. The sound of it suffused Zero's whole body, driving her heart like the gas pedal on an engine.

This was the hunt, and somewhere out there, Perp 35 might be hunting too.

"Any sign of 35?" she said into her throat-mic; a bone-conduction rig strapped to her throat. She'd already attached four tiny spy-cams to corners in the gantry's trusses, affording near 360-degree coverage across the club.

"Scanning for his physiology and gait," came her operator's response in her earpiece. All they had on Perp 35 was what they could glean from the snuff films he made of each girl's death. In those films he wore a pink baby-face mask to disguise his identity; but physiology and gait, or the way he looked and the way he walked, were each as unique as a fingerprint. You just had to match them up. "There may be a potential match in the southeast corner."

Zero's heart rate spiked. "It's him?"

Her operator took another moment to respond. Situated in a white panel van outside the factory, Zero's operator went by 'Armitage'. She was American, like Zero, and had a track record of prostitution on the streets of Boston, after a childhood spent in Catholic foster homes. Zero had recruited her from an online 'catfishing' group; good people who posed as girls on the Internet, in order to set up real-world meets with Pinocchios, or as they now liked to call themselves after a recent evolution, the 'Real Boys'.

"Could be," Armitage said, her voice lilting with her broad Boston accent. "The algorithm says he's a seventy percent match."

Zero moved.

Seventy percent was the best match yet, after two months of hunting. Three girls had died in that time, and it wore on her. She knew Perp 35 used date-rape drugs such as Rohypnol, also called 'roofies', to dose his victims. She knew it from watching the girls' slow rise back to consciousness in the videos, before he set in with his hammer. He wanted them awake enough to scream.

Now the horrors of those videos played on repeat in

Zero's head as she circled the gantry, loosening the stainless-steel dermal jet injector from its holster under her leather jacket. Loaded with four milliliters of her own supply of Rohypnol, the slim silver device only had to make contact with skin to push a high-pressure jet of fluid across the skin membrane and directly into the bloodstream.

Four milliliters was enough to knock out an average-sized woman. For a man like Perp 35, pushing six feet and two hundred pounds, it would render him insensible and compliant; exactly what Zero needed to lead him out to the van and commence her interrogation.

"Any Real Boy entourage?" she asked, heart hammering in sync with the music.

"If it's him, I read no security," Armitage replied.

"Good." That matched the pattern Zero had built for Perp 35. He liked to hunt solo. "Precise location?"

"Seventy yards, no, fifty, to your two o'clock, by the wall. He's got a girl with him already."

Zero's adrenaline spiked, heightening every sound and sensation as she sped down the clanging metal stairs into the churning masses. At once their sound, stink and motion swamped her. Elbows jostled, spinning faces sprayed sweat, drinks splashed, roving disco strobe lights flashed, feet stamped, and above it all boomed the consuming thump of the music.

Zero cut through the dancefloor like a shark. She was twenty-three and knew clubs, drugs and rave music like the back of her hand; all were prime hunting grounds. Thirty yards, twenty, and she could feel the perp drawing her in like chum in the water. Fifteen yards. Ten. The crowd opened and there he was before her.

He was squat despite his height, a mottle-skinned toad of a man squeezed into a too-tight silver suit. A pastel-pink shirt bulged outward at his belly and revealed a thatch of dark hair at the throat, where three buttons were undone. In the roving lights he looked sickly, with sparse dark hair combed sideways over a pronounced widow's peak.

In one hand he held a plastic glass filled with a blue cocktail. Zero recognized the shade; in the late nineties manufacturers added a blue dye to the tiny, powerful Rohypnol caplets, after bad press about their use as a date rape drug. That shade could easily be disguised, however, with a blue liquor like Curaçao.

On his other arm hung the girl. Her head was already lolling. She had bleached blond hair and wore a tight, sequin-sparkling maroon dress. What little Zero could see of her face suggested she was around eighteen, but subtract the effect of her makeup and she was probably fifteen max.

This had to be Perp 35

Five yards.

"Screens read clear," Armitage said. "No backup. It's just you and him."

Zero came on the perp from behind and pressed the dermal-jet injector into the greasy folds of his neck. The effect was instant as the chemicals flushed into his bloodstream, far faster acting than a spiked drink. His right leg wobbled and he let loose a piggish grunt.

Zero swiftly holstered the jet and caught the girl as she slipped from his grasp. She was close to ragdoll unconsciousness now, her eyes rolled back in her head. Zero laid her gently against a nearby wall, planning to come back for her after.

Perp 35 had staggered a few yards in that time, looking knocked-out standing up. She ducked under his limp arm and started walking him through the crowds toward the exit.

"Still clear, Armitage?"

"No eyes on yet."

He didn't resist as she pushed onward, scanning

constantly for any incoming Real Boys. She'd stumbled into nests of them before, and it hadn't gone well. A few pairs of inquiring eyes followed after her, but each time she plastered an embarrassed smile to her face and kept on, like it was so awkward to have such a drunk friend, until at last she emerged through the exit.

The night air outside GOMA-49 was humid and warm. Perp 35 was leaning against her heavily now, and it took all her strength to keep him walking. Across the front of the factory they went, then turned into the forest down an overgrown gravel track. On all sides lay the shadowy ruins of old industrial outbuildings, a labyrinth of partially demolished brick walls, half-filled in ditches and run-off channels, all obscured beneath the canopy cover of looming white pines and tangled up in thick green ferns. The air smelled of mud and sap, fresh after an evening rain.

In ten minutes she reached the van and pounded three times on the side.

The door slid open, spilling white light across the muddy clearing and haloing Armitage. She was a slight figure with wispy brown hair pulled back tight. Behind her lay the van's interior, their mobile supercomputer. There were two long racks filled with high-speed computer servers, connected via a flat satellite dish to the Internet; enough to run a hack on any modest-sized organization and win out. Enough to track Perp 35 via the digital signature left in his videos, and nail down his habits, and find him tonight.

"Hurry," Armitage said.

Zero grunted and let the perp drop. He hit the muddy ground with a wet thump. "We have Real Boys incoming?"

"Not yet. But that was a long walk, and I don't like it here."

"He's a slow walker," Zero said, rolling her shoulder. "But OK. Hammer, nails and tape."

Armitage had the tools ready and handed them over. Zero set the hammer and box of nails on a mossy rock then swiftly trussed Perp 35 with the tape, finishing with a gag over his mouth. He was too far gone to react in any way.

"Juice," Zero said.

Armitage ducked back into the van, rustled, then emerged with a drip bag trailing plastic tubing that ended in a needle. The bag contained liquid flumazenil, a temporary antidote to Rohypnol. On her knees, Zero expertly stuck the needle into the perp's right forearm, hung the bag off the van's wing mirror and turned the small red tappet on the drip bag. Clear liquid flowed into his arm, and after a few seconds she stopped it.

Already the perp was coming around, and began to writhe like a maggot in his duct tape. Zero looked up at Armitage, whose slim, bird-like features belied a core of steel, even if she couldn't stand this stage of the process.

"You don't have to watch," Zero said.

"Yeah, I'll pass, thanks. Just go as fast as you can. We're too exposed out here."

Zero nodded then rolled the slide door closed. Armitage wasn't good with pain, and it was better if she didn't watch. Inside, she'd put on headphones and go back into oversight mode, monitoring the various spy cams Zero had dropped in and around GOMA-49.

The van's exterior side lights came on, shining a spotlight on Zero and the perp. Now his eyes were brighter and his bound body churned up the mud.

Zero raised the hammer and he fell silent. It focused his attention completely. She leaned in and pulled the tape off his mouth, then spoke clearly and slowly.

"Do you know who I am?"

5

THREE QUESTIONS

Perp 35 stared at her. It took a long moment, but gradually his eyes widened. All the Real Boys knew her, after all. She'd been hunting them for nearly a decade.

"You're Girl Zero?" he whispered.

Zero smiled. "That's right. I'm going to ask you three questions. You're going to answer them truthfully, or you're going to experience pain like nothing you can imagine."

Immediately he began to struggle and beg. "Please don't do this, please, I can-"

"Question one," she continued, "how many girls have you killed?"

He blinked furiously. "What? None! I haven't hurt anyone. You mean in the club? That was just my girlfriend. She had too much to drink. I swear, I-"

"But you know my name," Zero interrupted, silencing him. "You know who I am."

He opened his mouth then closed it again.

"Answer the questions. Answer, or I'll do to you what you did to those girls. An eye for an eye."

The shock bedded in then, as he realized this was really happening. He began to cry. "Please," he whispered. "I can't."

"You can," Zero said. "Now talk."

"No!"

She reached up to the tape. He struggled, but he couldn't prevent her sealing off his mouth. Then she brought down the hammer. Four blows struck his calves and ankles, cracking and splintering bone. She chased that with two carpentry nails driven firmly into the meat of his thighs, directly into bone. His face turned red as he screamed into his duct tape gag. The sound emerged like a honking horse's bray.

It took perhaps five minutes for him to stop wailing and weeping and hyperventilating. Zero waited then pulled the gag away.

He vomited to the side.

"You've done much worse," she said softly, while he mewled and wet himself. "Haven't you? Many times. You've hammered nails into girls until they died. Now answer the questions and the pain will end. How many girls have you killed?"

He whined. She reached for the gag again and the truth spilled out of him in a long, wet sob.

"Eleven. I did it to eleven."

Zero watched. It was always the same. They started with defiance, but that soon became pain, tears and shame.

"Who were they? I want names, addresses, and the place you buried them."

He answered in a long, slithery moan. Zero took notes. She'd follow them all up. She'd visit the families and let them know justice had been done. She'd tell them where Perp 35 was buried, so they could come spit on his grave.

He shuddered as he finished. A vein popped out on his forehead, pulsing hard.

"Question two," she went on, "which other Real Boys do you know?"

Now his eyes flared indignantly, and the defiance came back. He shook his pale, rubbery face. "I can't tell you that. We're a brotherhood."

Zero said nothing. This, too, was a familiar part of the process; really just the flumazenil effect fading. False bravado came in as the pain diminished. So she turned the tappet for two seconds, giving him another swift dose and bringing the pain back to full.

"No," he gasped, still resistant. "Never!"

"Tell me or I start breaking ribs."

"I can't!" he barked, so she pulled his gag back on and went to work with the hammer. Three ribs broke. She held up the third nail over his crotch and he went into some kind of fit, shaking and jerking so hard he almost pulled the needle out of his arm.

It disgusted Zero. He'd done this eleven times already, to children. He'd enjoyed it. He'd taken paid requests off the darknet and then sold the videos, and this was all he could bear?

"Who do you know?" she demanded, and pulled the gag clear again.

He vomited the names of three Pinocchios and everything he knew about them. Zero took notes. All of them would be future targets. When it was done there wasn't much of him left. Blood stained his silver suit and pink shirt where the hammer had struck. His thighs continued to bleed where the nails jutted out.

But this was nothing. He'd pounded the girls full of nails before their ordeal was over. Perhaps he'd get by with only two.

"You're doing very well," Zero said, the encouragement failing to reach her eyes. "There's just one final question. The most important. Get this one right and I swear, I will let you live."

His eyes perked up at that. "You'll let me go?"

"I swear it. Now." She gave him another hit of flumazenil. "Where is my sister? Where is Hope?"

His eyes went wide and round. "What?"

Zero saved this question only for Boys who were about to die. There was no more private part of her life than this; no memory she clung to more tightly. "My sister, Hope. My father sold her sixteen years ago on the Blue Fairy exchange, when she was five years old. I want to find her."

Perp 35 jawed at the air in disbelief, then began to babble. "I don't know that! I didn't even know you had a sister. I swear, I don't know. I would tell you if I knew. I promise! Please!"

Please.

She'd heard it all before. It wasn't good enough.

"Her name was Hope," she said one last time. "She had straw blond hair and mischievous blue eyes and she was just five years old. My father said she was the first girl sold on the Fairy's exchanges. She had an Idaho accent. Think."

His eyes flickered around wildly, looking for an answer. "I, I, I can't tell you what I don't know! I swear. I like teenage girls. Not five-year-olds. I swear, not five, and not sixteen years ago! How would I know that?"

Zero gritted her teeth. That made thirty-five times, now, that she'd had this answer. "You're sure?"

"Yes! I swear it, yes!"

She considered driving the third nail through his crotch, but didn't think it would gain anything. The threat of that level of pain was as good as the execution, she found, and Armitage was right that they were exposed here.

Time to go.

"I believe you. Thank you."

His eyes bugged hopefully. "Then you'll let me go?"

"Yes."

Zero spun the hammer and brought it claw-side down on his forehead. It struck and shattered his skull, driving through to destroy his brain. One hit and he was dead.

"That's more mercy than you gave any of them," she said, and pulled back.

In the aftermath, the night was quiet around her, apart from the muted thump of GOMA-49 still pounding through the forest. In these moments after a kill, she felt nothing. Maybe emptiness. For seven years she'd hunted for Hope, changing her name and ID multiple times, scouring first the US and then the world, with thirty-five Real Boys killed, and still she had no real leads.

It was as if Hope had just disappeared.

She gathered up the tape, hammer and nails. Next up was the shovel for Perp 35's shallow grave. She was about to bang three times on the van door when Armitage's voice urgently called in her ear.

"Zero!"

Then something hit her in the shoulder, a pinprick punch.

She spun and saw a thickset figure dressed in black kneeling at the edge of the van's red taillights. He held a thick rifle jet gun to his shoulder, the kind that fired pneumatic hypodermic darts. Her focus shifted and now she saw the slim tube of glass and metal jutting from her shoulder. She stared at it for a millisecond, already recognizing the sudden rush of knockout drugs needling into her system, as familiar as a slap in the face.

The Real Boys had found her.

She reacted fast, plucking out the dart and thrusting herself away from the dead perp and into the dense vegetation. Something else struck her in the back just as she folded into the ferns, and she reached one hand to find another dart protruding from her right hip.

She yanked it out and fled deeper into the dark and jumbled industrial ruins, but the chemicals already had command of her system, instantly bringing on a mental fog through which it was near-impossible to think. She'd been here before, spent half her childhood like this, but that couldn't stop the knockout effects.

Her foot missed a step and she stumbled into a tight cluster of saplings, tumbling from one to another. A man appeared before her, maybe two, though she couldn't tell thanks to her doubling vision. His hand was reaching out with the glint of silver: a dermal jet.

She pulled her own jet and thrust it forward with everything she had. It hit him in the throat and discharged. He fell back and Zero stumbled on, hot and cold at once, her mind fogging and her legs giving out. Another man appeared and this time she fell against him. His arms clasped around her, even as she drew the five-inch black stiletto blade from her triceps holster and drove it into his kidneys three, four, five times.

He sagged to the ground and she barely stayed upright, sucking in breath.

"Armitage," she shouted, wheeling in the chaos of the forest. "Where are they?"

No answer came back and Zero staggered on, clambering through the ruins until she emerged by the GOMA-49 wall. They were already there; right in front of her, three men in black holding dart rifles.

The bass thump pumped from GOMA-49 like the devil's drums. Hellish lights flashed through the shattered windows above. One of the figures stepped forward and his lips moved as he closed the gap toward her, his words filtering into her brain as if underwater.

"You've been hunting us, Mona," he said, using her birth name. "Are you so surprised that we've been hunting you?"

She thrust out her stiletto blade, but the drugs made her slow and he pushed it easily aside. She sent out a knee and caught empty air. Hands gripped her arms and she glimpsed the future playing out ahead. She'd sworn she'd never be taken alive again, but now the moment had come. She jerked the blade back toward her own eye, but strong hands caught her wrist and wrapped it like the shackles of her father's torture rack.

"You're a rabid dog, Mona," he said, his face filling her vision as the drugs' dark curtain descended. "Time to put you in a cage, just like your sister."

6

DARK CURTAIN

Zero was drowning in darkness.

Hope was the only thing tethering her to the surface.

The man had mentioned her sister, and that thought kept bringing her up to fight for breath. In blurry snapshots she felt them loading her into the back seat of a vehicle, wedged in between two large men with her hands cuffed behind her.

The night was warm. She felt that much on her bare skin, breezing in through an open window. It did nothing to cut through the tranquilizer fog. They were talking and she snatched at words as the vehicle moved away, but it was too hard to pick them out.

It didn't matter.

These men knew her sister, and that thought spiked through her head like a nail. It kept her fighting with everything she had for the surface. Almost unconsciously, with painful slowness, her tongue rooted in her dry mouth until she located the hollow false teeth in the back of her lower jaw. There were four in total.

She'd prepared for a moment like this.

The right rear tooth contained a flumazenil lozenge; the antidote not only to Rohypnol, but also to diazepam, alprazolam and other benzodiazepine-based depressant drugs. It acted as a chemical blocker, cutting through the lethargy that depressants brought on. The right front tooth contained naloxone, an effective antidote against many opioids like oxycodone, morphine and heroin, which blocked the opioid receptors.

Recovery from either wasn't pretty. Zero tried hard to think. They'd shot her with pneumatic syringe darts; most likely they'd contained a mixture of opioids and benzodiazepines. She'd become a connoisseur as a child, and could distinguish the compositions from the effects they brought on.

This numbing fog she was currently in, matched with the nauseating, out-of-place euphoria, felt like both in combination.

Her tongue worked over to the left. Both teeth there contained cyanide capsules. If the worst came to the worst, she'd crack and swallow them. Death would be near instantaneous.

But she wasn't there yet.

She tried to still her wandering thoughts and focus on the moment. Opening her eyes was a task too far, but she knew the best time to escape a kidnap was early. Soon the Real Boys would have her manacled into a breaking frame, and all that remained then would be the cyanide.

She stretched harder for some measure of control, until she got a sense of her own physical position. There was a chill across her belly, thighs and shoulders; most likely they'd stripped her naked. That meant all her concealed blades were gone, along with her phone. Her hands were also bound behind her back. Did she remember them cinching metal cuffs? She hoped they were plastic zip-ties. Her beaded bracelet was still in place on her left wrist, though, inscribed with her sister's name: HOPE.

Their mistake.

She pried with her tongue and steadily worked the right two teeth out as the vehicle rumbled on. They swirled in the pocket of her gums. Carefully, slowly, she bit down on both until they cracked, releasing their antidote lozenges.

"Did you hear that?" one of the guards said.

One of them grabbed her by the cheeks and twisted her face side to side. She didn't react, her eyes didn't open, and there was no pain at his rough touch; the drugs saw to that.

"She's out," he said. "Dead to the world."

He let go and Zero slumped back, sucking silently on the pills. Each was a small dose, and could not compare to the amount of drugs already circulating in her system. They should bring her up from the depths, but for only fifteen minutes or so before their blocking effect wore off.

It felt like a long ascent up from a deep, dark well. She tried to count the minutes as sensation gradually returned: her feet and fingertips tingled; her hearing sharpened; the fog swamping her thoughts cleared; her hands tightened into fists. She wouldn't be strong, she wouldn't have fast reflexes, but she had the element of surprise.

That would have to be enough. She cued up a schedule of actions like she was programming a computer hack, then hit execute.

With the fingers of her right hand, she clasped the beaded bracelet around her left wrist. It took a dozen fumbling seconds to locate the catch and release it. The bracelet opened and the beads slid free, pressing into the soft seat behind her. Only four were left at the bracelet's tail, fixed into position on the leather thong. One-handed, she screwed the top two against the bottom two, and steadily the oiled threads twisted away.

What remained was a tiny razor-sharp blade; barely an eighth of an inch across and an inch deep, with an inch of beaded handle. She almost dropped it, nicked herself once, then managed to get it against the plastic zip-ties and push.

"She's squirming," one of the guards beside her said.

Someone answered from in front. Zero didn't catch what they said. Time was running out. She worked the tiny blade against the zip-tie until the plastic sheared.

"She's still doing it," the guard said.

"So give her a slap," the man in the front passenger seat said.

He did. The blow came hard and rang her head off the seat, bloodying her lips against her teeth. She tasted copper and reacted by bucking forwards and spraying blood into the guard's face.

Everything happened fast after that, as Zero executed the program she'd prepared. The man reeled back and she followed him, her right hand rising and raking. The tiny blade sank an inch-deep into the side of his throat like it was soft cream cheese and tore sideways. He cried out and shoved her hard away.

She landed in the lap of the other guard, who brought his fists down on her back and grabbed at her arms. Her ribs creaked under the blows and he managed to catch her left arm, but her right arm snaked free to slide beneath her body and up between his legs to stab and slice across the interior of his right thigh.

Blood gushed at once from his femoral artery, and he jerked instinctively upward with his knee, driving Zero against the side window. She hit the glass headfirst, cracking it with a sound like a gunshot, then fell back across the first guard's lap as he aspirated blood from his open throat. The SUV fishtailed as the brakes kicked in, both men up front shouting and turning to see. She had only seconds until-

A real gunshot rang out, as thunderous as the bass speakers in the club, and the leather seat beside her head tufted open in white wool. She rolled and tucked, tumbling into the footwell. More bullets discharged, taking out the back and side windows, and gunpowder smoke stung Zero's eyes as she rooted at the guard's ankle, finally coming up with a snub nose pistol.

It felt strangely heavy in her blood-slick hand. She twisted, pressed the muzzle up against the back of the driver's seat and fired three times.

The driver cried out, the vehicle lost control and slammed up a high verge then crashed into a tree. The guard on Zero's left thrashed open his door and staggered out into the night, hands clamped to his right thigh as his life's blood poured out. The guard above her was down to short wet wheezes, holding his throat like he could patch up his slit carotid artery.

Then the door opened beside her and the man from the passenger seat appeared. Three more bullets fired, but Zero couldn't tell if they were his or hers. Long seconds passed. She didn't feel anything, but then she wouldn't.

"You little bitch," the man murmured, then dropped where he stood; two spreading dark stains on his chest.

The gun fell from Zero's fingers.

Already she felt her fifteen minutes were winding down as the fog climbed back in. She just needed to…

She roused briefly on the roadside, dragging herself along. Her knees and elbows scraped on the raw blacktop but she barely felt it. Four Real Boys dead, but were there more? She could barely see a thing for the gray walls coming down. Perp 35 had been a trap. They'd been watching. More could be coming any moment.

Darkness grayed her out until she rose up what felt like the final time, clutching to the thought of Hope. The only people Zero had ever mentioned her sister to were the men she'd killed herself. But these Real Boys had known Hope's name.

Maybe Hope was still alive.

She was on her knees, damp in amongst thick ferns. Her hands were numb, her whole body shaking. There were trees all around, dark and blurry in the night. It took everything she had to rustle deeper into the patch of ferns before the knockout drugs bit through the naloxone/flumazenil cocktail and dumped her back into the black.

7

NOT YOUR FRIENDS

Zero woke with a splitting headache and a bone-deep ache in every part of her body, in a place she did not remember falling asleep.

It was a bed.

She jerked alert at once, ignoring the pain and scanning for a weapon. The Real Boys had Armitage, and she had to get her back. The large space around her looked like a basement, with bare wooden rafters overhead, a concrete floor coated with a few tattered Persian rugs, and slim windows inset high into the walls through which wan white light rinsed.

She was lying on what looked to be a foldout sofa bed, covered with a quilt decorated with bright superhero figures. There was a coffee table to the side with a space heater glowing orange beside it and floor-to-ceiling shelves fixed to the walls.

There were no cuffs on her wrists or ankles, but that was their mistake. She bounded up and padded to the nearest rack of shelving, just catching herself on the frame. Nausea made the world swirl but she pushed it back, sorting through the plastic crate until she found a junior-size baseball bat.

Only then did she notice her clothing. At some point in the night she'd been dressed in what looked to be a man's striped pajamas.

It didn't matter. Whatever fantasy was playing out here, the Real Boys were going to regret it. She ran to the wooden stairs and took them two at a time, expecting the door at the top to be locked, but it wasn't, and she slammed through, bat raised, to see something quite unexpected.

It was a calm breakfast scene; two young girls seated at a breakfast table in the middle of a spacious kitchen with bowls of cornflakes before them. Large windows admitted more pale light. Standing at the kitchen counter with a knife in one hand, a spatula in the other, and an apron hanging around his chest that depicted a muscular torso, was a man in his early thirties.

Zero stared.

The man gazed back at her with some modicum of surprise. He was a shade over six feet and looked to be in shape, with gray flecked through his rough stubble and at his temples. Slowly, steadily he raised both hands above his head and said something in what had to be Polish.

Zero only stared.

"Nie?" the man asked, then tried again. "Not … Polish? Maybe English?"

"American," Zero said.

"Ah," he said, and raised his arms a little higher, a smile appearing at the edge of his lips. "Baseball. Yes. We surrender."

Zero looked at the bat raised over her head. Vertigo hit and her vision doubled. She'd killed several Real Boys with bats. She refocused on the table and now saw all three of them had their hands up. Milk dripped from the spoon of the elder girl, maybe eight years old, and into her hair. She flinched and began to giggle, which set off her little sister.

Zero lowered the bat as the girls laughed and the father smiled.

"It's OK," he said gently. "But this isn't a baseball diamond. We aren't the New York Yankees." The little girls laughed even harder. "No, girls please, this is bad behavior." He gestured to a fourth place laid at the table. "Young lady, you are not well. I think you have a bad headache, yes, some dizziness too? Join us."

Zero's eyes darted from side to side. She had both a headache and dizziness, but if this was a trap, it was an elaborate one. Her first thought was to just run. Get out of there, head for Krakow and melt back into invisibility. But the man seemed to read her expression and raised a full cafetiere.

"I have coffee. Also better clothes, um, than this. Sorry." He pointed. "These are my, what is the word, pajamas?"

A pang of anger pushed through Zero's confusion. "You dressed me?"

"We had to. You were freezing. But it's OK, my girls did most of it."

The elder girl pointed her spoon at Zero and said something in Polish.

"She says this is a good look for you."

The girls laughed. The man shrugged and laid his knife down beside a pile of chopped strawberries. "Truce, yes? You are American, so you like coffee. This is a well-known fact."

Zero didn't know what to say. This was another world from the one she'd just left, where hammers and nails did the talking, and Armitage had been taken, and-

The abrupt honk of a horn sounded outside, and the girls immediately tossed their spoons into their bowls and hopped up out of their seats.

"School bus," the man said. "One minute, please."

Zero watched while they hustled and bustled around the

kitchen, snatching up a lunchbox here, swapping bags there, putting on a hat then swapping it for another hat, speed tooth-brushing into the sink, until after a whirlwind few minutes all three of them hurried to the door and filed out without a further word.

Zero was left in the silence of the kitchen. The knife lay on the counter still, alongside the cafetiere. Her head swirled as she strode forward. First she took the knife, then she drained a tall glass of orange juice, wolfed down a banana and two pieces of jam-slathered toast and chased it all with a glass of ice-cold milk.

It helped a little, and she was back in her place by the basement door by the time the man came back, shaking his head and smiling.

"My girls," he said, "always late."

He picked up the cafetiere, paused for a moment looking at the counter, then sat back at the table and poured.

"Do you like cream?"

"How did I get here?" Zero countered.

He looked up and gave her that slight smile again. "It isn't my habit to find young women shivering in the bushes and bring them home. This is only the second time it has happened."

Zero's eyes widened. "The second time?"

"It's a joke." He smiled. "Of course I know there is a club nearby, in the old factory? Police sometimes come, but young people have to dance somewhere. I tried to call the police for you, perhaps an ambulance, but you said no. You were very clear. So we came here. My girls dressed you. That was five hours ago."

Zero checked a clock that hung over the fridge. It was nearly 10 a.m. Five hours ago would've been around 5 a.m. She'd captured Perp 35 sometime before midnight, which made for five hours spent nearly naked in the forest. If it had been winter she'd have surely died. In total it was ten hours since she was drugged, which meant the effects were still an ongoing concern. Rohypnol alone could take a day or two to fully recover from.

"Where did you find me? Near here?"

"Yes. Behind my house. I could not see where-"

"Were there any men?"

His eyes narrowed. "Men?"

"Looking for me. Did you see a car on the road? An SUV, maybe, crashed."

He puzzled over that for a moment. "No. The nearest through road is ten minutes' walk." He pointed. "Did your car crash?"

Zero considered. She couldn't remember the fight for control clearly, but then knockout drugs played havoc with your memory.

"Perhaps. I'm not sure. I was drugged."

"Drugged? That's terrible. I'm sorry. You should go to hospital. I'll take you now."

He stood up.

"Take me to the road."

"You want to go to the road?"

She thought fast. "To look for my car. I think my friends were in it. I want to check they're OK."

His expression shifted. "And will you take my knife to look for your friends?"

She thought for a moment, then spun the knife from its concealed position behind her forearm and set it on the table. "You know what they say. Never trust a stranger."

He watched closely as she stepped back. She could see the processes working behind his eyes, and she didn't blame him. He wasn't a Real Boy, though, of that she was certain. He was just some guy trying to help.

"My name is Gabriel," he offered, "and you're already wearing my pajamas. I don't think we're strangers anymore."

Zero weighed the price of giving him this. It wasn't high. She had a large number of fake names and fake IDs, bought through contacts on the dark Internet. Any one of them would do. She had a favorite amongst them, though, and it seemed fair to give him that. "I'm Clara."

He nodded. "It's nice to meet you, Clara. And the people in that car, they weren't your friends, were they?"

"Let's go," she said, and started toward the door.

8

GABRIEL

Gabriel produced a pair of faded blue jeans, a black t-shirt and white socks, along with a big yellow jacket and a pair of insulated boots.

"My wife," he said, by way of explanation as he handed them over, then appeared to catch himself. "Or ex-wife. I never know what to say. She died last year. I'm a widower."

Zero didn't care. "I'm sorry."

"You can change in the bathroom."

Zero did. Gabriel had even thoughtfully folded in underwear. Fully dressed again, Zero surveyed herself in the mirror.

The same wide, ice-blue eyes gazed back at her, forever intense but quizzical, like she was searching for something and perpetually angry about not finding it. Now they were shot through with red. Raver's eyes, she thought, blitzed from an all-night party, high on Rohypnol.

She snorted, and her black hair bobbed around her eyes in thick feathers. It was a wild mop, too long since she'd had it cut, hanging down around her jawline and barely obscuring the splashes of blood on her face, partly cleaned away.

Gabriel must have mistaken them for mud. It looked from

the swipe pattern like he'd done it carefully. She pulled her t-shirt back and saw the swiping ended at her collarbones. That was good, too.

"You OK in there?" he called.

"One second," Zero called back. What she really needed was a shower, a full-body detox, a spa treatment, but there'd be no time for those things until she found Armitage. She remembered the men creeping up on the van. They'd have her. Zero just hoped she was still alive, and settled for splashing her face with hot water, tying her hair back with a band and squeezing a line of toothpaste onto her finger and running it around her mouth.

The two gaps on the lower right of her jaw felt alien to her finger and tongue, where the antidote pills had been. They'd saved her life. The two hollow teeth containing cyanide on the left remained, as sturdy as ever.

It all helped. No use going off half-cocked. She felt a little better and stepped out of the bathroom. For a moment Gabriel just stared at her before he blinked and looked away.

"I'm sorry," he said. "It's just, you look like her. In those clothes. I didn't think-"

Zero shrugged on the big jacket. It was a decent fit, heavy and warm if a little too bright for her taste. The boots were sturdy and comfortable. She went to the door and pushed through.

The morning air was cold and crisp and smelled of rain and trees. There were pines on all sides of what looked to be a decent-sized home, with a gravel track running across the front of a yard decked out like a Japanese garden. There were two gravel patches raked in uniform lines, several heaped rocks coated with moss and the small-scale figure of a red shrine gate.

"My wife was Japanese," Gabriel offered. "I keep it up for the girls. Uh, this way."

He led her off the gravel track and into the woods. Everywhere water dripped from a rain that must've recently ended. The light had that same pale quality and the earth was spongy and soft underfoot, shrouded with a thick layer of ferns.

They walked in silence. It wasn't comfortable, but Zero didn't care. Comfort didn't matter. What mattered was finding the Real Boys who'd set her up. It was all getting clearer now. They must've been watching Perp 35 in case she showed up. They'd arrived less than an hour after she'd taken him, coming in force from somewhere nearby, which meant they'd known she was in Krakow.

How many low-level perps had they been watching, hoping to catch her out?

Now they had Armitage.

"If you don't mind, can I ask why you didn't want me to call the police?" Gabriel asked over his shoulder.

"I mind," Zero answered.

"It's just, I've worked with addicts sometimes. I'm not saying you are one, of course." He turned halfway as if to reassure her he was sincere. "But it was part of my job. I think in America you would call me a 'pastor'? Here I am a '*kaplan*'. Or was."

"I'm not looking to get saved, Gabriel."

"I am not trying to save you. Much, anyway. But I couldn't help see your scars."

Zero stopped in her tracks.

There were scars all over her body, courtesy of her mother and father. Some she'd obscured with tattoos. Some she'd had dermabraded away. Some, though, would be with her for life.

He stopped too, then turned. "I'm sorry. I shouldn't have-"

"No," Zero said firmly. "You shouldn't have. This is not what you think it is, Gabriel. I don't need your help, at least not like that. Now listen to me." She took a deep breath. "I appreciate what you've done for me. You might have saved my life. But no more questions. Let's go to the road. I owe you plenty, but I don't owe you answers."

He gazed at her. The sadness in his eyes pissed her off.

"It's just that I've seen scars like these before. I know what they mean. I am very sorry, Clara, because-"

"Start walking now or your girls will grow up orphans."

The threat came out before she could stop it. He eyed her, then nodded heavily, turned, and the walk continued in silence.

Within five minutes Zero heard the road. In moments they passed through an outer screen of bushes, branches and ferns, and stepped down onto the siding of a two-lane backcountry road.

Cars zipped by doing at least fifty. She scanned both ways but there was no sign of the SUV, though there was a pattern of sparkling glass on the blacktop fifty yards to the left. She strode over.

They were cubes of shattered safety glass. Nearby the verge had been deformed by tire tracks, and there was a fresh rectangular gouge cut into the bark of a tree.

Zero remembered the chaos as she slit men and shot them, as the SUV had slammed to a halt. One man had escaped, she remembered that much, the one whose thigh she'd slit, and she dropped to one knee to study the blacktop. There were no bloodstains though; the rain would have washed them away. With his femoral artery slit he couldn't have gone far, but perhaps a hundred yards or so, before he bled out.

The rest of the scene had obviously been cleared up: the SUV, most of the wreckage, the bodies, though it certainly wasn't by the police. If it was, everything would still be in position. There'd be a major investigation in process.

No.

The Real Boys had sent more men to clear all this up. She

tallied the numbers; that was four dead last night, plus a handful more this morning with a tow truck. The scale of the operation was expanding.

How thorough had they been, though?

She turned to find Gabriel peering over her shoulder.

"This is where you crashed," he said helpfully. "I think the police have already come. Or were the people in the car fit to drive?"

Zero weighed up his involvement. He had two daughters. He seemed like a nice man.

"You should go home, Gabriel. Thank you for everything you've done. It means a lot to me. But I'll take it from here."

He looked confused, then just nodded. "I have some money. Please, take it. As for the clothes, I needed to get them out of the house anyway."

He fumbled in his wallet and held out some rumpled bills, concealed within which was a card with his name and number on. Zero took the bills but separated the card and offered it back.

"In case," he insisted. "Please. I will think about you, now, and worry. Like my daughters. My wife, she died in a hit and run. It's not the same, but I wasn't there. I didn't help. I..." He trailed off for a moment. "If I can help you at all, please let me."

Zero sighed, then pocketed the money and the card. She had no intention of calling him, but it was a nice gesture. "I don't deserve it. Now go home, Gabriel. Don't think about me anymore. I'll be fine. This is what I do."

He looked at the shattered glass and the gouge in the tree, and the way Zero's gaze kept wandering into the deep forest, and simply nodded. Maybe he had some sense of what she meant.

"I understand. Good luck, Clara. There's a bus stop half a

mile that way." He pointed. "You can get into Krakow. Well. Stay safe."

He turned and started trudging away. Everything about him seemed sad. But Zero didn't have time for that.

She had a dead Real Boy to find.

9

CORPSE

It was clear from the raked-up trails through the underbrush leading from the road that others had been searching for him; at least three, most likely in the night. Zero imagined them calling to each other in the dark, perhaps fearful of Girl Zero leaping out of the shadows to skewer them.

Depending on the severity of the cut to his femoral artery, her target could have covered hundreds of yards in any direction. At night and fearful, they could easily have overlooked him.

Zero had two advantages: the light and her experience of man-tracking.

For one of her kills back in the woods of Vermont, a Pinocchio who'd specialized in locking children in cupboards for extraordinary lengths of time, she'd learned how to track and read the trails left by men: the occasional lucky footprint or cracked branch; compressions in the ground cover, where his careful passage had pocked the surface layer of dust; depressions in leaves and scuff marks on rocks and branches; dullings in the morning grass, where a footfall removed the gloss of dew.

She'd eventually caught her prey in an old forestry cabin that appeared on no maps, surrounded by large wooden cupboards. He must have carried each one there by himself over the years, and each one contained the corpse of a child. Some were skeletons, some midway through the process of decomposition. He was simply sitting in the center of the cabin when she'd approached, like a monk at meditation.

He had no chance to offer resistance, as Zero shot him with a needle dart that knocked him out in seconds. When he came to, she'd already emptied out his cupboards, laying the bodies and bones reverently outside in body bags, ready for the FBI to come find them.

The man fouled himself when he saw her face. He blabbered and babbled excuses, about his awful childhood and the cruelties he'd know, how he genuinely loved the children and this was the sign of his adoration, but Zero had no time for any of that. She'd asked her three questions, but he'd known nothing worthwhile. The anonymity of her father's darknet was too complete. He'd taken videos of the children spaced hours and days apart, moaning and begging in their cupboards, then uploaded them to the darknet for cash, and that was all he knew.

He hadn't known anything about other Pinocchios. He knew nothing about Hope.

She locked him in one of his own cupboards. It took him an impressive five days to die. Longer than Zero's mother. She took video of him at regular intervals and uploaded it for the other Pinocchios to see. At first he screamed and threatened, then he moaned and wailed, then he begged and bargained, then he sobbed and groaned, then he was quiet, then finally he died. She left him there, placed an anonymous call to the local sheriff's office from a nearby payphone, and disappeared back into anonymity.

Three false trails ran through the undergrowth before her,

but only one continued onto the open needle-bed of the inner forest.

Zero dropped to all fours and lowered her head side-on to about two inches above the ground. The height differential between her eyes, with one closer to the ground and one further away, allowed her to pick out the 'ghost-scale' of 'dullings' and 'compressions' in the mat of needles coating the forest floor. The dying man's meandering trail was faint but there, and she followed it: a hundred yards further through the forest, across a gravel track and into a bank of ferns, which was where she found him.

He lay pale and silent as a shroud, curled up around his injured thigh. He wore dark jeans, black boots and a gray shirt that was coated in bloody palm and fingerprints. His face was hard and angular in death, but unfamiliar, his vacant eyes staring up.

Zero kneeled by his side and patted him down. His thighs were damp still with the spill of blood, and even the rain hadn't washed away the coppery scent in the air. In his right pants pocket she found a sodden wallet. In his left pocket was a simple touchscreen cell phone.

She opened the wallet. It contained a slim wad of green hundred-zloty notes, the currency of Poland, each showing a stern-faced king with long flowing hair, alongside another wad of hundred-euro notes. There was no ID or anything else.

Next was the phone. There was no PIN lock to open it and only three calls in the history; number withheld, with no messages. A burner phone. She hit redial but the call wouldn't go through. Instead she scrolled through the app icons to the camera and took photographs of the dead man's face. There was some kind of tattoo around his neck, so she peeled off his jacket and shirt to get a closer look.

Blurry black prison tattoos covered his torso: a large Virgin Mary clutched the baby Jesus in the center of his chest; twin mermaids with skulls for heads were painted low on either side of his belly; a long dagger was seemingly pushed through his throat, with the grip on his right clavicle and the tip on his left. There were words written in the Russian Cyrillic script, in twin semi-circles above and below the Madonna and Child: 'бог против вора, вор против бога'.

Zero didn't know what any of that signified, but it certainly wasn't Pinocchio or Real Boy symbology.

She photographed it all then sank back on her haunches, intent on hacking his phone. There was some Internet connection, if weak. His battery was down to twenty percent, so she worked fast and economically; downloading the anonymous Tor browser along with the SudVPN Virtual Private Network app that would disguise her location. Protected by both, she keyed in the location string to a private online portal she kept on the darknet.

No one else knew about it. Not Armitage, not her operator who'd died in Tokyo, not anyone. It linked directly to a remote supercomputer she kept in the concealed basement of a rural Kansas duplex, always switched on and ever ready to crunch data for her.

She was about to upload the photographs to initiate an image search through every international criminal database she had hacked backdoor access to, when she stopped.

Her thumbs poised over the screen.

Was the Kansas computer secure?

That was a question she couldn't answer. She'd never told anyone about it, but she'd never told anyone about her hit on perp 35, or about Hope, but still the Real Boys had found her. It was possible she'd left some trackable route from the van's servers to Kansas, and with Armitage in their hands, she had to consider the van compromised. It was even possible Armitage had been compromised, before the strike.

Was that how they'd found her?

She didn't think Armitage would ever sell her out, but how well did she know her, really? They'd only been working together a few months; both women operating under fake names, catfishing Real Boys. How hard would it have been to catfish Zero too?

She pushed such thoughts aside. In any case, the Boys had the van, so they could've cracked her Kansas computer too. If so, they'd have eyes on anything she ran through its processors. They could feed her false information and lead her into another trap.

Zero cursed loudly and killed the connection.

The screen resolved to black.

The Real Boys were likely inside her digital fortress, and that was a violation of everything she'd built since leaving the Idaho pig farm behind. It knocked her queasy and off-balance. She was an excellent hacker, and her defenses were top of the range, but she wasn't the best. There were cracks in her security that any one of a dozen elite could break through.

Two sprang immediately to mind. Their names were Hellion and B4cksl4cker, and they were trouble. Zero had history with them and it wasn't always good. The last thing she wanted to do was call them, but Hope was on the line.

She restarted the VPN and placed the call.

10

PYRAMID ERADICATION

The phone was answered by a female voice with a clipped Bulgarian accent.

"Pyramid Eradication."

For a moment Zero thought she must've dialed the wrong number. Pyramid Eradication? Then she heard the sound of keyboard keys clattering at an impossibly fast pace in the background and understood.

This was 'Hellion', just using a cover company name. Hellion was a twenty-three-year-old hacker savant, one of the greatest in the world. She was part of a do-gooder team called the 'Foundation', helmed by a pseudo-cult leader called Christopher Wren. Wren was an ex-black-ops CIA officer who'd spent years battling domestic terrorists in the United States; his path had crossed Zero twice in the last three years.

The first time had been galling. Zero had only been 19, still ramping up her catfishing endeavors to track down, capture and kill Pinocchios across America. They'd managed to entrap her in Detroit, and shipped her off for a ritualistic sacrifice in front of a livestream for all the Pinocchios to enjoy. It was only Christopher Wren's intervention that had saved her at the end.

She didn't like that she owed him.

The second time had been even more galling, when the Pinocchio trail led her to the Real Boys, operating in the sewers underneath Tokyo, Japan. It was her first time operating international, and she was out of her depth. She'd done what she could to uncover the hotbed of Real Boys, but simply didn't have the infrastructure or assets to take them on. so she'd called in Christopher Wren and his Foundation, by writing his name on the dead bodies of Boys she'd killed.

He'd arrived, almost got himself killed several times, and only survived when Zero saved him. That made accepting his help go down a little easier. She didn't exactly hate him. They'd been a pretty good team. But she didn't exactly trust him, either, or his foundation.

As for Hellion, or indeed her partner B4cksl4cker, she'd barely exchanged two words with them. She knew, though, that they were both wunderkind hackers who had, in their day, held large corporations and even a few nation states to ransom, making millions in the process. Now they rolled around Europe in a vehicle convoy, white-hat hacking for the Foundation. While Zero herself was a skilled hacker, they definitely put her in the shade.

"It's Clara Baxter," she said, gritting her teeth as she spat out the name they knew her by. "I need your help."

A long silence passed, broken by bursts of keystrokes as Hellion no doubt checked her out.

"Clara Baxter," Hellion said, her voice turning cold and methodical. "This is same Clara Baxter who manipulated and endangered Christopher Wren many times previously? Also manipulated and endangered Foundation at large, thinking only about herself. Is correct?"

Zero's jaw tightened, but she couldn't argue with any of that. It was true that she'd manipulated Wren before. She'd dragged him into her last strike against the Real Boys in

Tokyo. He was like a caveman's club, inflicting massive blunt force trauma wherever he went, and sometimes that was more useful than a stiletto.

"Correct," Zero allowed. "I apologized for that."

Hellion laughed. "Apology. Very nice. Very generous. Now you are calling me, like naughty girl after misbehaving. Is this new attempt to manipulate Foundation?"

There was only so much Zero was willing to take. "It's not. Now call me 'naughty girl' again and see what happens."

Hellion laughed louder. "Is this asking for help or threatening, Clara Baxter? I am not clear."

"Call it both. I may not be as good a hacker as you, but you won't stand a chance if I come for you. Nobody will save you, and you'll never see it coming."

There was a brief silence, punctuated by a handful of loud keystrokes. "You are in forest of Poland, south-east of Krakow, talking on stolen burner phone. Interesting. Many photos of dead man on this phone. Tattoos of skulls, knives and baby Jesus, very dark. Also three calls coming in, yesterday only, no number to track. Yes, you are in trouble, most fearsome assassin."

Zero bit back an angry retort. Hellion had just hacked her phone, but there was no point expressing anger about invasions of privacy with an uber-hacker like Hellion. Just by calling her, Zero had abdicated her privacy rights.

"If I did come for you, it wouldn't be with a phone you can track. I'll be a hitchhiker by the roadside. You'll never see me until it's too late."

Hellion just laughed. "Perhaps. Now, you wish for my attention, yes? You have it for one minute. What help do you want, Clara Baxter?"

She took a deep breath. She'd never been good at asking for help. "You're right that I'm in trouble. I'm hunting some Real Boys who set a trap for me last night. I don't know how they did it, but they must have been camping on some of their worst members. When I turned up, they came in force. I barely escaped, but took a couple of them with me. One of them's the dead guy with the tattoos; this is his phone. Now they've got my operator and I need to find her."

Seconds passed. Zero suspected she'd been muted. When the line clicked back on, all sign of humor was drained from Hellion's voice.

"You are lying."

Zero frowned. "Lying about what?"

"About everything. Who you are. Price of my help is truth, Clara Baxter. For years you are killing Pinocchios. Real Boys. Again and again. Sometimes castration. Torture. These are necessary acts, perhaps, against Pinocchios, but what is reason? I do not like such sadism. I do not like you close to Christopher Wren. Your network is compromised? Good. You are poison. You can die. Unless."

She left that hanging. Zero's heart pounded harder. She had a suspicion about what was coming next.

"Unless what?"

"Unless you show me you are more than killer. Vengeance, yes, killing, very nice. But it is not Foundation way. Christopher Wren does not approve. I do not approve. This is simple question. Why should I help you?"

Zero opened her mouth then closed it again. The answer was simple. Hope. But the only people she ever mentioned Hope to were the men she killed. It was the only way to know their answers were true, not just telling her what they wanted to hear.

Did she dare trust Hellion with that?

"I killed my father, but that didn't finish the job," she offered instead. "Now I'm taking out his network."

"Not enough. That is vengeance. Five seconds, I am

hanging up. Come hitch-hike beside me, we will see who dies. Four."

Zero's mouth went dry.

"Three."

Zero didn't know what else to say. This was why she'd always worked alone, keeping her network at arm's length, using fake names, sharing nothing with anyone.

"Two."

"It's none of your business."

"Correct. One. I am now hanging up."

The line clicked then died.

Zero was left in the forest, kneeling over a corpse alone.

Her head swirled. The task ahead loomed large, and somewhere along the way she'd made a mistake. Maybe she'd trusted the wrong person. Now her operator was captured, her network was compromised and Hope was ebbing away like a tide.

More trust wasn't the answer to that. She didn't trust Christopher Wren or his do-gooder 'Foundation'. Trust made you weak. If she'd learned anything in her life, it was that there was only one person you could rely on.

Yourself.

She squeezed her eyes tight and dropped back into planning, like she once had under the pig farm. There were things she could do without a supercomputer. Her mind began to whirr and she brought the phone up again.

The battery indicator had dropped to seventeen percent. It should be enough.

11

IOTA

Zero fired up the commercial search engine 'Iota' and tapped through to image search. Her thumbs flew over the small screen, opening multiple search tabs and setting basic parameters for each.

Sixteen percent battery.

Into each search tab she uploaded the photographs and hit execute. She opened an additional tab and opened fresh accounts with two services, TruthSeeker and SubterLets. TruthSeeker was a legitimate data harvesting operation that expedited public access to criminal records in the United States. SubterLets was illegal but widely known, and hooked her into Interpol's massive Nlets database, composed of the data from some 18,000 different international agencies. She dumped the dead man's photos into each.

Fifteen percent.

While those compiled, she ran parallel searches on Iota with a customized string of requirements: Russian tattoos; gangs in Krakow; Real Boys in Poland.

The search graphic spun.

Fourteen percent.

Zero cursed again as the searches turned. If she had her

Kansas supercomputer, working with her usual suite of hacking tools and pre-existing backdoor access codes, all this would come in seconds, direct from the actual databases. She would further design an intelligent algorithm to track the Real Boys via traffic data from near GOMA-49 in the last twenty-four hours: CCTV records from speed or dash cams; satellite, drone or weather overwatch; cell phone GPS tracking data.

But she didn't have any of that.

In seconds the phone chimed; down to thirteen percent now.

She refocused on the screen as search results came in from Iota. There was nothing on 'Real Boys in Poland', little on 'gangs in Krakow', but plenty on Russian tattoos. One site was titled 'Gulag Tattoos' and she scanned it swiftly. Apparently these tattoos were a blurry blue color because they'd been made with ball-point-pen ink using improvised needles, which was all that the prisoners had access to.

Each image carried a different meaning: the Madonna and Child was a standard for thieves and criminals, perceived as watching over them; the dagger through the throat meant this man had killed in prison and could be hired to do so again; the mermaids signified he was a child abuser and the skulls implied he'd killed the children in the process.

Zero looked down again at the man. In death he looked innocent, but they always did, drained of life. He was a killer and abuser and he'd deserved what he got.

The phone chimed as one of her other searches found something. She brought up the SubterLets app and saw the dead man's face looking back at her from an FSB record, Russian's Federal Security Bureau. A mug shot was written in Russian Cyrillic. She grabbed the file and dropped it into a translation app, and results came back rapidly.

Twelve percent battery.

His name was Ilhev Rostak, 37 years old, and he was,

apparently, a carpenter who lived in Yekaterinburg, Russia. He'd been in jail once in 2017 for a DUI and that was it. There was no mention of his prison tattoos, his presence in Poland or any Real Boy affiliation. According to the records SubterLets had turned up, he was still running his small carpentry business out of his home.

She cursed loud enough to startle a grouse out of the woods. So the Real Boys had falsified the records of the FSB? That was no easy feat. It was the kind of hack that left a trail, but not a trail she could track in amateur hour on her phone.

She stood and started walking, swiping through the phone to download an anonymized ride-hailing app. She input codes to a digital cryptocoin wallet she kept, then summoned a taxi. She had one lead right now, and Gabriel had said it himself; GOMA-49 wasn't far away. The van might still be there, and along with it some further clue to where the Real Boys were.

She saw Armitage's face again, just before she'd closed the van door. 'Go fast if you can, Zero,' she'd said. 'I don't feel good here.'

She'd been right. Zero wished she'd listened.

The phone chimed one final time as she closed in on the road.

'Translation received'. She tapped through; the search engine had transliterated and translated Rostak's tattoos. The writing across Rostak's belly was definitely Russian. 'бог против вор, вор против бога' meant 'God against everyone, everyone against God.'

It sent a shiver up Zero's spine. It was the motto of a man who'd given up on any kind of morality. Her ride was two minutes out. Her battery was down to ten percent. She broke into a run.

12

GOMA-49

The taxi was waiting for her, a little putty-colored sedan with a maker's badge she didn't recognize. She climbed in and the driver said something in Polish but Zero ignored it, watching the pine trees whip by on either side. Her heart pounded and her fists balled up in the pockets of Gabriel's big yellow jacket.

His wife's jacket, killed in a hit and run. An unbidden picture of his two daughters at the breakfast table came up, and she couldn't help feel the anger mounting. That should have been her and Hope. The Real Boys had stolen it from her.

In ten minutes she signaled the cab to stop on the road's verge, five minutes from GOMA-49. She stepped out of the cab into long grass. The driver barked something angrily but she ignored him and he ripped away.

She covered the remaining half-mile on foot through the pine forest, until she came to the edge of the tree line, where she kneeled to survey the grounds. The turn-off to GOMA-49 lay fifty yards ahead, blocked by a great heap of discarded industrial equipment: ruptured conveyor belts, an assortment of large rusted gears, at least two skeletal forklift trucks and half a mile's worth of crumpled pipe. Beyond it lay the parking lot, now slathered with weeds and spotted with burned-out vehicles, and beyond that reared the factory itself, five stories tall against the white summer sky, dressed in red brick and largely windowless.

The worn structure was still and silent by day, but Zero could almost see the flashing lights beaming through its many eyes and feel the ghost thump of its rave pulse carrying through her skin.

There were no obvious Real Boy sentries patrolling the grounds. There could be spy-cams anywhere, though, or men posted in the woods or the factory. Zero brought up Rostak's phone again, flicked to camera then downloaded and opened the same app she'd used the night before to scan the crowd.

In real-time it analyzed every pixel for signs of anything out of place, like human movement or the glint of light off a spy cam lens. Everything came back green. It didn't mean they weren't watching, though.

She tapped through to Bluetooth status. The spy cam network she'd placed herself last night, attached to corners in the club's walkway gantry, had a near-field radius of two hundred yards, boosted to five hundred by a relay. The batteries were long-life, good for twelve hours continuous recording with transmission, with an auto switch-off in the absence of movement. They should still be live.

The signal they produced was obscured within a standard radio frequency, but Zero tapped the exact frequency into the phone's finder and there it was. Her mouth went dry as she brought it up. The cams had local storage, and she spun back through the record all the way to the moment she grabbed Perp 35. It was subtle, clean and barely noticeable.

But had somebody followed her? It was hard to tell, but on watching from different angles she realized it was true.

Perp 35 had a sitter without realizing it. She even saw the moment he brought a phone to his ear, calling it in.

Girl Zero.

She tried to zoom in but the image was too grainy for detail. He left, and after that she spun forward, keeping one eye on her battery. Down to eight percent. The club kept raving until around 5 a.m., at which point the crowds thinned. The smoke stopped pumping, the lights died out and the clean-up crew moved in, stripping their equipment. By 6 a.m. they were all gone and the factory fell still as dawn light crept in. The cams shut off until 9 a.m., when a man in a deep hoody came in through a side entrance.

Around that time, Zero was unconscious in the bushes. This man patrolled the club with a device of some kind. Scanning for her spy-cams? He didn't seem to find them, though, and brought out a phone. He held a brief conversation in the center of the dance floor, surrounded by the anodizing vats and heaps of broken bottles and crumpled plastic cups, then at 9:14 he climbed up the stairs to the gantry himself.

Zero leaned into the screen, switching between cams to track him. He went to two spots along the walkway, near to two of the cameras she'd placed, and lingered at each for several minutes. Zero zoomed and tried different angles, but couldn't see anything definitive. One thing she could be sure of was that he hadn't taken anything down.

The answer seemed clear. The Real Boys had rigged GOMA-49 with interior cameras. Her detection app hadn't seen them, but that wasn't surprising. His device hadn't spotted her spy cams either.

At 9:29 he descended the walkway and left the factory. Shortly after that the cams died again.

Seven percent.

Zero rocked back on her heels, taking a deep breath. This was a thorough Real Boy operation. They'd rigged the factory before she came, and now they'd left the cameras in place. There was only one reason for that; they thought she might return. It was another trap, but one that Zero now knew about.

A plan began to form in her mind. The only thing better than evading a Real Boy trap was reversing it.

13

TRAP

Zero pulled the bills from the pocket of Gabriel's yellow jacket, along with the kitchen knife she'd palmed again on the way out. She slipped the bills into the dead man's wallet and stuck it into her rear jeans' pocket, then wrapped the knife's blade in leaves and tucked it into her front pocket.

Next she stepped up to the edge of the tree line and started working her way around toward the factory. The goal was to be seen, while looking like she was trying not be seen. The bright yellow jacket was a big help with that. At the last stretch she took a deep breath, ducked her head low and made a beeline directly for the factory.

She crossed the corner of the rubble-strewn lot in ten seconds and leaped at the factory's red-brick wall. One kick off the lock plate of a sealed double door sent her shooting upwards, a second off the door lintel propelled her sideways and up just enough to snatch the bottom rung of a rusted fire escape ladder, some fourteen feet high.

The ladder's rusted rungs were unable to pierce her hard palms, callused from the last seven years spent redoubling her grip strength through climbing, and in seconds she was at the top. She peered down through an empty window arch into the factory's church-like interior. Bands of light poured through the gloom of that vast, decrepit hall, spotted with heaps of shattered bricks, broken bottles and powdered cement.

Zero stepped through the window and onto the gantry from the night before. She knew that she would be within the range of their spy cams now, and could almost hear the Real Boys mobilizing. How many had they kept close, though? She was banking on it being a manageable number.

She swiftly vaulted the railing, slid down the pole to the factory floor then sprinted across the 'dance floor'. There were no open doorways, so she swiftly scaled the opposite interior wall up to the third floor then exited through another broken window. Outside, the thick canopy of the forest blocked her view, but she knew the van's approximate position, hidden several hundred yards away. If she knew the Real Boys, then they'd be staking it out. Hopefully, if they were as arrogant as every other Boy she'd met, they'd break formation and come directly for her, now they knew she was here.

She was counting on that, and immediately began 'bouldering' sideways, climbing horizontally along the factory's pocked brickwork. At a hundred yards' distance she stopped and descended into a tight scrum of pine saplings, bamboo shoots, Japanese knotweed and flowering rose bushes.

She was off-line. The Real Boys would be expecting her on a different vector. That was just the first part of her improvised trap, though. She took off the bright yellow jacket and bundled it up, then plunged into the forest. The undergrowth here was every bit as dense and grown up as she remembered from the night before, atop an uneven landscape of half-demolished brick walls and partly filled-in ditches.

Zero used the cover as if she'd known it all her life, using all four limbs to propel herself through gaps in tumbledown walls and between interweaving trees with a free-runner's abandon. Her heart pounded as she circled wider. The van had to be some hundred yards to her east when she heard the first whispered shout to the south; words in Polish or Russian or some other harsh Slavic language, though there was one English word she recognized.

'Zero.'

The intonation was off but she'd recognize her name anywhere. They'd taken the bait and peeled off the van, and now they had no idea where she was.

Time to give them one. Zero dropped immediately, and hung the hood of her bright jacket off a low column of stone. From a distance it should look like she was kneeling down. She brought up Rostak's phone and set a five-minute timer on her phone then dropped it into the jacket's pocket.

After that she slowed down, spiraling around tighter on the Real Boy's position. They continued speaking amongst themselves in Polish or Russian; maybe arguing about where she should be, perhaps even debating the wisdom of coming for her directly.

Soon she was directly behind them, thirty yards off and still couldn't see them through the dense vegetation.

Twenty.

At fifteen the alarm went off. It rang loud through the forest, disturbing a flight of birds and drawing curses from the Real Boys. They barked into bleeping radios and crashed through the undergrowth toward the phone.

Zero followed. At ten yards she got her first clear look at the broad backs of the two large men hunting her. They were dressed in tactical black and carrying large-bore dart rifles.

She closed the final yards in near-perfect silence, any sound covered by the percussive sound of their dart rifles discharged into a glimpse of yellow jacket. She surged up from a two-foot-deep brick channel behind the trailing Real

Boy, and her kitchen stiletto blade landed with textbook precision, entering the *foramen magnum* gap into the back of his skull, where the spinal nerve entered the brain. The blade thrust through soft tissue and gristle so forcefully that it made a sharp thunk on the inside of the Boy's skull, like the knock on a far-off door.

He dropped instantly, dead on the spot. His partner spun in time to see him fall, spraying darts in a panic, but not fast enough to see Zero as she dropped back into the channel. He shouted and fired blind into the forest until he exhausted his magazine, darts pattering harmlessly through the canopy, then Zero's blade met his ankles and slit both Achilles' tendons in one savage slice.

He toppled like a dumb log. His head hit the far side of the brick channel, his neck snapped and he was dead by the time he hit the ground.

Zero squatted over him. He had reload magazines on his belt and the dart rifle in his hands. She snatched an extra dart magazine and the rifle from his slack grip then plunged back into the forest, reloading as she went.

Her alarm was still ringing out in back. She dropped at a concealed spot overlooking the dead Boys and waited, rifle beaded on the direction of the van. In twenty seconds one man burst through the ferns directly ahead. Zero fired. Two shots took him in the chest, but he managed to get off a few return shots. By wild luck one took Zero in the shoulder.

She instantly plucked it out, just as he plucked both from his chest, but it was too late. Already she felt the effects, just as his right leg betrayed him and he went down. As if in sympathy, Zero dropped to one knee.

14

EYE FOR AN EYE

Somewhere her phone alarm cut out mid-chime. The battery had died, she figured, as she staggered through the forest. A second dose of knockout drugs so soon after the first was bad.

Very bad.

Already she felt her heart rate spiking to dangerous levels. The chemical load could kill her. Her heart could burst. Her system could simply shut down. There were many ways that-

The forest peeled back and the van appeared before her. She slumped against a tree as the scene around it overwhelmed her, clamped in the embrace of a tight clearing.

It was a wreck.

The van's sliding side door had been wrenched off and cast aside, with the interior guts of computer server racks ripped out and scattered around the tight clearing. Bright sprays of colorful wiring lay in mud churned by many feet, amidst a low rubble of smashed black plastic shards.

It looked like they'd stripped the hard drives. Her heart pounded manically. That was bad news. Combined with Armitage's security codes, they could have burrowed even deeper into her fortress. Not all the way, but deep enough to…

She fell forward and caught herself in the wreckage. Her hands came back bloodied from sharp plastic. There was no time. She scrabbled up into the shell of the van, where it was dark and stank of blood and baked dust. She ignored the sawn-off racks and dropped to the front, where she fumbled to slide a concealed panel aside. Her hand patted in the dark space beyond, then came back with a slim black case.

She had seconds left and barely the coordination to pop the clasps. Inside were two long, thick glass syringes nestled in shaped foam: one contained flumazenil, the other naloxone. Hidden away for emergencies, in large enough doses to resurrect a one-ton bull. She took a breath then stabbed the first into her forearm. It wasn't a good shot clean into a vein, but there was no way she could manage that coordination now.

She squeezed barely a quarter inch down then let up. Too much and she'd space out into unconsciousness then death. She pulled it out and went for the next, repeated the process, then fell to her back as the intravenous delivery brought on an instantaneous effect.

For a second her breathing stopped. Her pulse halted. She couldn't move and couldn't think, like she was frozen in time as the two sets of drugs battled over her nervous system, then there was a jolt like a car crash and she was instantly hyper-aware.

She jerked to her feet, feeling like her head was stuffed full of TNT. Too many chemicals, too much manipulation, and the blast was coming soon. She snatched up both syringes and surged from the van, with the thunderous memory of GOMA-49's bass speakers pounding in her ears, only to stumble sideways into a scene she hadn't seen earlier.

Armitage lay before her on the forest floor, naked, bloody

and spread-eagled with maybe a dozen long iron nails spiking from her body. Her fragile, bird-boned features had been smashed. Zero weaved in place, trying to comprehend, but there wasn't much to grasp.

Her operator was dead, killed in the worst way possible.

Not compromised, then. Not a sellout. Zero regretted ever considering that.

Either way, Armitage had known little. Whatever she had known, she would have spilled on the first threat of pain. She was strong, but she was also bad with suffering. It made her choice to work with Zero all the braver. It made her death another cross for Zero to bear.

That lit the fuse on Zero's anger. They'd killed Armitage like this not to gain more information. They'd killed her like this for fun.

The spark ran down and the TNT in her head exploded.

She sprinted and the forest crashed around her. The sound of engines roared from somewhere but she ignored it, racing until she was back at the one surviving Real Boy, lying catatonic where she'd left him, staring upwards. The engines grew louder as she thumped down to straddle his chest, pinning his arms by his sides.

He had tattoos peeking from the loose collar of his shirt. Zero reached down and ripped the fabric open, revealing a dagger through his collarbones, and skulls, and another large Madonna and Child.

Without any words she pushed the first syringe in through the pupil of his open right eye. It carried over an inch deep until the tip clunked against the sphenoid bone in back, where she discharged half the chemical load.

He didn't so much as twitch. She took the second syringe and pushed it through his left eye and squeezed the plunger.

It took perhaps thirty seconds for him to start screaming. It began as a whimper, breath sucking in hard as the antidote dose pushed back against the knockout drugs, then rose to a wail.

"Listen to me," Zero said, forcing speech through the slurry of drugs. "Answer my questions and I'll pull them out. Is that what you want?"

He tried to nod between gasping breaths. It was hard for Zero to focus.

"Use your words," she insisted.

"Da!" the man cried. "Yes, yes!"

"Good. First question for your right eye. Where is Hope?"

"Ya ne znayo!" he wailed in Russian. "Do not know! Ovi ne govoryat mne! They do not, uh, tell me!"

Zero took hold of the syringe and pushed it a little deeper, piercing the fragile sphenoid. "Where?"

"Do not know!!" he roared. "Ask other question, please!"

Zero blinked. She'd heard many men beg for their lives and believed him. "Who's hunting me, then?"

"Da, yes! Is, uh, osobyy, special! Pakhan Anatoly!"

"Pakhan Anatoly, who's that?"

"Is not name! Pakhan. Is title! Like, ah, captain? Please, now, take out!"

Zero frowned. As far as she knew, the Real Boys didn't have a formal leadership structure, at least not with titles. The 'best' amongst them simply rose up and took command. "Captain in what? The Russian army?"

The engines growled closer, merging into time with her racing pulse.

"Nyet," he moaned, face writhing as if he could push the syringes out with his cheeks. "Bratva."

Zero stared. That was a word she just about recognized. "You mean the Russian mafia? This Anatoly's a captain in the Russian mafia?"

"Da. Please, take out!"

"Bratva are working with the Real Boys?"

"Da, yes, take out!"

Zero's mind reeled. Suddenly Ilhev Rostak's Russian prison tattoos made sense. As far as she knew, the Russian mob were huge. Maybe they had the power to falsify FSB records. And this Anatoly was a part of both? The possibilities blurred like a poison gas. Had the Real Boys hired the Russian mob, or was this something worse?

Was it some kind of merger?

The slam of a car door carried through the forest like a rifle report, and she jerked back to the moment. She was out of time, and refocused on the man beneath her, begging her still.

"Where are they based?"

"Ya ne znayo, do not know, please take out!"

"Did you stop when Armitage begged?" she hissed, and didn't wait for an answer before depressing both syringes the whole way then plucking them out of his eyes. A promise was a promise, after all. He cried out and began to thrash, but there was nothing he could do now. The battling overdose would kill him within minutes.

Gunfire ripped through the foliage. Zero swiftly checked his pockets and came up with a phone; the same make and model she'd taken from Rostak. She stripped the battery and SIM card, tucked both into her pocket then stumbled up and ran, half-blinded by the chemical war waging in her head; over walls and ditches, weaving between trees. With every step her body flushed with hot and cold chills. The pulse in her throat slammed like a countdown clock. Her face felt like it was ballooning while her vision blurred and doubled.

Bratva.

Real Boys.

Soon the sound of gunfire fell into the background. Minutes and miles flew by in a flurry of bark and roots and leaves, until what felt like a lifetime later she reached a road that looked to her addled senses like a river. She dipped her toe against the blacktop then skated swiftly across. A vehicle screamed by, horn blaring. She searched the sky for some sense of direction but there were two suns overhead now, spiraling madly.

Then she was there.

A gray space lay before her, raked into perfect parallel lines. There was a small red gate and two bright pink scooters by the door, and -

She dropped to her knees. The world spun and she barely managed to bang on the window before she fell. His voice came from above. She tried to look up but only tipped herself sideways into the little red gate.

"Clara," came his voice again, "what happened to you? You're covered in blood. You need to-"

"Not my blood," she murmured.

"What? Not your blood?" Now he was on his knees beside her. "Then what is this? Really, you have to go to-"

"No hospital," she managed. "They'll kill me."

"They'll help you! Clara, this isn't-"

"Drug me," she hissed, head lolling, "kill me. Sorry. Please. Said you'd help."

A long moment passed, then she felt his arms in the hollows of her knees and behind her shoulders. His grip was strong and he scooped her up and carried her into the house then back down the stairs to the basement, where he laid her on the pull-out sofa bed she'd only left an hour or so ago. Her head hit the fabric and she was out like a light.

15

REST

When Zero surfaced next, he was there, sitting on the opposite sofa in the dark basement, lit by the orange glow of a camp lantern and turning a cellphone steadily in his hands.

Gabriel.

With his stubble and tartan jacket over a faded AC/DC t-shirt and baggy jeans, he seemed like a natural part of this place: the old, beaten mauve sofa, the tattered rugs, the floor-to-ceiling shelving stacked with the detritus of four lives, now reduced to three.

Zero thought of her own loss; sweet, shy Armitage, so afraid of other peoples' pain, now dead in the forest. She thought of Hope, and Bratva, and a man called Viktor Anatoly.

"You're awake," came Gabriel's soft voice.

Zero pushed herself up and opened her eyes. "What time is it?"

"10 p.m. You've slept through the whole day, Clara." He paused, like he was taking stock. "How do you feel?"

She tried to sit up straighter, but the movement set off

alarm bells of nausea and she gave up. Every muscle felt like it was hollowed out. "Sick."

He nodded, but didn't say anything further, just kept turning the cell phone in his hands and looking at her.

"You called the police?"

"Not yet."

"But you will?"

"We'll see."

Zero tried to put herself in his position. It wasn't a pretty picture. "You're angry at me."

He snorted. "Of course I'm angry. You're a liar."

"I didn't lie."

Now he laughed, but there was no humor in it. "You've lied three times. I've been sitting here for hours, counting them. Weighing them."

She blinked. Even the lantern's soft light hurt her eyes. "What lies?"

He raised his left hand and counted off one finger. "First, you said it wasn't your blood. But there was really a lot of blood, Clara. All over you. In your hair, on your clothes." He pointed. "But I couldn't see any injuries. So where did it come from?"

She opened her mouth, but thought better of lying again to cover for the lie. He nodded like this was all the answer he needed.

"Second, you have a man's wallet in your pocket, filled with zlotys and euros. You didn't have that when you left here this morning. I didn't give it to you either. So where did you get it?"

Zero's eyes narrowed. Rostak's wallet. It wasn't a lie, but she didn't object.

"Third, and worst of all," he went on, "I lied to my daughters for you. That's what I'm most angry about. I told them nothing happened today, when all day I've been sitting here waiting to see if you woke up or not. To see if I was a party to your overdose." He took a breath, turning the phone in his fingers still. "I couldn't let them see you like that. But now you're awake. So. Those are the three lies."

Zero grunted. There was no point debating about how only one of those was even her lie. She understood it wasn't easy to lie to people that you loved, although she'd spent most of her life lying to everyone.

"I'm sorry."

He shook his head. "Sorry's not enough, Clara. Is that even your real name?"

She grimaced slightly. "It's one of them."

"Give me one good reason I shouldn't call the police."

Zero couldn't think of any. "Because you don't want to. You haven't called them yet."

"I'm getting closer."

Somewhere in the rafters above, the central heating ticked on. Pipes began running with a low rushing sound.

"Can I get some water?" Zero asked. "Maybe something to eat?"

He stared at her, then sighed and stood up. He pointed over to the side. "The baseball bat's over there, if you want it." Then he leaned over the back of the sofa and came up with an old double-barrel shotgun. Zero's eyes widened slightly. As far as she knew, Poland had strict gun laws.

"I hunt," he said, by way of explanation. "We cull deer every year. I am a good shot." He gave her a pointed look then went to the stairs.

Zero lay still, thinking about the shotgun. About how he'd had it behind the sofa all that time, where he could reach it if he needed to, but it wouldn't alarm her upon waking. In an odd way, that was comforting.

But she had no time for comfort. She had to recover and get back on the hunt. She needed a phone. She knew nothing about Bratva. She'd never heard the name Viktor Anatoly. She had to-

Gabriel's footfalls came back down the steps. He set a plate and glass of milk down firmly on the ring-stained wooden coffee table between them; some kind of crusty pie with green vegetables, giving off fresh wisps of steam.

"This is leftover beef pie from tonight. My daughters liked it. I saved it for you."

The smell was intoxicating, driving thoughts of Bratva from her mind. A rich and meaty gravy oozed from beneath the crust. He'd heated it up for her. "Are your daughters asleep?"

"Yes. I told them fairy stories, as always. Also, lies. I don't like to lie to my daughters. I want this lie to be worth it."

There was the anger pushing through. The phone was still in his hand.

"I'll be gone by tomorrow morning."

"Not good enough, Clara."

She frowned. "So what do you want?"

"The truth."

"What truth?"

"Why you are here. Why there is blood. Why you have money. Why I should help you anymore?"

He stared. She stared back. "It's better if you don't know."

"Then I am calling the police," he said, and started to dial.

Zero waited for the bluff to end. The line rang then connected. A voice spoke on the other end in Polish.

"OK," Zero blurted.

Gabriel said something more in Polish, it sounded like an apology, then hung up and stared at her. She opened her mouth then closed it. There was no good lie to tell.

"The truth," he pressed. "Now."

She grunted, considering where to begin. She'd lied

already and it hadn't worked. Maybe some version of the truth was best.

"There's a powerful man who wants me, Gabriel. Last night he drugged me in GOMA-49. His men took me, but I wrecked their car and escaped." She took a breath. "Just this morning they tried again, and this time I fought them. That's where the blood came from."

He just stared at her. The phone remained in his hand. "Who is this man?"

"He's dangerous. He has contacts in the police. In hospitals. I'm not safe anywhere."

The moment stretched out. His gaze didn't waver, though his grip on the shotgun tightened. "It was a lot of blood, Clara. Did you kill someone?"

Zero met his gaze head on. "You don't want me to answer that question, Gabriel. Really."

His eyes bored into hers. A silence stretched between them. The pipes rumbled overhead then shut off as the house's automated systems went through their cyclical motions.

"Your scars," Gabriel said at last, his tone heavy. "They are from this man, yes? He's a criminal. A drug dealer."

Zero didn't say anything.

The phone stopped turning in his hands. Slowly, he set it down on the table without breaking eye contact.

"I know about drug dealers, Clara," he said. "Before my daughters came. Some were violent. Some caused scars like yours." He said nothing for maybe twenty seconds, just gazing at her, or perhaps past her. "I learned there are two types of addicts. Those who can see a life beyond their addiction, who want to escape, and those who can't." His gaze grew distant, like he was gazing into the past. "The first usually recover, Clara. They escape. They find purpose and move on with their lives. The second, however, do not." He took a slow breath. "Many of them die. Some died the same week I saw them. Some months or years later. Overdoses, sometimes. Sometimes, murder."

He stood up, shotgun crooked across his folded arms.

"I look at you, and I think I see the second type. It may not be drugs, but I know an addict when I see one, Clara, and addicts who cannot see beyond their addiction die." He pocketed the phone. "You are safe here tonight. But I want you out by the morning. Is this understood?"

She nodded. He looked at her a moment longer, then padded over to the stairs and headed up. She heard his progress through the creak of the boards above, walking across the kitchen to a point by the wall, where his weight settled and remained still.

Standing guard at the window.

She reached for the milk. Perhaps her hand felt steadier, but inside she felt like something had been lost, though she wasn't sure what.

16

LOOKING BEYOND

Gabriel's words echoed in Zero's mind as she ate and drank methodically.

She knew she was an addict. She already knew every Real Boy she killed bought her more tickets in a lottery she was one day bound to lose, but she couldn't quit. The stakes were too high.

Hope.

But for him to see that and throw it back at her? She didn't like it, so she pushed it aside. What mattered now was Viktor Anatoly.

Who was he? She had no idea, but he'd come the closest of any Real Boy to capturing her in years. He was a pakhan, or captain, in Bratva. He knew about Hope, and he wanted Zero alive.

She started listing her priorities out in her head, the same way she had as a child in her cell, plotting her parents' downfall for all those years.

First, she needed a new computing rig. That would begin to unlock the answers she needed: Viktor Anatoly, the Real Boys and their link to Bratva.

Second, she needed gear: weapons, comms, armor. All of

that should be available through the darknet, once she had a fully anonymized rig up and running.

Third, she needed to kill Anatoly and find Hope.

Flashes of Armitage's frail body came back to her: her kind, shattered face; her bird-like arms staked into the ground. It brought the rage right back to the surface, but watery and sickened. She'd done nothing to save her. She'd only-

"Did you like the pie?"

Zero blinked back to the moment. Two little girls were standing over her, looking down curiously. It took her a long moment to recognize they were Gabriel's daughters, dressed in their pajamas.

"Where's your father?" she countered.

"Papa is in the garden," the elder girl answered in slow and thoughtful English. She had light red hair and freckled cheeks. Perhaps she was eight years old, and her pale blue pajamas were spotted with bright strawberries. "He is walking with his gun."

Zero grunted. So Gabriel was out on patrol. "He told you not to come down here, right?"

The girl's face screwed up. Her little sister, maybe six, pulled on her shirt and she looked down. They spoke in Polish briefly.

"She says, it's our house. We can come in our basement if we want to."

Zero couldn't argue with that. "Shouldn't you be in bed?"

"I wanted to be, but Hanna kept biting my toes."

Zero frowned and nodded at the smaller girl. "She's Hanna?"

The little sister hung her head. "Yes. I was hungry."

Zero frowned. "You're joking."

"It's not a joke," the elder sister said. "She bites very hard. Papa saved the extra pie for you, so she's hungry."

Zero couldn't tell if they were teasing or not. "That's how you knew I was down here? Not enough pie?"

The two looked at each other again and spoke in low Polish, then the elder turned back to her.

"Yes. Pie. Also all the shouting you both did. But why are you here? Again? Is it because you like my Papa?"

Zero snorted. "No. I mean, well, yes, he seems a nice man. But no, it's not why I'm here."

"It's OK," said the little one generously. Hanna. "We can share him."

"He is lonely," said the elder sister. "He misses Mama."

"I miss Mama."

Zero didn't know what to say to that.

"You look like Mama, a little. Here's a deal. If you come here one more time, you have to kiss Papa."

Zero frowned. "Where did you get that idea from?"

"It's a rule!" Hanna hooted, suddenly cheerful and tugging on her sister's shirt again. "Zuzanna told me."

"And you're Zuzanna?"

"Of course I am," the elder girl answered carefully. "Hanna is six. She doesn't know anything about boys."

Zero found herself smiling despite herself. "Good point. But I don't think your father and I are going to-"

"I heard about it at school," Zuzanna interrupted. "For the first time, you eat together. You did that. It's called a date. For the second time, you hold hands. I think you did, because he carried you down here. For three times, you kiss."

Hanna hugged herself tightly. "Kiss! He's the prince. You're the princess." Her head then tilted slightly to the side. "We can play school, if you like?"

Zero couldn't help but laugh. She'd spent very little time around children. She protected them, she hunted the men who hunted them, but she didn't spend time with them. "I don't think that's a good idea. What time is it?"

"Almost time for school," said Hanna brightly.

"You mean morning?"

"It's nearly midnight," Zuzanna whispered. "It's late."

"It's probably better if we all just go to bed, don't you think?"

"I can't," Hanna said. "Not without school." She crossed her arms, sucked in a big breath and held it.

Zero turned to Zuzanna.

"She does this. She's very good at it."

They both watched the little girl. Her face began to turn red.

"Sometimes she passes out," Zuzanna offered.

"Stop it," Zero said, but Hanna didn't. "Tell her to stop it."

"She doesn't listen to me. But if she passes out, I'll have to get Papa, and we'll all be in trouble then, and-"

"OK fine," Zero said, noting a blue tint creeping across Hanna's chubby little freckled face. "We'll play 'school' for five minutes."

"Ten minutes," Zuzanna countered.

"Eight," Zero bargained. "And I'm thirsty, so you get me some water too."

"Nine!"

"Now it's seven minutes."

"OK, eight! But can it be a long eight, please?"

Zero couldn't take her eyes off Hanna. The little girl's eyes were bugging out. "There's no such thing as a long eight minutes. Eight minutes is eight minutes."

"But a looong eight minutes?"

"OK, yes! Then you have to go to bed. Now tell her to breathe!"

Zuzanna nodded solemnly. "I'll get the blackboard."

Hanna finally breathed out then sucked in a big gasp of air, after which she smiled and patted Zero's hand. "That was easy," she said. "I like you."

Zero didn't really understand everything that followed. It took over eight minutes to get everything situated, which included paper and pens for everyone, a chalkboard and chalk, two sheets of rubbery bubble push poppers for rewards, and a 'naughty hat' for punishment.

Zero drank her fresh glass of lukewarm water and played along. It didn't involve much. Zuzanna ran the class firmly, and had her students take down lines, some of which were simple math calculations. Zero completed the tasks, and helped Hanna, and then was rewarded with one of the bubble push poppers.

"Well done, you're the head girl!" Hanna said.

"What's your name?" Zuzanna asked, drawing a large golden chalice on her piece of paper. "I need it for the trophy."

"Clara," she said. "Really, it's bedtime now, isn't it?"

Zuzanna took her little sister's hand and went to turn, but Hanna didn't budge; instead she looked up at her sister with big, winsome eyes. Zuzanna looked down then sighed.

'What is it?" Zero asked.

"She wants to sleep here with you."

"No."

"Upstairs is so cold. Mama used to sleep here sometimes, too. Can we? We'll be quiet. You won't feel a thing."

"Absolutely not."

Hanna was already climbing up onto the sofa. Zero tried to marshal her strength to shove the child off, but she was weak and Hanna just rolled Zero's arm over her like a blanket, then snuggled in like a hot little glow bug and closed her eyes.

"Goodnight moon."

Zero looked at Zuzanna. "I don't agree to this."

Zuzanna shrugged. "It's OK," she said, then jumped onto

the sofa, dived for the crack between Zero's back and the cushions and sank in.

Now Zero was sandwiched in position; no easy way to move without squishing a child on either side, and barely the strength to do it. It wasn't at all how she'd seen this day closing out.

"Goodnight," Zuzanna's warm breath whispered in her ear.

"Goodnight," Zero answered, then closed her eyes, unable to banish the one thought she didn't want to revisit.

Maybe this was what it had felt like all those years ago, curled up with Hope in the fallout shelter of their Idaho farm.

17

UPON A STAR

Mona was back under the farmhouse, back in her old cell surrounded by all her Pinocchio friends, back when it was all just an exciting new adventure.

The first night in the dungeon. The first night to sleep apart from her little sister, and now Hope was singing.

Her sweet young voice floated through the cell like a warm spring breeze, but there were sad notes in the melody, and Mona had to find out why. She got up and went to the metal grille door. It opened easily. She went back along the concrete passageway that she'd helped her father dig with his backhoe, through the hall with its padded leather walls and up through the trapdoor into the living room.

It was so dark, and moonlight lit the floor in silver. From the fields nearby the pigs grunted and snuffled, but above that was Hope's sad little voice, singing the song they'd decided was theirs: When you wish upon a star.

It was coming from upstairs.

Mona started up. The old wooden steps creaked and she was afraid her parents would wake up. Their door lay to the side, slightly ajar. She thought she could hear her father snoring.

She reached the landing and padded softly down the hall, where the song only grew louder. It seemed impossible her father hadn't heard. She had to get there and hold Hope until she quietened a little. Maybe she didn't understand that the adventure was only for one night. That it was supposed to be fun. It wasn't worth making their father angry over…

She rounded the corner. Ahead the door to Hope's room was closed, and she laid her fingers on the round knob, turned it so quietly until the lock clicked.

The singing stopped.

The door swung open and Mona stepped through into an empty room. There was no bed, no desk, no wardrobe, and no Hope.

The room was completely empty.

Zero's eyes opened.

It was light in the basement, and Gabriel was standing before her. From the pockets of cool at her front and back, she knew the girls were gone. Had their father seen them?

"It's time to go, Clara," he said. His eyes looked red and tired. Perhaps he'd really patrolled all night. "Can you walk?"

She pushed her hands beneath her, and her arms responded. The hollowed-out feeling in her muscles was still there, but much less than before, like a faint watermark on paper. Her strength was coming back.

"I'll be fine," she said, as the trails of the nightmare dissipated. She'd had some version of it ever since she was seven years old, and it was worn and familiar. "Thank you for letting me stay."

"Breakfast's on the table. You can use the shower, whatever you like. The bus comes every twenty minutes on the main road. I think you can see yourself out."

She nodded. He looked at her for a moment longer, like

there was something more that he wanted to say, but he didn't say it. Maybe something about addicts, Zero guessed. She knew hers was a hopeless case.

"Where's my phone?" she asked.

"On the table. I charged it for you, but the SIM's out. Don't put it in until you're far away from here. Is that understood?" She nodded. "Then goodbye, Clara."

He turned and left the basement. She heard his footsteps cross the kitchen then the thump as the outer door closed. He was giving her privacy, which was kind. He hadn't had to do any of this.

She rose unsteadily to her feet. Her legs trembled but held, and she could feel the hangover of the drugs in her system still, but the effect was fading. A hot shower helped. Fresh clothes were left on the sofa: another pair of loose blue jeans with a cool checked shirt. The fit was good, again. Up the steps, she found a wonderful breakfast laid out on the table. It didn't look Polish in the slightest. Rather, there were waffles, crispy back bacon, maple syrup in a jug, glistening strawberries and blueberries, and a steaming copper cafetiere of coffee, alongside a smaller jug of cream.

Zero felt touched. He hadn't had to do this.

The clock over the cupboards said 10 a.m. He'd let her sleep in again. The girls must be off to school, but they'd left something for her on the only placemat that had been set, alongside her stolen cellphone and wallet stuffed with bills. It was a crayon drawing, scribbled hastily, of what was probably Zero standing with two little girls either side of her.

She picked it up. Maybe they were throwing a frisbee to each other? Or was that the sun? She couldn't tell.

NICE TO MET YU, ran the text underneath it in big untidy letters.

Zero crumpled it up and tossed it in the trash. Next she folded two rashers of bacon into a waffle with maple syrup poured on top, glugged down a fast shot of coffee mounded with four spoons of sugar and a generous dollop of thick cream, popped a strawberry in her mouth, retrieved her phone and wallet and strode out of the kitchen.

In her wake, the cafetiere steamed. In the trash can the drawing uncrinkled slightly. Vapor rose off the bacon.

In a moment the door opened again, and Zero stood at the doorway, seemingly uncertain. Her eyes flickered, then she strode to the trash and plucked out the drawing. It smoothed out nicely, and she folded it neatly into her pocket. She also went for a second pass at the coffee, chomped all the berries in half a minute, polished off the waffles and bacon with a generous helping of maple syrup, then stood to survey the empty table.

This was what she might have had as a child. This was what she should have had. The drawing from the girls burned a hole in her pocket, like an unanswered song in the night. She cast around, found a sketchpad and a single red biro pen, and drew a quick sketch.

She'd rarely drawn before. Her father hadn't given her pencils or paper in her cell, but she'd spent years tracing the shapes of the figures on her walls. Now she sketched out a smiling Jiminy Cricket and wrote 'Nice to meet you too' underneath it.

Then she left, and this time didn't come back.

18

KRAKOW

Outside it was a bright and sunny day. The sky was blue and the strong sunlight filtering through the forest canopy threatened to bring on a headache. Zero kept her head down, trying not to think about how Armitage had looked nailed to the forest floor. She paced alongside the main road under cover of trees, in case any Real Boys were on patrol, then waited near the bus stop until one came. She rode it for twenty minutes into central Krakow, where the air thickened with age and culture.

She got off at the Main Market Square, an expansive stone-flagged space encircled by four-story pastel-painted townhouses. There was a tall red-brick clock tower to her left, a tiny, beautiful domed church to her right, while ahead lay a long, town-hall-looking structures replete with Gothic sandstone arches. Crowds of tourists passed her by, licking ice creams and holding out their phones on selfie sticks. Little children pattered on, parents fussed, young lovers swung their held hands as they promenaded from coffee shop to museum to church and back. The air was rich with the sweet, buttery scent of donuts frying in a one-man cart.

It was a different world. Zero didn't belong, and swiftly snapped her new stolen cell phone together.

For a few brief seconds they'd be able to track it, but in the crowd it wouldn't matter. She used those seconds to redownload the Tor browser and SudVPN. Both were up and running within a minute or two.

She walked fast from the square, thumbs flying over her cell phone screen as she ran Iota searches on 'Bratva', the 'Real Boys' and 'Poland'.

Wikipedia came up first, giving her a decent overview of Bratva. The name itself meant 'brotherhood', and encompassed over a quarter million criminals spread across the world, from Moscow to New York, Cape Town and Sydney, but focused primarily in Russia and Eastern Europe. They dealt in drugs, human trafficking, murder, robbery, smuggling, and just about anything you could imagine.

She scrolled on through the search results. There were plenty of articles about Bratva's immense drug empire; a vast logistical enterprise that martialed and connected producers, manufacturers and distributors around the globe. One article dived into the example of opioids: production began via sprawling poppy farms in the 'Golden Triangle' of Burma, Thailand and Laos along with Afghanistan and Iraq; manufacturing took place in equally vast factories in a spreading halo of low-wage, low-oversight countries throughout Southeast Asia, Russia and the Middle East; while distribution, or 'trafficking', spread around the world, with one major market being the USA.

Zero skipped ahead. Another article talked about the 'hydra-headed' nature of the Bratva infrastructure; every time Interpol, working in concert with local forces, brought down a major node in their infrastructure chain, others spun up immediately to replace it. It then took months if not years to hunt down this new farm, factory or trafficking node, during which time Bratva raked in billions and set up their next set of replacements. They had it down to a highly orchestrated checklist, like a corporate franchise model operating on 'Just In Time' principles, allowing them to swiftly plug any holes in their distribution chain.

A car honked nearby and she looked up; there was a gorgeous Baroque church beside her, and ahead lay a long and narrow swathe of wooded parkland. Cars streamed by, honking seemingly at random.

Zero crossed the street like a New Yorker, holding out her hand to halt traffic, then turned left underneath the cover of trees. If Anatoly had managed to track her phone to this area, he could have eyes on her from above already. Time spent under the cover of a foliage canopy would help obscure her passage.

People walked dogs. Joggers jogged. Life seemed so different here. A sign in English gave the place a name: Planty Park.

Zero dived back into her search, though this time she changed the Iota search settings; requesting only results that included both Bratva and Real Boys, leaving out Poland for now. Iota came back with an instant response:

'Your search did not match any documents.'

She grunted. It made sense, though it was disappointing. The Real Boys were a secret new evolution of the Pinocchios, after all, and unlike their prior incarnation did everything possible to keep their name off the open web, likely employing digital scrubbers. Zero tried again, this time using 'Bratva' paired with 'Pinocchios' and/or 'Blue Fairy'.

Now the search results populated. She scanned the listings, which included a CIA World Book reference, several government white papers on crime and terrorism prevention as well as a range of blogs and conspiracy theory sites, but quickly realized there was nothing substantive. As far as she could see, the only times Bratva was linked to the Pinocchios or Blue Fairy was when they were being compared, usually to draw a contrast. She scoured the example snippets:

"... the Pinocchios terror organization, unlike a criminal cartel such as the Russian Bratva, is driven not by the money motive but by an ideology. This can be seen..."

"The primary Blue Fairy tactics of digital terror were designed to effect a mass shift in governmental policy. To compare this to the tactics of an Organized Crime Gang such as Bratva or La eMe would be a mistake, as..."

Zero kept scrolling and walking. It wasn't until she hit the fifth page of search results that she found an old article on the Gazeta Wyborcza newspaper linking the two in a meaningful way. It was a report about an anonymous whistle-blower who was widely believed to have once been a high-level Bratva captain. Three years ago he'd testified against Bratva in a closed-door deposition which included mention of the Pinocchios, then been shifted into witness protection.

Zero stopped in her tracks.

What was the connection?

"Hey!" someone called behind her, and there was a crunch of wheels followed by a tall young guy with floppy hair whizzing by on roller blades; shirtless, tanned, wearing shorts. He spun and skated back right at Zero, only stopping inches apart. Elevated as he was on the blades, her eyes came up to about his mid-chest area.

He shouted something at her in Polish, which she ignored, so he swiftly shifted to English, growing red-faced as he leaned in closer.

"Stupid Yankee bitch, watch where you're going or go back to-"

He stopped talking when his feet abruptly kicked out behind him. It was a stupid thing to do, starting a fight with wheels on your feet. All Zero had to do was deliver a short, firm push to his feet.

He yelped and fell, bound for a headfirst bellyflop to the blacktop. Luckily for him Zero had already taken hold of his floppy hair, and used it to slightly slow his fall. His chest still contacted the ground with a lung-busting thwack, but she was able to lay his head gently down.

"You should watch where you're going," she said in a concerned tone. The guy batted at her hand but she'd already withdrawn it. He pushed himself to his knees. There were raw scrapes now on his bare chest, palms and knees.

"And wear a shirt when you're in public," she added.

His face reddened and he fought to his feet, but now the wheels slid awkwardly underneath him. He opened his mouth and started shouting again, more 'bitch' and other curse words while his hands flapped closer to her face, so Zero just gave one of his feet another push.

This time it sent him spinning. She caught him again by the hair, a balletic grab, and dragged him into another tumble to the ground. This time he came down hard on his back, grazing it to match the front. Again she guided his head down, but let it drop the last inch or two with a smack to the blacktop. She was left with a few generous tufts of his hair in her fist.

"Stay down, dumbass," she said, then blew his hair in his face and walked on.

He did. It put a spring in her step. After a hundred yards she exited the park walk to the right, already dialing the number for the Gazeta Wyborcza.

19

GAZETA WYBORCZA

"Gazeta Wyborcza," came a harried-sounding female voice.

"Yes, I'm looking to contact one of your journalists, I think I may have something for them."

A second passed. "Yes, who would you like to speak with?"

"That's just it, their name isn't listed on the article. It's about Bratva and a group called the Real Boys."

A few more seconds passed. "I'm afraid we're not interested. Please don't call again."

The call ended. That was curious.

Zero found herself in front of a small, cool-looking indie coffee shop. It had a succulent wall of small leafy plants growing up the front, with gaps only for the door and large windows. There wasn't even a sign.

Zero stepped in and ordered a 'handcrafted' vanilla latte with all the cream, syrup, chocolate dusting and toppings they could manage. She needed sugar to think, and this was the closest they had to a milkshake.

She sat down outside with her phone up, sipping the latte in the sun.

The Iota search engine said that Gazeta Wyborcza was the largest newspaper in Poland by circulation. They'd clearly published that article, and were equally clearly not interested in writing any more.

Bratva threats? Real Boys threats, maybe? Anything was possible. Which raised the question, why hadn't they taken down the original article?

She opened the article again, then tapped on the URL bar. It brought a dropdown menu, on which she selected 'View Source Code.' The screen altered, becoming a page full of multicolored code. Some of it was html, come CSS and some JavaScript, reflecting a backend programing language that was probably a combination of C, C++, Python, Java, Node and Go.

Zero could read and write in all of those. She scanned it, swiftly spotting fields where the author name should be. It had been erased, however. There was evidence they'd deleted the article itself numerous times, but then reinstated it. She scrolled further and found the answer to that puzzle in a series of date-coded programmer notes.

The entries were in Polish but the tags were clear, and it was a simple matter to grab the text and run it through a translation program:

Reinstated by court order.

That told an interesting story. Most likely the article had drawn Bratva threats and the Gazeta had taken it down. But a court order had been filed forcing them to put it back up. It seemed that process had happened several times.

Interesting.

Zero sipped her hot, sweet latte. She thought about how Armitage had looked, nailed to the ground beside GOMA-49. It set her body into a low-burn rage, fueling her on, and easily explained why the Gazeta would have pulled the article down. But the scrubbers hadn't been thorough. They hadn't followed up, at least not yet.

Zero downloaded the Venom Decompiler app, one of a suite of publicly available hacking tools, and set it loose on the Gazeta's page.

Almost all websites were protected by a ranged of locked software doors. Hacking just meant uncovering those doors and getting through them using a suite of 'cracking' programs and techniques, just like any home-invader came prepared with a pry bar, lockpicks and ladder.

There were countless open-source cracking programs available for download: some designed to seek out weaknesses in code or physical architecture, some seeking out stray passwords and logons floating for sale around the darknet, some capable of brute-force guessing passwords, and some designed to 'phish' negligent employees for their data.

The Venom Decompiler was one such tool; not advanced or cutting-edge, but solid, reliable and untraceable. Many hackers wrote their own master programs, combining various such tools into automated decision-tree structures. Advanced hackers incorporated narrow-field AI programs, or simple Artificial Intelligence, into these decision trees, crafting algorithms that had a narrow form of 'intelligence'. The best of these algorithms were capable of hacking at the speed of light, while also learning from their mistakes and successes.

Zero kept an established stable of such algorithms that she called her 'dogs'. They'd been 'bred' for years via accelerated machine learning. Knowing which one to send out on any given hunt was half the skill of a hacker.

But she didn't have her dogs now. They'd all been left behind in the van's servers, now currently in the hands of Viktor Anatoly. It meant he knew how she worked, how she thought, and how she hacked.

So she was doing this one solo, from scratch.

While the phone churned its little digital brain against the Gazeta, Zero polished off her latte and watched cars pass by on the narrow street outside. This was the old world, she figured. So different from America, where the oldest buildings dated back a hundred, maybe two hundred years. She'd been to Japan recently, and it had been the same; everything sleek, modern and shiny.

Not Krakow. Even the cobbles underfoot looked like they'd been laid half a millennium ago. Some of the wooden buildings leaned out over the street, dating back to an era long before prefab timber frames and plasterboard, back when everything was built as bespoke as her hand-crafted latte.

The phone chimed. She brought it back up. Half her battery had drained, but Venom had done its job. The Gazeta had some basic security locks; she'd need more than a phone to crack them, but fortunately that wasn't necessary. She didn't need to get into the system and make changes.

All she needed was access to the 'Changes' track concealed in the programming language. They'd clearly deleted the name of the author in response to the Bratva threat, but had they fully erased it from the underlying code? Most content management systems, like those used by a blog or a newspaper, kept a record of every alteration unless it was manually deleted.

It took a few minutes of scanning for Zero to find out. The answer was no. The journalist's name was right there. Maja Kominski. It even had her email address attached.

The Real Boy scrubbers had let this data point slip through their net. Zero stood up. She was going to make them pay for it.

20

MAJA KOMINSKI

Zero re-downloaded the ride-hailing app and summoned a taxi. One came in minutes, a burgundy Kia Forte whizzing along the slim street. Zero dropped in, ignored all attempts by the driver to make conversation, and after a ten-minute westward run was delivered to the offices of the Gazeta Wyborcza in Cystersów district.

Cystersów turned out to be a cool, young area packed with start-up tech companies and coffee houses, and the Gazeta Wyborcza office fit right in; a four-story red box split almost into vertical thirds by a three-story glass-filled arch in the center. The arch was framed with shiny sprung steel supports, making for a fresh industrial look, and revealed a spacious lobby as well as multiple mezzanine floors within.

Zero puffed the collars on her shirt and strode in like she belonged. The lobby was tall and wide but not deep, with an excellent view of the many floors within, where journalists worked at pine desks like stacked layers in a wedding cake. The floor was tiled in slashes of bright colors; red, yellow, blue and black. A single young man stood at what looked to be the reception desk. Improbably, he wore a green beret.

"I need to speak to Maja Kominski," Zero said.

He gave her an interested look. "Is she expecting you, Ms…?"

She didn't supply a name. "No. I've got something to tell her about the missing girls. Poland's dungeon girls? There's a whole level of lewd criminality nobody's even imagined yet."

The young man's eyes widened slightly. Zero knew the story was still front-page news; it was lurid, outrage-inducing and on the minds of all Poles thanks to Perp 35's perversions.

"Could I ask your name, and how you came by this information?" the young man asked, picking up a pen.

"No. I'll talk to Kominski only. But this won't wait. I can always go to Fakt or the Super Express. Either way, this news is coming out."

That lit a fire under him. "I'll contact her right now."

He picked up his phone and started talking in Polish. Zero looked around, trying to spot Kominski on the layers. After a few seconds a woman on the third floor hopped to her feet and hot-tailed it down the stairs.

"She's coming now," the receptionist said, uselessly. Zero was already striding over to the security gate to meet the journalist. Kominski soon appeared, straightening her vibrant red locks. She was maybe Zero's age, with high cheekbones, threaded eyebrows that were barely there and an intense look in her pale blue eyes. She was wearing a snug long-sleeved black blouse over a matching pencil skirt, and walked with a practiced, elegant gait.

"I'm Maja Kominski," she said in perfect English, holding out a hand to shake. "I understand you'll only speak to me?"

"Let's sit," Zero said, ignoring the hand and pointing to a row of Lego-looking bright plastic benches and coffee tables in the window. They were coated with squares of colorful notepaper, adding to the rainbow jumble.

"All right."

They sat. Zero took a moment. Sitting Kominski down might give her a few seconds more of her attention.

"In your own time," the journalist said, though she clearly didn't mean it.

Zero took a breath. "Have you heard of the Pinocchios, Maja?"

That took her aback. She froze for a second, then continued like Zero had said nothing. "I was told you want to talk about the missing girls?"

"Perhaps you've heard of a woman named Mona Gebhart? They call her 'Girl Zero'."

Kominski's ghost eyebrows pushed closer together. There was recognition there, as well as distaste. "What is this? I thought-"

"You've heard the name. I know, because you wrote that article about ties between the Pinocchios and Bratva."

Kominski stood up sharply, like the seat had scalded her. "I think you need to leave."

"I'm Mona Gebhart," Zero pressed. "It's me. Girl Zero, in the flesh. I can show you my scars, if you like."

Kominski stared. Zero could imagine the thought process in her head, trying to figure out what on earth was going on. She didn't walk away, though. "What do you want? And why did you say this is about the missing girls, when it's clearly not?"

"It is. It's all linked. And I need information, Maja. First up, a freebie. There'll be no more missing girls. The man who was killing them is dead."

"And how would you know that?"

Zero said nothing, just let her firm gaze answer for her.

"I'm leaving now."

"He's dead, Maja," Zero said. "I found him in GOMA-49, an illicit club south of Krakow, based in an abandoned rubber factory."

"You found him in a club," Kominski repeated, clearly disbelieving. "What does that mean?"

"It means he's dead; that's what matters. Now I'm hunting the man behind him. He's a top-tier Pinocchio, or Real Boy. In turn, he's hunting me, and he's not alone. Like you wrote in the article, it seems the Real Boys are working together with Bratva now. That's something that should terrify us all. If you could just-"

"That whole article was erased," Kominski interrupted. "My name is nowhere near it. As for dead men in factories, I can't even get started. How did you tie it to me?"

Zero shrugged. "I'm a hacker. I learned from my father. All I want is a name, and I've got plenty to trade."

"What?"

"There are more dead bodies in the woods south of Krakow, Maja. They might have cleaned some of them up, but at least one remains. His name is Ilhev Rostak and he's thoroughbred Russian Bratva."

Kominski stiffened. "Dead gangsters is hardly news. Not news I want to be involved in."

"In the coming days there's going to be a lot more of them. Bratva, the Real Boys, the missing girls, it's all connected. It's the story of the century, and if I break it open I'll give you an exclusive."

"And if I don't want it?"

Zero smiled. "You do. I can see it in you. You wrote that article in the first place. Your interviewee was ex-Bratva, a boss level pakhan. This is bigger. This is clickbait money and Pulitzer fodder at the same time."

A long moment passed. Kominski shifted her weight from foot to foot, then slowly sat back down.

"So you're really Mona Gebhart."

"I go by Clara Baxter now. The old name has a lot of weight."

"Also Girl Zero? I thought she was an urban myth."

Zero spread her arms. "Here I am, in the flesh."

Kominski leaned in, lowering her voice. "And you'll give me an interview."

"Out of the question."

"I need it."

"You're not getting it."

"If anything you're saying is true, this is extremely dangerous. You would know that, if you really are 'Girl Zero'. If I push for this, it needs to be rock-solid. Enough to initiate mass police action. A Pulitzer's no good to me if I'm dead."

Zero couldn't argue with that. "I'll go on background. I'll wrap it all up in a bow for you. You just need to write it up."

Kominski leaned back. Perhaps playing it cool. Perhaps genuinely cooling off.

"Maja, these people killed my operator. They tortured her to death in the forest with a hammer and nails. I know the man who did it. I just need to find him."

"You said he's dead."

"Not the same man. That one was a two-bit player at best, and he is dead. This one's worse. I could tell you his name, but it won't mean anything without a location."

Kominski snorted. "And you think I know where he is?"

"Of course not. But your contact might. In the whole Internet, he's the only one tying Bratva to the Pinocchios. I need to know what he knows."

Kominski looked around, as if checking to see whether anyone was watching her, then refocused on Zero. "That's privileged. He's a whistleblower. Bratva will kill him if they find him. They've made threats against me twice. I can't risk his life."

Zero looked around too. Nobody was near. It felt strange to talk about subjects like this in a sunlit, brightly colored lobby. She lowered her voice. "If he can help me, I'll end the threat. Including the hammer and nails guy, I've killed eight in the last twenty-four hours. I've killed more before, and I'm going to kill a lot more in the future, including the man behind it all. It's in everyone's interests that I talk to your source. It's in yours."

A sheen seemed to come down over the journalist's eyes. "You killed eight people?"

"It's what I do," Zero said. "Now, I need your contact's name."

Kominski shifted. It was a massive breach of journalistic ethics, but Zero could feel her bending. After maybe thirty seconds, she plucked a square of colored paper off the table and scribbled something on it. She folded it, then paused.

"How do I contact you?"

"You don't. When it's over, you'll know, and I'll reach out to you."

Kominski hesitated, then dropped the paper onto the bench and stood. "I didn't give this to you."

"Of course."

They eyed each other a moment more, then she turned and started away.

"Don't run a search for them on the Internet," Zero called after her. "They're probably looking for that."

Kominski's gait wobbled slightly, but she didn't turn or say anything, and passed smoothly through the security gate without looking back.

Zero picked up the slip of folded paper and walked out.

21

JOAS LEVI

The whistleblower's name was Joas Levi. That was his old name, prior to witness relocation. A quick search on Iota told Zero he'd been a Russian telecoms oligarch who'd helped Bratva build out their digital infrastructure in Poland, moving their black-market operations further into the darknet. At a point three years ago, he simply disappeared.

There was no Internet trail after that, but the intel from Maja Kominski gave Zero everything she needed.

Levi's new name was Jakub Wozniak. Improbably, he'd taken the funds he'd managed to extract from his Bratva accounts and used them to found an art academy in the vicinity of the old Auschwitz concentration camp, now known as the Auschwitz II-Birkenau State Museum. It was called 'Wszyscy Razem', which translated as 'Everyone Together.'

Zero was reminded of the tattoo on Rostak's belly: 'God against everyone, everyone against God.' Levi's academy was clearly his response to that.

She checked the academy's website. It was open every day, with a busy schedule of art and reflective tours conducted through the museum. The next tour began at noon, led by Levi himself. His picture was included, but he must have had substantial cosmetic surgery done, as he looked nothing like the man he'd once been.

It was just past 11 a.m. Zero brought up a map; Auschwitz was around fifty miles away to the east. If she set out now, maybe she could meet the tour at the halfway point. She hailed a cab and it pulled over within four minutes. A Toyota Prius. She grunted at the driver, an old guy who grunted back, then settled into the rear seat.

The cab pulled away.

Zero sat silently, watching out of the window as thoughts raced through her mind: Armitage, Gabriel, Anatoly and now Levi. She'd fought for so long to get a lead on Hope, and it felt strange to finally have one, like the lull before a storm. The world seemed unusually still around her, cocooned by the Prius' quiet hum. Even highway 79 around Krakow was quiet and serene, with few cars out on the road on a mid-week morning.

Soon Krakow paled into the rearview mirror. On all sides there was green beneath a hazy blue sky; trees, grass, occasional hills topped with white-walled chateaus with terracotta roof tiles.

She'd never been to Auschwitz. Of course she knew about it; a complex of vast concentration camps where the Nazis had systematically wiped out over a million Jews, Poles, Romanians and others. She'd never been to school, but she'd learned about it from the books her father provided, giving her a fictionalized sense of what other kids were doing at the same time, somewhere out there in the world.

She just hadn't been part of it.

Nothing much had changed since then.

She had her parkour group, and her climbing group, and she'd trained intensively for six years in Paranza Corta, the

Italian fighting art focused on the use of stiletto and throwing blades, but it wasn't the same. She'd learned to fake small talk and social niceties the same way she'd learned so many everyday skills, like driving, cooking and ordering food in a restaurant; by studying WeStream videos and practicing, practicing, practicing until she had it down.

But it wasn't the same.

She had no commonalities and no shared life experiences with most people. All the stories she shared were made up. Nobody wanted to know the truth about her past, and she didn't want to share it. It wasn't a fun coffee shop story, or something to trot out on a second date.

Her real skill had always been the ability to focus with an intensity none could match. That same intensity had kept her sane through nine years underground in her father's cell, where all she'd thought about every day for years was increasing the strength of her grip.

So it had been with climbing, parkour, Paranza Corta. She'd sought out experts and masters and trained harder and deeper than any student they'd ever had. Whenever she'd exhausted their knowledge, she found new masters; at first within a reasonable radius of the pig farm, then spreading wider and wider, using darknet funds 'inherited' from her father.

Now she had peers, and masters, and people she fought with and trained with and climbed with, but there'd always been an impenetrable wall between them. Zero understood it was one area where intensity of focus wasn't going to help.

The cab ate up the miles, and the sky progressively grayed out. A fine rain fell then became a downpour as civilization built up around the road again, like blood clotting around a wound. There were gas stations and low, single-story malls, coming blurry through the rain. Soon the cab turned left into a lot, ran along a long stretch of stores then came to a halt.

The driver said something in Polish. Zero got out to stand in the rain.

Joas Levi's art studio was fronted in chrome, blond wood and glass, like a modern cell phone store. The name 'Wszyscy Razem' glowed with white backlights. In the floor-to-ceiling windows hung large artworks; one was a wholly red square marked by slight variations in tone. The other depicted a giant thumbs up, with a head in place of the tip of the thumb. Zero didn't get it, and strode in.

A girl sat on a high stool at a narrow booth. She was tall, thin and wore her hair in a slicked back mullet. Zero approached. "I'm looking for Jakub Wozniak," she said.

The girl studied her for a moment. "Are you a Seeking Soul?"

That was the name of the tour group. "Yes. I just made a booking under Alison Briers. I know I'm late."

The girl sucked her teeth and studied her tablet screen. "Mrs. Briers. Yes, you are late. Normally we don't-"

"I'm only in town for today," Zero pressed. "It would mean a lot. Can I get in still?"

The girl considered, then gave a tiny shrug, like it didn't affect her life much either way. "They're not here, of course." She reached under the hood of the booth and came up with a map. "Here is the itinerary." She tapped the paper with her pen, then started adding circles and Xs. The title said it was a map of the Auschwitz II-Birkenau State Museum, built atop the Nazi concentration camp; a roughly oblong shape with one corner cut off, filled with regimented lines of long buildings. It looked like the schematic for a server circuit board.

"Here," the girl said, circling the entrance on the east side,

"Mr. Wozniak started the tour one hour ago. By now they will be discussing prisoner art. Have you heard of Dina Babitt?"

"No."

The girl looked bored. "She was a prisoner. Josef Mengele, the SS doctor who ran lethal medical experiments in the camp? He let her live in exchange for a series of paintings she made of Romani prisoners. He wanted a more accurate take on their skin tone than the photographs of the day could provide. These paintings now are on display. You will see them and discuss what art made under threat of death means."

"I see."

The girl pointed. "Go out and turn right. It's only a few hundred yards further to the museum entrance. You'll find them somewhere in the middle."

"And Jakub Wozniak is there?"

She frowned. "Of course. Where else would he be?"

"Of course. Thank you."

Zero left the building and turned right. The rain was easing up a little. She walked a few hundred yards until the entrance to Auschwitz II-Birkenau became clear through the rain. A railway line ran out of an overgrown verge to her right, continued across grass on a bed of gravel chips until it led into the long red building that fronted the museum. There was an archway in the middle just big enough to fit a single-width train carriage through. Barb-wire fences ran to the left and right as far as she could see.

People and groups were milling along the train tracks. Some were on their knees, shoulders shaking as they sobbed.

Zero set her jaw and walked on.

22

AUSCHWITZ II-BIRKENAU

The camp was vast and flat, largely laid to grass that allowed sightlines all the way to the far fences maybe a mile away. Zero felt different as she passed through the turnstile entrance, though she couldn't say how. Ahead the train track stretched straight like the course of a bullet. To either side more fences ran in parallel some fifty yards off, further subdividing the camp, and beyond the fences lay block after block of largely demolished buildings.

People were spread all along the train track, individually and in groups. There wasn't much sound, as if she'd entered a dead zone; even the burr of traffic from the nearby roads seemed strangely muted.

She walked on, scanning each group for 'Jakub Wozniak's' distinctive white goatee beard. He'd never had a beard back when he was Joas Levi; just another part of his new, lifelong disguise. She passed a tour group wearing dull colors and holding uniform gray umbrellas, listening to a guide speak in low and guarded tones.

"... roughly the size of six thousand football fields. At its peak it held some hundred and twenty-five thousand prisoners. There were one hundred and seventy-four barracks, and each barrack held up to a thousand prisoners, affording each person a total space of one meter square to sleep in. Prisoners had to sleep interwoven in stacked wooden cots, with their heads on each other's legs. The punishment for being found out of their assigned cot was severe; if not immediate death by dogs or firing squad, they would be put in the standing prison, a one-foot-wide cavity between brick walls, where they would be left on their feet, unable to shift position, for days. It's been said-"

Zero continued on, her stomach churning. The camp stretched away on either side; more fences, more gates, more demolished barracks that had once held thousands. The heaviness of the place began to weigh on her. She passed another group where many were openly crying.

"-are the crematoria," this guide said. "Each comprised of a dressing room, a gas chamber and the furnaces. Two to three thousand people were forced to strip and enter the gas chambers, on the pretense they were to receive a delousing treatment. The chambers were frequently at capacity; standing room only. The doors were sealed and Zyklon B pellets, originally a widely used pesticide, were dropped into each of these long chambers, immediately began to produce hydrogen cyanide gas. The cyanide in these pellets made absorption of oxygen impossible at a cellular level. The people in these chambers fell into fits, then comas followed by heart attacks. Death was thought to come within two to twenty minutes, and-"

Zero hurried on.

Already she wanted to leave. The weight of the place was bringing things out in her that wouldn't help. The same old boiling frustration. The same old reckless rage. Viktor Anatoly was no different from the evil men who'd run this place. The Real Boys, Bratva, they all lay on a spectrum, and Zero just wanted to slaughter them all.

Then she saw him. Jakub Wozniak, or Joas Levi. He stood to the right, a diminutive figure at 5' 7", with a white goatee beard and dressed in a solemn gray suit. He genuinely looked like a different man, with surgical alterations to his nose, ears, chin and cheeks. His eyes were the same, though. His group of 'seeking souls', about fifteen people, listened rapt in a circle around him.

Zero stepped in amongst the group. Despite his slight frame, Levi had an aura of command about him. He registered her arrival with a slight smile and nod. Zero watched and waited as he spoke; barely listening as the rain fell and people around her broke out in tears. It was like the air of the place exacted a tax, and Zero could feel the tears vying with the rage.

After a few minutes Levi set them into groups to discuss the issue of forced art. Zero took her chance to approach him, putting one hand on his arm and speaking in a low voice.

"Joas Levi, I know who you are. Can we speak privately?"

She pulled back and watched his face transform. At first it was to shock, but swiftly that shifted; not to anger or even fear, which she'd half expected, but to something like resignation. He gave another slight nod then refocused to address the group. "I'll be back momentarily."

He then started away without looking back. Zero followed. Some hundred yards on he halted by the fence and turned to face her. The resignation had worn deeper into his features. He took a deep breath.

"If you've come to kill me, I only ask that you don't do it here. This place has seen too much death already."

Zero shook her head. "I'm not here to kill you. I need your help."

His eyes narrowed. "Help? I can help you with art discussion. My old life is over. I am no longer that man."

He reached up to his shirt collar and pulled the open throat wider. A large oblong patch of skin on his upper chest was unusually pale, signaling a skin graft. He'd had his tattoos removed, of course. There were other methods of tattoo removal, though; this one seemed extreme.

"Bratva," Zero said. "You hate them now."

He closed his shirt collar and shook his head. "Not hate. Regret is a better word. Deeply. It's why I'm here. It's why I do this." He gestured at the art group.

"I get that. 'Everyone together?' It's the opposite of a tattoo I found on a dead man's belly. 'Everyone against God, God against everyone.' The Bratva creed. And you turned against them. You blew the whistle in court, and you spoke to a journalist for Galeta Wyborcza called Maja Kominski."

He frowned. "How did you find that out?"

"It doesn't matter. What matters is what you told her. Bratva are hunting me right now, Levi. It's some kind of joint operation between them and a group called the Real Boys. I need to know everything you know about that partnership."

At the mention of the Real Boys, Levi's face soured. Perhaps there was even a hint of anger in the beetling of his white eyebrows. "I know the Real Boys. They're one of the reasons I left. They've been polluting the brotherhood for a decade, back when they were still called the Pinocchios."

That took Zero aback. "A decade?"

Levi said nothing.

"The deposition was three years ago. Now you're saying Pinocchios were partnering with Bratva as much as *ten years ago*? What for?"

Levi opened his mouth to speak, then paused a moment and turned, slowly scanning the camp around them. The various groups of people were blurry through the rain, just dots of color on a landscape of green and grey.

"Tell me what you see here," he said.

Zero shook her head. "I'm not interested in the Socratic method, Joas. I want answers."

He fixed her with a sharp look; it must have instilled fear when he was a Bratva boss. "Humor me."

Zero reined in her frustration and looked around. She saw the fences and the barracks and the weeping groups under the gray, hopeless sky. She thought of what she'd heard, about bodies shipped in on trains and crammed into gas chambers in their thousands. "I see a machine built for killing. I see industrialized death."

Levi nodded. "That's a good phrase. Industrialized death. And it's why I finally quit Bratva."

He said nothing more for a moment. This time Zero was silent, waiting.

"You're good," he said, and shot her a small smile. In that smile she glimpsed the piece of humanity that had somehow survived his time amongst so many cold-hearted killers. "Bratva has become more like what this place once was. Call them industrialized crime; a machine for making money at the largest scale possible, regardless of the cost." He took a breath and refocused on her. "When you picture Russian gangsters, you probably think of thugs with tattoos following the direction of some patriarch thug. Something like the Godfather or Sopranos?"

Zero shrugged. She'd seen the Godfather once. "Maybe."

Levi shook his head. "It's not like that. Bratva's a corporation now, one of the biggest in the world, and in many ways they act like it. You may find this ridiculous, but even ten years ago we were holding regular conferences where expert speakers gave talks on how to expand the business, whether that was through political action, bribery of authorities, streamlined logistics, expanding markets in the developing world or via disruptive tech. There were seminars, lectures, even keynote speeches at these events, just like in any other industry."

Zero frowned. "That does sound ridiculous."

"Doesn't it?" There was the smile again. "But this is the nature of industrialization. In our early years, fifty years ago, perhaps we were like the Corleones. We fought amongst ourselves for turf and power, carving out spheres of influence. Strong men ruled. But now those spheres are settled and strength is not enough. Now we own office blocks in respected neighborhoods, where decisions are taken by corporate-grade CEOs, as informed by white-collar analysts. Data drives Bratva. Profit and power come not through conquest anymore, but through growth into new areas. We battle not on the streets, but over first-mover advantage. This is what Bratva is today. A modern, highly competitive corporation whose industry is crime."

"So you're serious about those keynote speeches?"

Levi sighed. "I am. I never joke in this place."

"But what's this got to do with the Real Boys?"

The smile flashed. "You're impatient. I like that. Picture the Real Boys, or the Pinocchios, coming into that rewards-based, money-focused environment. Imagine them bringing the same kind of amoral, single-focus vision that built the barracks we see here, and the train lines, and the gas chambers. Imagine the focus that mined gold from the teeth of dead Jews, and wove the hair of dead Jewish women into socks for the SS." He paused a moment, calming himself. "The Pinocchios brought expertise in this new market."

"You're talking about children," Zero said, her tone growing colder.

Levi's face paled faintly. "Yes. We'd always dealt in the market, of course, via human trafficking, but never with an explicit focus. Some in Bratva rejected the move to exploit this new market fully. I was one. Bratva was a brotherhood, but also a family. There was some sense of values. But values cannot survive against the profit motive. There were those who did not object. They chose to partner with the Pinocchios, and they profited from it enormously, rising to positions of power."

Zero felt sick. She worked the logic through. "They industrialized the market."

"Exactly," Levi said.

"What were the terms of the partnership?"

"We had the infrastructure. The reach into every country in the world. We could access the raw materials, and ship them and package and distribute them."

"Raw materials means children," Zero said angrily. "Just say children."

Levi gritted his teeth. "Yes. Children. Thousands of them. Supply had to meet demand, and there was always more demand from the Pinocchios. We provided the product they wanted on a scale to rival what was done here. We scooped children from wherever we could. War zones. Starving countries. Unfit parents."

"And what did the Pinocchios bring to the table?"

Levi shook his head. "They brought the market and the means. Through their Blue Fairy darknet, they had already captured the core audience demographic. Tens of thousands of hungry buyers. The demand was overwhelming. As soon as we started to fill it, it just grew. The growth was incredible, the profits immense. That money brought first-mover advantage to us, and nobody's touched us since."

Zero felt the anger surging again. "And you did nothing."

Levi laughed low. "I testified. Much good that it did."

"Your testimony was on this cooperation?"

"Yes. I couldn't take it anymore. But it achieved nothing. It was quashed at the supreme court. Bratva have people everywhere, and I destroyed my old life for nothing. The brotherhood may be a corporation, but it still runs on blood. The men in charge now, they have abandoned any sense of values we once shared. They will never forgive me for turning against them."

Zero grappled with her anger. She had little pity to spare for this man. His testimony had clearly released him from the lifetime he should now be spending in prison. And it wasn't such a bad life.

"I'm hunting them," she said. "The Real Boys. Bratva, now, too. A man called Viktor Anatoly. Do you know him?"

Levi shook his head, even as there was a spark in his eyes. "No. But I already knew you were a hunter. A *vor*."

"What?"

"Vor. That tattoo you saw, 'God against everyone, everyone against God?' In the original Russian it's 'bog protiv vora, vor protiv boga', and it doesn't mean 'everyone.' It means thief. Vor. The Corleones would call you a 'made man'. A killer." He paused, eyeing her. "I think you are a killer."

"I need to find Viktor Anatoly. Where is he?"

Levi looked at her for a long moment, then turned to look through the fence's chain links. "Do you know the story of Dina Babbitt?"

"I don't care. Tell me where to look."

Levi turned back. "Dina Babbitt was compelled to paint that butcher Josef Mengele's victims before they died. He experimented on his victims to the death, via successive amputation, live vivisection, all manner of horrors. She painted his victims before that happened, because she had no choice. Because he would do the same to her, if she hadn't. Now the paintings are kept here, like a testament. Nobody asked Dina Babbitt if she wanted them back. Does that sound fair?"

"Where do I find Anatoly, Levi?"

He ignored her. "Dina Babbitt's dead now, but back in the

seventies she asked for her paintings back. The museum said no. Babbit's paintings were owned by Mengele, then by an Auschwitz survivor who'd found them, from whom the Museum bought them. She kept asking, and they kept saying no."

He fell silent. Zero searched for an answer in the story but couldn't find one. "So what?"

"So even the best institutions compromise their values under threat. This Museum is a beautiful organization, existing to keep the story of the Holocaust alive. To honor the victims. But when it came to Babbitt, they couldn't do both, so they chose the path that helped them most."

Zero thought about that for a moment. "You're saying Bratva compromised. They're hardly an institution with values, but I get it. How does it help me?"

He smiled. "They did more than compromise. If anything, they've become an extension of the Real Boys. A decade ago, it was my job to help set up server farms across Europe to service the massive Pinocchio demand. Have you heard of the Blue Fairy exchanges?"

Zero felt her face drain of blood. "What?"

"I see you know them. Perhaps you lost someone to them?"

Zero felt herself vibrating, ready to shred this man. He nodded, like he saw what was coming.

"I would deserve it. But you won't, because I can help you. If there is a hinge the Pinocchio-Bratva relationship is built upon, it's the Blue Fairy exchanges. And where are they? Hosted within Bratva server farms. We have hundreds. I set up one in Krakow. It may still be there, though they've no doubt moved its geographical location. If you look I'm sure you'll find it." He turned back to her. "If this Viktor Anatoly is truly the current lynchpin between our two organizations, then you will find him in there, in the data if not in person."

Zero felt the world spinning around her. This man deserved to die for who he'd been and what he'd done.

"My sister," she said, barely choking out the word. "She was sold. She was the first."

"The first? Well. That explains everything. I think, if you choose to kill me now, I will deserve it. I won't fight."

Zero couldn't speak for the anger surging through her.

'I do not know her though. The first? I wasn't there for the first. They brought me in to industrialize. To expand. And I hated it. But that is no excuse. Like many of the guards in this place, I followed orders. I did as I was told, because the alternative seemed worse."

Red tinged Zero's vision. It was worse that he didn't know. That there'd been so many that he couldn't remember.

"Whatever you decide, be careful, little vor," Levi went on. "I think I know who you are, now." He mouthed the name. He didn't have to say it out loud. *Girl Zero.* "If they catch you, they will surely industrialize your death too. You will make them billions, and the exchanges will burn with your passing."

Zero didn't know what to say.

"Perhaps trillions. Who can say what they have planned? But that's all I can do for you. I can't help anymore, and please don't come back. I have become a coward, and I hate it when people hold up a mirror to that."

He started away and didn't look back.

23

CLARITY

Zero rode back to Krakow with her head in pieces.

Joas Levi's shame blurred and confused her. He'd helped build the exchanges. He'd helped industrialize the Blue Fairy. She'd even told him about her sister, and said Hope's name, and somehow he wasn't yet dead.

She didn't understand it.

For every other perp she'd ever met, she'd killed them for far less. She'd tortured them to death one after another, and here she'd let this man live, simply trusting his word for what was true.

It made no sense.

Now he could sell her out to Bratva. Perhaps she would be his way back in. Her gut churned.

Would he?

The cab drove on, as inexorable as a missile. She could stop and go back. She could kill him in any of a dozen ways. She could make it clean or painful, but for some reason something was stopping her.

His story of Dina Babbitt reverberated in her head. Him calling her a vor. A killer. But if she was letting men like him live, what did any of it mean? Was it enough that he'd stopped committing his crimes and made some token effort to atone? That he'd offered some answer to her questions? Was that enough to earn forgiveness?

There were no answers behind her. Maybe ahead there would be. She stared out at the bland gray landscape passing by, imagining the fate of those million victims of the Nazi regime shipped on trains like carrier freight, fated for industrialized death.

Within an hour she was back on the outskirts of Krakow. It was nearly 3 p.m. and she knew what to look for, a Bratva-Real Boy joint venture server farm, but it didn't seem real. She needed to shake off this gray haze.

The driver stopped at the drop-point she'd requested through the app, a gas station on highway 79. Vehicles raced past nearby. The driver said something, then said it again louder, and that brought Zero a little way out of her fugue.

She looked around. The cab was a five-seater; not nearly big enough for what she needed to do. She got out and stood on the grass as a hard rain fell, then hailed another cab on her phone, this time a seven-seater.

It came within ten minutes, a large Toyota SUV. Zero was soaked to the skin by then and shivering, which helped bring on a fresh clarity. Levi was in the past. The future was Anatoly. She climbed into the front passenger seat and looked at the driver.

"You speak English?"

The young female driver looked back. She had three piercings in her nose and one in her cheek. "Some. Why?"

"I want to hire you direct for the next four hours. Take the SIM out of your phone and I'll pay you double your normal rate. We're not going far, but it'll take time. Do we have a deal?"

The woman's eyes narrowed. "Double? That's a bad deal. There are penalties when I go private."

"Triple, then."

"A five times multiple. It's not cheap. Can you afford it?"

Zero pulled out her wallet and fanned the bills. "Cash or card, it's up to you."

"Mmm, cash. Yes." She leaned forward and pushed several buttons on her satnav phone, switching it off. "What's the destination?"

"SIM out. Not just powered down."

The woman grunted but complied, fiddling to take apart her phone.

"Good. Let's go…" Zero scanned the map on her phone. She found what she was looking for within five miles and pointed to it. "There."

The woman frowned. "There? This is not a tourist location."

"I'm not a tourist."

"This is a computer store. You are buying computers?"

"That's the other thing," Zero said, thinking about Real Boy oversight. They knew she was a hacker, and after they'd stripped her van, they'd surely be looking for her to resupply. "You're going to go in and do the shopping for me. On the clock. Every second adding up."

The woman stared, then shrugged. "Fine. OK."

The cab pulled into traffic.

It took a little longer than three hours to do all the shopping, as they bounced between big box stores picking up portions of everything Zero needed from each, ensuring there was no single obvious bulk purchase the Real Boys could key into.

As they shuttled from place to place, filling up the back seats with boxes of top-spec monitors, hard drives, servers and server racks, cooling fans, additional RAM and processor motherboards, Zero set up the short stay rental of a new location.

Four hours after setting out, around 7 p.m., they arrived. Her new safehouse was located in a backlot warehouse on the southwest edge of Krakow, a district called Skawina, in the shadow of the Elektrownia Wodna coal-fired power station. A pall of coal smoke hung thick in the air, fuming in great gouts up from the station's three tall stacks. The approach road was a clay track churned with deep wheel ruts and lined with large transformer arrays on either side, crackling with electricity.

"Nice place," the driver said. "You want to get cancer?"

Zero said nothing. The coal smoke was a problem, potentially getting into her circuits and cross-wiring the high-spec gear, but she'd already bought enough plastic sheeting to wrap an elephant, or reinforce a temporary 'clean room' tent, along with air purifiers to suck the dust out of the air.

The cab pulled up at the open loading bay to her warehouse. The nearby units looked half-dead; either abandoned or little-used. Being this close to the power station ruled out a lot of commercial operations. There were a few signs of cloud computing companies nearby in the lot. Zero's Iota searches had unearthed several large unmanned computer arrays; most likely other server farms that provided processing capacity for one of the big online shopping services.

Maybe one of them was Bratva. It was unlikely, but possible.

There were no people around and no open doors. Every roll shutter was bolted or padlocked.

It was perfect for Zero's needs. The powerful electrical output of the factory, combined with the intense data churn of the server farms, would mask the large power and information pull of her new computer array. If the Real Boys were hunting for a new electrical spike on the grid or an IP suddenly sucking down large quantities of data, they were going to fail.

The driver killed the engine. "You want me to help bring all this inside?"

"Yes."

The keys were waiting in a key safe with a four-digit PIN. The roll shutter slid up, revealing an empty warehouse that was some thousand square foot in size, far bigger than she'd need, and it was largely bare. The floor was raw cement, the walls mildewed plasterboard broken by 'panes' of opaque polycarbonate plastic that admitted little light. Down one long side were stacks of tables, chairs and old server racks, all smothered in a thick layer of dust. It seemed the previous occupant, perhaps a failed dotcom bubble business, had left some time ago.

Once the shipping back and forth from the cab was done, her pile of brand-new equipment looked incongruous in the center, barely a molehill in that huge space.

"We're finished?" the driver asked.

"Those three tables," Zero pointed, "that chair. Right here, inside the tent."

Together they unspooled and built the ten-person tent frame, then set the tables up in a U-shape around the chair inside it, situated above a power outlet and data strip embedded in the concrete. Under Zero's guidance, they unpacked all the boxes and set up the server rack; a tall metal frame with thirteen horizontal server slots. They slotted in the server computer cores, wired and loaded them, then set up the fans and the air purifiers via slits cut and duct-taped through the tent's reinforced plastic skin.

At the end they were both sweating, closing in on 8 p.m.

"Now we're finished?"

Zero handed over a wad of zloty bills. The woman counted them and nodded, then shot Zero a probing look.

"Anything else you need?"

Zero recognized what that offer was, or at least the outlines of it. An offer of drugs, maybe. Maybe some company to enjoy them.

"I'm all good. Thank you."

There was the faintest look of disappointment on the woman's face. Zero took that as a compliment.

"Your call. Enjoy camping out with your computers."

She left. Zero went back to work.

Food arrived shortly after by courier. She knocked back a burger and fries as she began to program the array to work in harmony. It was important to get everything running before she started the hunt.

As she worked, her head cleared from the fog Levi had put into it. Things were simple, really. Bad men died. Maybe he wasn't such a bad man anymore. That was why she hadn't killed him.

Occasionally she thought about Gabriel. Those moments in the basement seemed like a lifetime ago now: how he'd looked both concerned, angry and disappointed in those final moments; how he'd kept the shotgun out of sight; how he'd laid out the table for her final breakfast in his home.

The drawing the girls had done burned in her back pocket. One time she took it out thinking to toss it away, but that didn't seem right, so instead she tucked it back in and kept working.

Sometime around 10 p.m., it was all done and she stepped back, zipping her improvised 'clean room' closed behind her. It stood in the middle of the warehouse, a large tent wrapped in plastic sheeting with holes cut through for the purifier fans, patched up with silver insulating duct tape. The computer array inside was lit up and humming, currently downloading a fresh RedHat linux operating system and an essential hacking app suite off the darknet.

Her own miniature server farm, capable of hosting, processing and transmitting large volumes of data.

There were many searches she could focus on: algorithms to reconstruct the movements of Real Boys and Bratva in and around GOMA-49 based on CCTV captures, dashcams and GPS monitoring data; drawdown hacks on the criminal databases of numerous countries, seeking out Rostak or Anatoly or others she knew by name.

But this server couldn't handle more than one primary task, and none of those were the priority now. She was searching for the Blue Fairy exchanges. The lynchpin between Bratva and the Real Boys.

Time to start the hack.

24

REX

The rig boasted three 27-inch screens in a side-by-side array, powered by a rack of twelve Dell servers with Hexa (6) Xeon dual processors slotted into a lightweight steel chassis. It was capable of 1.15 petaFLOPS, or one quadrillion floating point operations per second; around ten times faster than the human brain, and pretty much what the best supercomputers in the world had been capable of circa 2008. Not bad for a jerry-rigged machine built within hours.

Zero cracked her knuckles and laid her fingers on the keys. Her AI hacking dogs were lost, so it was time to build a new one.

Rex.

She began by downloading open-source cracking programs: some designed to seek out weaknesses in code or physical architecture, some seeking out stray passwords and logons floating for sale around the darknet, some capable of brute-force guessing passwords, and some designed to 'phish' negligent employees for their data.

These she started building into a narrow-field AI, composed of automated decision-tree algorithms capable of accelerated machine learning. As the parameters of the task became clearer to her, she coded and recoded Rex's priorities, learning and evolving in real-time, just like him.

They were looking for a large building with a server farm's signature, something with huge power uptake and data flow, though likely disguised, much the same way she'd buried Rex with the power plant and other server farms nearby. That required access to all manner of data locked down behind Internet firewalls: construction and rental records for warehouses newly built or rented under fake names and shell companies; access and usage rates from companies such as PGE Polska Grupa Energetyczna and Emax-MT, Poland's largest power supplier and largest Internet service provider respectively; unusual traffic flows in and out of industrial areas signaling abnormal usage; signs of intermittent large power and data spikes tied to big moments on the Blue Fairy network, like the moments popular video streamers such as Perp 35 went live with a victim.

All of that data when crunched, recombined, cross-correlated and compared should help isolate an illegal server farm.

Her fingertips hammered the keys and the Internet steadily gave up its secrets, firewall after firewall falling to Rex's expanding arsenal of cracking attacks. In-between guidance, when Rex was brute-forcing a key log or phishing for access codes, Zero ran Iota searches to get a better sense of the scale of what she was up against. Search terms including 'Bratva' and 'server farm' turned up a range of articles on the Russian mafia's alleged huge investments into darknet black markets.

The dark Internet comprised vast portions of the open, or 'clear', Internet that were only accessible through encrypted sites with no indexable address, or via a specific app. They sold drugs, weapons and industrial secrets, trafficked men, women and children, and posted kidnap and kill contracts, constituting a trillion-dollar black market.

Ever since the popularization of such markets by the darknet site 'Silk Road' in the early aughts, where they sold and same-day delivered drugs, weapons, stolen vehicles, government intelligence and violent services, there'd been a chaotic land grab for market share.

It was the world's biggest growth industry, a trillion-dollar evolution in anonymous crime, as darknet black markets were well-concealed, anonymous and impossible for authorities to pin down. In some cases, thanks to the difficulty of applying twentieth-century law to twenty-first-century problems, darknet server farms weren't even illegal anyway, as they simply allowed data to 'pass through' them, rather than hosting it directly.

Bratva's huge investments in the darknet had allowed them to steadily dominate it, launching a swathe of online white-collar crimes in addition to black market sales, including money laundering via untraceable cryptocurrencies, phishing attacks against civilians, hack-and-hijack blackmail attacks on multinational corporations, as well as political influence and disinformation campaigns via social media and email. Several articles suggested Bratva had already been paid to sway the outcome of numerous elections, including the UK, Hungary and even the US.

Zero didn't care about any of that.

What she cared about was the darknet's anonymity, which meant they had no way of knowing that any orders placed came from her. You could buy anything on the darknet, and Zero built out her shopping list: a wide range of blades, from stiletto to throwing shuriken; stab-proof para-aramid Kevlar body armor, flexible but sturdy enough to block hypodermic darts; a fresh in-ear device and wireless router to stay in touch with Rex remotely; a printed security card; a uniform; and last of all, a motorbike.

Zero finalized her list, boosted all her packages to same-day delivery via criminal couriers and paid with cryptocoins from a digital wallet.

Then she dived back into the hunt. Rex was getting closer, and the possibilities mushroomed with every source added to his data matrix. If she really could locate the site of the Blue Fairy exchange, she could potentially shut it down tonight. She might have Hope with her before the night was over. She might even be able to slave Bratva's entire darknet to her own purposes, converting all their secret data to ammunition she could use to bring the Real Boys crashing down.

Her fingers flew on the keys and Rex churned by her side. She was in her element, feeling fast and wild and dangerous. Neither the Real Boys nor Bratva were going to like what happened next.

25

DARKNET DELIVERY

By 1 a.m. Zero and Rex had isolated the Bratva server farm. It was located in the Nowa Huta industrial park on the eastern side of Krakow. There were no official listings stating the building was zoned for data transfer or hosting, and city records had it marked up as construction supply storage, but together Rex and Zero had charted its power and data output; they were off the chart.

It was Bratva, no doubt.

By 2 a.m. they'd run a successful brute-force key log attack on the farm's external security, enough to slip a purchase order into their outgoing order stream. By 4 a.m., Zero had placed and received rush darknet orders on a new ID card with spoofed magnetic stripe and a courier's black box backpack. By 4:30 her delivery of a stolen Kawasaki Ninja ZX-25R had arrived.

It was an incredible-looking bike, jet black and sporty, with a liquid-cooled, in-line fuel-injected 250cc engine that boasted 43.5 horsepower. She stowed a few blades in the backpack box, straddled the bike's precision-tooled chassis and kicked off the soft courtyard clay.

The Ninja was a smooth, powerful ride, galloping along Highway 79 at a hundred-ten miles an hour. The night was dark still, with the moon hidden behind thick clouds, and streetlights were few and far between, leaving her single beam headlight as the sole source of illumination as she weaved between the red taillights of commuters.

None of them knew who she was. None of them knew where she was going or what she was capable of.

But she knew, and with every swerve her anger grew. Flashback images blared across the darkness: Armitage lying spread-eagled, eyes staring up into nothing.

The exit came up on her left and she took it hard, braking onto a ring road that switch-backed under the highway and ran along the edge of an empty commercial park.

"Rex, do we have oversight here?" she asked.

The in-ear mic caught her speech and transmitted it back to Rex, where speech-to-text software transliterated it and fed it in as a command, just like the virtual assistant on any cell phone. Rex's servers churned as he assessed the request and came back with an answer in seconds.

"There are no satellites overhead," he answered, speaking with a light California accent; the voice Zero had chosen for him. "I have access to CCTV on the highway but nothing in the parking lot."

Zero grunted. Rex was smart, but he couldn't operate in a vacuum. She ran the Ninja along the lot's edge, looking out for sentries or visible security cameras. The server farm lay to the right, a windowless block structure with corrugated aluminum walls, some two hundred yards in length. It had two large shipping doors on the left and an access door on the right with a security light and a CCTV camera. Nearby was a large black van, sitting in darkness.

Zero guessed this was a security contingent of Bratva vor.

Maybe Anatoly had stepped up security, with 'Girl Zero' on the loose. She considered circling away for a different approach, but didn't consider it for long.

Anatoly could be here right now.

She pulled into the lot and rolled slowly past the van, heart pounding. No doors opened but she glimpsed dark figures inside, watching. She parked by the entrance, eased the bike onto its kickstand and stepped off. Her whole body felt alive, muscles tingling with anticipation.

From the back of the bike she lifted the large black delivery box. Along with her heavy black tactical leathers and helmet, she could easily pass for a darknet courier shipping in new computer parts. Server farms notoriously burned through their gear in record time, requiring constant replacements.

She walked up to the door and held her fake ID card to the scanner.

The scanner flashed red.

Zero's heart skipped a beat, and she scanned the card again. This time the scanner flashed red three times then beeped orange. An intercom line opened and Zero heard a buzzing sound on the other side. Within moments a weary voice came through the speaker in Polish.

"Co chcesz?"

"English only," Zero said swiftly. "I have a shipment just in from Brussels, special order for Pakhan Anatoly."

A long moment passed.

"Understood," said the voice. "Checking your manifest."

Seconds ticked by. Sweat beaded down Zero's back. One of the van doors behind her opened but she resisted the urge to turn. Killing vor in the chaos of the forest was one thing. Killing them in the middle of an open parking lot was another.

"Scan your card again," came the voice. "You say the order's for Pakhan Anatoly?"

Zero held her card to the scanner. Her hack on the purchase order system had been necessarily hasty; Rex had been able to insert the purchase order into the outgoing system, but not the initiating order form. That was a different system and would've taken longer to crack.

"That's right. The Pakhan. I heard he's here."

"I don't care what you heard. The order's been filed wrong. You can't do it this way."

He said nothing more.

Footsteps slapped across the blacktop behind her; sounded like two men. Zero readied herself to fight. Probably she could spin and take one with a thigh-drawn stiletto through the throat, distract another with twin shuriken flung from a concealed halberd down her left side, at least temporarily eliminating two men in seconds. But that would do nothing for any others in the van, drawing their weapons.

After that it would be a crapshoot.

"Sorry about that," Zero offered. "I'll get it right next time."

The voice snorted something in Polish before swapping back to English. "Come in. But you're installing it yourself."

She nodded eagerly. The footsteps in back halted maybe five yards off. The door buzzed and opened, spilling white light, frigid air and the ozone smell of burning dust. Zero recognized the man inside from Rex's exhaustive searches of local CCTV footage and social media. His name was Dmitry Korsakov, and he was a computer engineer, seemingly sucked into Bratva by happenstance. Server racks rose ten-feet high behind him.

"Helmet off," he said, his tone long-suffering. "Come on, you know the drill."

Zero raised one hand to her helmet as she stepped through the threshold. Dmitry stepped out of the way. The door began to close. The helmet lifted clear just as the door clicked closed, sealing her in alone with Dmitry.

Now he saw her face and his eyes flared wide.

"You're her," he whispered.

She stepped close, smoothly palmed a knife and pressed it against his throat. "I am. And I have questions."

26

SERVER FARM

Cold air from the extraction fans blew down the server aisle. With the door closed, the hum of so many processor boards churning black market data sounded like a swarm of bees. Green lights blinked all along the racks.

"Turn," Zero said in a low whisper, and Korsakov complied. She zip-tied his wrists behind his back. "Who else is in the building?"

"It's just me," Korsakov answered. "They're going to kill you for this."

Zero spun him back around and pressed the blade to his throat again. "Nothing new there. And bullshit you're alone. Where's Viktor Anatoly?"

His eyes narrowed to a frown. "You mean the Pakhan? Why would he be here?"

"The order's for him. You took receipt. He's here."

Korsakov laughed but the sound was strangled. "Every order comes for him. Every order comes from him. He's God in this place. He's watching right now."

He looked up and to the right over Zero's shoulder. She

turned; there was a CCTV camera trained on the door. She waited for maybe ten seconds.

"But no alarm yet. No vor at the door. How long until someone checks that footage?"

He smiled. "It could be minutes. Any second."

Zero headbutted him, hard and square on the nose. He rocked back against the servers in a burst of blood, gasped in one suck of breath ready to scream, but Zero had already followed up with a punch to his solar plexus, which drove all the wind from his lungs and momentarily paralyzed him.

No shouting, no crying out for help.

"How long?" she pressed. "This place is a clean ship. You must have a schedule. There'll be a security room. How long, and how do I stop that from happening?"

She gave him a minute to recover. Still no knock came at the door.

"Every hour," he croaked eventually, tone muted from his broken nose. "You could loop the feed. But they will kill me if I help you."

"Die now or later," Zero said. "I'd take my chances."

He stared at her for a moment, swallowed blood, then nodded. "This way."

He led her into the thick of the servers, tall racks stretching away like a digital labyrinth. He turned left then right then left, weaving between the lights and sound, until a one-man booth appeared ahead, secured with a digital touchpad.

"Four five three eight," Korsakov said. Zero tapped the code into the door and the locks clanked back. Inside there was a five-by-five bank of monitors displaying CCTV feeds. She scanned them rapidly: there was the van outside in the lot, with its *vor* inside; there were many screens of empty rack servers, and one screen showing a woman on her knees, working beside a partially disassembled rack. There was no sign of Viktor Anatoly anywhere. There was no sign of anything other than servers.

Zero dropped into the seat. The user interface was written in Polish but she was familiar with the design, and swiftly set up a rolling loop of footage on the cameras where she'd passed. She hit execute then turned back to Korsakov.

The blood down his lips and cheek was starting to dry. He licked them tentatively.

"So where's Anatoly?"

"I don't know. I have seen him only once in three years. He doesn't come here."

Zero stared. "Are you lying?"

"Of course I'm not lying. You could kill me. Why would I lie?"

She grunted. Maybe she'd got her farms wrong. That was OK. She nodded out to the server racks.

"Do you know what data's passing through those lines?"

He just stared back at her defiantly.

"I asked you a question."

"Yes, I know."

"Are you a Real Boy?"

"Am I a what?"

"A Real Boy? A Pinocchio."

He looked puzzled. "You're just saying words."

"Have you ever heard the name Hope?"

"Hope?"

"She's my sister. Have you seen her?"

"I see no one," he answered. He was talking faster now. "Anatoly's men, only. I don't use the servers. It doesn't interest me."

Zero nodded slowly. Perhaps that was true.

"I'm looking for Anatoly. Where is he?"

"I have no idea."

"You must know something."

"I don't. You need to understand. I'm a computer engineer. He's the *Pakhan*. I come to work here. I maintain the servers, here. I follow orders. That's all. I don't see them. I don't talk to them. They don't talk to me."

"You maintain the servers," she repeated slowly, like a mantra. "You follow orders. Sounds like something the Birkenau Museum guards said."

His eyes bugged. "What? You mean Auschwitz? No. I'm not… "

Zero ignored him. There were a lot of other questions she could ask and threats she could make, but there was no point in any of them. Korsakov had made his bed. She'd been merciful with Joas Levi, but that was a special case for a man who was trying to make amends. Killing him would have achieved nothing.

But Korsakov? It would send a message.

While he kept babbling excuses, she smoothly pulled her five-inch stiletto knife and pushed it into his chest. It passed between his third and fourth ribs like a steel corer into a roll of soft cheese, spearing and stilling his heart. His eyes widened slightly in an expression of mild surprise and he looked down, then he died.

Zero let him drop, pulling away from the blade. His blood pooled on the floor and his legs kicked.

There was no drama to it. No fuss. As easy as switching off a light.

She turned back to the bank of monitors. There really only was one other person in the whole farm, it seemed; the woman on her knees working on the servers. Zero recognized her from the research she'd done. Her name was Anastasia Wojcik.

She pushed open the security booth door and strode out, leaving bloody footprints behind.

Wojcik didn't see her coming. Under questioning, she

knew nothing more. Less, even. Her death came a little more raucously, though. After three questions she ran, and Zero was forced to bring her down with a thrown shuriken blade, three inches long and perfectly weighted. It took her in the back and must've pierced a lung, because by the time Zero reached her she was aspirating blood.

"I … swear…" Wojcik gasped. "I don't know."

"It doesn't matter," Zero said, pulling the shuriken blade free.

Wojcik cried out. "I have children!"

"They'll be better off without you." Zero needled her chest with the stiletto, and she fell still.

Zero watched the blood spread for a moment, wondering. So Anatoly wasn't here in person. Maybe he never came here, but that left everything else. The data.

She went back to the server Wojcik had been working on, where her laptop was still attached via a high-speed data cable. Zero produced a flash drive from a zipped pocket and slotted it in. At once the screen flushed with the icon of a barking dog. Rex.

"Sic 'em, boy," Zero muttered, and darted her fingers across the keys, opening a single port to let the full force of Rex in. In moments the system buckled.

The local Bratva darknet was hers for the taking. Maybe the whole thing.

"Working," Rex said in her ear, as the data began to churn.

By the time she stepped out of the server farm, back in her helmet, she was utterly calm. In the zone. Nothing else mattered but the work. The courier's box was on her back again. Her knives were sheathed. Her feet still left bloody marks, but nobody would see that in the dark.

She approached the vor in their van.

She'd taken a closer look at them in the security room,

winding the footage on the CCTV display backward and forward. There were three of them, sometimes getting out of the van to stretch their legs. All big guys. Tough guys. They had lots of tattoos, including some mermaids, some skulls, some daggers through the throat.

Killers. Rapists. Child abusers. The world wasn't going to miss them at all.

The passenger side door opened before she reached it.

"Kakiye?" the man asked. It sounded like Russian.

She just smiled and kept coming. "Delivery for Viktor Anatoly. They couldn't handle it inside."

"Pakhan Anatoly?"

She slung the box off her shoulders. Five yards now. She opened the top and reached inside as she covered the final stretch. The man's hand was at his waist but that was all. He wasn't worried about her. He'd already dismissed her. That was his mistake.

"Yes, Pakhan Anatoly," Zero said, and smoothly pushed the stiletto blade into his throat.

There was no sudden movement. Nothing to signal to the men in the cab beyond what exactly had just happened, as long as his body blocked their view. He made a single gulping sound, like he was trying to swallow the metal away, but that was all.

"Chto eto za khren?" called the man in the middle.

"He just really loves his present," Zero said, climbing up into the van as the first man sagged out. "He wants to share."

The one in the middle didn't stand a chance. Wedged in, he didn't even realize he needed to draw his weapon before Zero's blade found his throat and tickled his spine.

Only the third realized in time. He scrabbled for his gun, smacked away the knife once as Zero licked it out, then toppled out of the door. Seconds later he came up with his gun drawn, but it was too late. Zero had the middle man's gun and fired first.

The report rang out like an explosion in the cab's contained space. Zero's ears sang like she was back in GOMA-49. The man fell.

She followed. She dropped by his side.

"Where's Anatoly?"

The man's eyes were rolling and his body bucked against the blacktop. She'd hit him in the side of the head and splintered his skull. There was no coming back from that.

"Ah," Zero said, as he began to foam at the mouth. For a moment she thought about putting a second shot into his head and ending his misery, then thought better of it. The misery was the message. Instead she climbed into the van and found the radio. She lifted the receiver and spoke into it.

"This is Girl Zero. Get me Viktor Anatoly."

27

ANSWER

No answer came.

Zero waited. She checked her phone. Rex was 78% done with locking down the server farm. It was an unstoppable process now. He was through the back door and in their network, shutting them out. 22% more and the whole thing, complete with however many millions of dollars' worth of transactions and data, would be wrapped up in her own unbreakable encryption.

It was a hack for the ages. She felt proud.

Next up came the export. The amount of data in the server farm would be vast and there was no way she could download it all. For the moment locking it down would suffice, while Rex scanned for anything of value to download into his own memory; perhaps one thousandth of one percent of the total data.

At last a voice spoke in her ear, dragging her back to the moment. "If this is Clara Baxter, prove it."

She laughed. "I just killed five people at your server farm. Three yesterday. Four the day before that. How's that for proof?"

Seconds passed.

"What is your father's name?"

That pissed her off. "I have no father."

"You did. You killed him. Slowly. Painfully. We do not forget. What is his name?"

"I've just locked down your darknet," she countered. "That's millions of dollars. You can come for me. Capture me. Torture me, kill me, it doesn't matter. You're not getting that money back unless I want you to. So put Viktor Anatoly on the line or I flush it all."

The radio crackled.

"It is OK. Keep darknet. We have spare."

The line went silent.

Zero stared at it.

Spare?

There was a theory about the Real Boys, that they were steadily phasing out their use of the darknet that floated beneath the open Internet. It was too hazardous an environment, with all the regulations coming down. Instead they'd started laying their own separate optical fiber lines, upon which they could run their own version of the Internet. On Zero's last hit, in the sewers beneath Tokyo, Japan, she'd stumbled upon confirmation: Real Boys laying fresh fiber lines.

Were those lines confined to Japan, though, or had they spread via underseas cables? That was a major logistical undertaking, but it was possible. It had been done many times already by countries and corporations, beneath all the oceans of the world; it could be done again.

Had the Real Boys circumnavigated the globe by now? Were they poised to shift all their traffic off the darknet and onto this 'shadow' line?

Nobody knew. There'd been no further confirmation.

"You're talking about the shadow line?" she asked.

No answer came.

"It's not just money. I've got your data. I'll give it to the police. To Interpol. The whole thing will come down."

Another long silence passed, but this time it was capped by an answer. "This is doubtful. You will incriminate yourself. Many deaths."

She snorted. "So you do believe it's me. Get Anatoly."

A pause. "What is your birth name?"

She cursed. He wanted her to say 'Mona Gebhart', the name her father had given her, but she hadn't answered to that name in nearly a decade. "Get him now or I roll on to the next server farm. Let's see how many spares you have."

There was another long silence.

"This will not be necessary. You will have our answer soon."

The line clicked and died, leaving only static.

But there was the sound of engines.

Zero looked up. Two vehicles were coming down the exit road off highway 79. Three vehicles: two large black SUV Escalades trailed by a low silver Porsche. She was surprised; that was far faster than she'd expected.

"Find me some overwatch, Rex," she ordered, as she kicked open the Escalade's door and ran back to her waiting Kawasaki. "A weather helicopter, commandeer a drone, satellite coverage, whatever. I need real-time top-down assessment of my options."

"I will try," Rex said in her ear.

She kicked one leg over the bike, twisted the ignition and revved the throttle. The Ninja ripped away like a bat out of hell, almost tossing her off the back, but she leaned in and weathered it like a bull rider. The parking lot had one exit. The Bratva cavalry were almost there.

The windows of the SUVs rolled down and hands emerged through, wielding automatic rifles.

Zero redirected away from the lot's exit just as they

blocked it, skidding into a sharp right turn and giving the bike full throttle. The engine heaved between her legs and shot the bike up to fifty miles an hour in a cloud of scorched rubber.

Gunshots sang out behind her like fireworks. The edge of the lot whipped closer; a raised verge of grass and dirt broken by thick concrete bollards rising four-feet high, three feet apart. She hit eighty miles an hour and at twenty yards out yanked the front wheel up; a second later the back wheel hit the curb and bucked hard. She was almost thrown but clung on, and the bike shot between the bollards. The front wheel slammed down on the far side and she ripped away, accelerating past a hundred in seconds and through a red-light intersection, curving up into a quiet residential road lined with tall houses boasting leafy green lawns.

Her heart pounded and the bike thrummed. It didn't feel real.

"I have passing overwatch from a 747 undercarriage camera," Rex said in her ear. "Pursuit has stopped."

Zero kept on for another ten seconds before the words finally pushed through her racing mind. She chanced a glance backward and saw nothing.

It was an empty neighborhood, lit by soft glowing orange streetlamps. There were long green lawns, front rooms with the blinds drawn and TVs flickering within, but no SUVs chasing her, no Porsche.

She slowed down. "Rex, are they taking an alternate route?"

"Negative. All pursuit has halted."

That made no sense. The Ninja dropped to thirty. It was good there was no pursuit. It was also a puzzle. They outnumbered her. They had the weaponry.

"Why are they stopping?"

"I cannot answer why," Rex answered.

Zero cursed. Of course he couldn't answer why, because

he was narrow-field AI. He couldn't draw inferences about human motivation. She eased the throttle and hit the brakes, drawing the bike to a dead stop in the middle of the road.

There was no sound of pursuing engines. No gunfire. Only the dim grind of cars passing on highway 79 half a mile away.

"Where did they stop?"

"In the parking lot," Rex answered after a second.

That didn't make any sense. What had she missed? Zero stared back down the residential road. "What are they doing now?"

"The three vehicles are motionless. Five figures are standing in a half-circle. Two are on their knees."

Zero's eyes widened. "What?"

Just then a gunshot rang out; the whipcrack sound clearly recognizable even from half a mile away.

"A weapon was discharged," Rex offered.

"I heard it, thanks," she said faintly.

Another gunshot followed, carrying over the distance with after-echoes.

"A second weapon was discharged. Now the jet is transiting out of range. I am losing oversight capacity."

Zero couldn't grasp it. Two gunshots and two men on their knees. It sounded a lot like an execution, but why?

She clamped the front brake and revved the engine, spinning the Ninja in a rubber-burning half circle.

"Can you ID any of them, Rex?"

"Working. They did not look up. This is unlikely. I would need better angles."

"Let's get you one then."

Zero released the front brake and the Ninja took off back the way she'd come. Streetlamps whipped by like strobe lights in a club, then she was out of the green enclave and crossing the intersection again, right back to the edge of the server farm's parking lot.

She skidded to a halt at the verge, overlooking a scene that defied explanation. The three vehicles were parked in a semi-circle barely fifty yards away, headlights illuminating three men on their feet and two sprawled out on the floor. Automatic rifles lay next to their bodies, and their heads were haloed by red pools of blood.

Two of the standing men held handguns, but neither aimed them at Zero. No doors opened in the vehicles. The engines purred low but didn't budge. With the bollards between them and her, there was no easy way for them to give chase.

She stared at them and they stared at her.

Zero flipped up the visor of her helmet. "What the hell is this?" she called.

The three men didn't answer. They looked at each other. The two with guns holstered them. A third reached to his belt and pulled out a radio transceiver.

"I have now taken control of one hundred percent of the server farm," Rex said in her ear.

"Lock it down," Zero said, then pulled her phone and fired off several quick photos of the men in the lot. They didn't shy away or try to hide their faces. "Can you access these photos, Rex?"

"I see them."

"It's the same men from the jet's belly-cam. ID them for me, please."

"Yes ma'am."

Now the third man was holding up the radio. He advanced ten yards toward the edge of the dirt verge.

"Stop right there," Zero ordered.

He stopped, set the radio down atop one of the bollards, then backed away with both his hands up. After ten yards he turned around, as if Zero no longer mattered, and pointed at the dead men on the blacktop. The other two men moved. They picked up the one on the right by his wrists and ankles and carried him dripping to the rear of one of the SUVs. The trunk door opened upwards and they shoved his body in.

Zero watched in fascination as they moved to the second man and loaded him in the same way. The SUV's trunk door closed and the men filed back into their vehicles, one to each of the driver's seats. The third man turned to look at Zero and held her gaze for a moment.

"Do not wait here, Zero," he said in Russian-accented English. "Police are coming. Five minutes."

He didn't wait for a response, only walked over to the Porsche and climbed into the passenger side. The engine revved and the vehicle reversed, made a smooth three-point-turn then started away. The SUVs followed.

Zero just watched, not comprehending.

Maybe four minutes remained of the five he'd allotted. She looked all around, but there was no sign of an impending trap. There was no one anywhere near. Their convoy was already rejoining the flow of the highway. Maybe that was the sound of police sirens, wailing closer.

She kicked one leg off the Ninja and advanced tentatively to the bollards. The radio looked like a radio. It didn't seem likely they'd packed it with explosives. She picked it up and held it to her ear.

"Viktor Anatoly," she said.

"Mona Gebhart," came a man's voice, as smooth and rich as champagne. "Shall we discuss terms?"

28

ANATOLY

"What terms?" Zero asked.

"Of your surrender, of course."

She frowned. "I'm not the one executing my own people. I just took your darknet. What makes you think I'm going to surrender?"

He chuckled. The sound was warm and comforting and repellent. "Aren't you executing your people already? Do you even know the real name of your deceased operator?"

Zero gritted her teeth. "You're not a force of nature, Viktor. She's not 'deceased', she was murdered. Her death's on you, not me."

"Her name was Alyssa," he responded smoothly. "Alyssa Credence. A sweet girl, but then, so many are when they face their deaths, don't you find? The begging stops. The intimacy begins. The love, even. Soft touches then mean so much."

"I wouldn't know. I only kill Real Boys, and I'm not looking for soft touches when I do it."

"And Hope?" he asked.

A cold shudder ran up her spine like an electric shock. "What about Hope?"

"Your sister. Surely you remember her?"

Rage exploded in Zero's head. She barely heard the sound of the incoming police sirens, barely saw the flashing lights. All that mattered now was Anatoly; on getting him on her interrogation bench and wiping that sick smile off his face.

"What do you know about Hope?" she asked, low and dangerous.

He laughed again. "Memory's a tricky thing, isn't it? The right sound or smell, the right song playing in the background and everything will come flooding back. I hear your voice, and I can just picture you and Hope, huddling in the fallout shelter in the midst of all those pigs, dreaming about the day you escaped Idaho."

Zero couldn't believe what she was hearing. The words felt like a violation; like he was reaching into her past and scooping out her most treasured memories. "You don't know anything about that. You weren't there."

His smile widened. "Wasn't I?"

Zero said nothing for a long moment, fighting a battle inside. It was repellent. It made her feel sick.

But maybe it was the truth.

"You were there."

Anatoly said nothing.

"You were there in Idaho, when I was a little girl? How old were you then, barely twenty?"

"You were a good girl, Zero. Mona. And do you know why?" He leaned in, his breath fuming hot across the table. "Because of how well you loved your sister. Little Hope. Always upstairs. Always in danger. And all the things you would do to save her? It was truly beautiful. Heart-breaking, even."

Zero reeled. She'd carried the memories of what she'd done to protect Hope all her life. They'd haunted her. The only times she ever slept without nightmares were the nights after she executed a Pinocchio. She'd done such awful things to try and spare her little sister those same atrocities, but in the end she'd spared her nothing, because her father had lied and sold her anyway.

Nausea bloomed inside her and she gagged.

"I see I've offended you," Anatoly said. "But Mona, my child, we're just getting started. If you want to know about Hope, about where she is now, about how you can keep her alive, I suggest you surrender yourself immediately."

The explosion reverberated through Zero's body, dislodging decades of pain. "You're saying *you* have Hope?"

"She'd be twenty-one now, wouldn't she?" Anatoly mused. "Two years your junior. You worked so hard to protect her then, didn't you? Will you protect her now?"

"Prove it. Show me you have her."

He laughed once more, louder and longer than before. "Oh Mona. I could show you any twenty-one-year-old, and you wouldn't recognize her. You knew her when she was five. Now she's a woman. So who is Hope? Where is Hope? Your obsession is laughable, really."

"DNA test," she said.

"Now you want her blood?"

Zero growled; an automatic reaction she couldn't control. "You don't have her. This is bullshit. You're toying with me."

He sighed. "Perhaps. If I was, then it's easier than I expected. The notorious Zero? I'd thought you'd be harder to break. But there is a lever on your heart, Mona, and I hold the handle. There always was, and I always will." He paused a moment. "Just like your father."

"I killed my father. Maybe you've seen the video?"

That provoked a spark of anger in his eyes. "We've all seen the video, Mona. We all remember. But I'm not him. I may have learned at his feet, back when I was barely a man myself, but I've evolved, and so has the Blue Fairy."

Zero's heart skipped a beat. "You're talking about industrialization. The shadow line."

"Someone's done their homework. But what do those words mean, Mona? How do they take you any closer to Hope?"

She had no answer for that.

"I remember the first time I saw you both. I was transfixed. From then on I watched every moment of your life, Mona, or at least all the moments that mattered. And I learned so well. I've followed your father's vision in all things, and when I see that look of loving intimacy in your eyes a final time, his legacy will be complete. Your father's wishes will be done."

Zero's mind raced. The sirens were getting cacophonous and maybe she had a minute left only. "That's why you killed your own men, isn't it? Were they Bratva only, Viktor, not dual-purpose Real Boys like you? They should never have fired weapons at me. Only dart guns. Because you need me alive. That's poor discipline for a captain."

"Very clever, Mona," he said, and now there was a hint of annoyance in his voice. "You always were smart, for such a stupid girl. I am Bratva. I am also a Real Boy. I am so many things. Just like you."

Zero's blood ran cold. "What does that mean?"

"You'll see soon enough. You contain universes, and it will be my honor to show them to you."

The first police car raced down the exit road and ran right over the far verge into the lot. It was heading for her.

"What universes?"

"You should run now, little girl. The police only belong to me in part. I think these ones will not be kind."

The police car pulled to a halt where the Escalades had been. Men got out and shouted orders at her in Polish.

"I'm going to rip your face off, Viktor," she said. "You're already dead. You just don't know it yet."

She dropped the radio and backed up. The cops came toward her, weapons raised, but not fast enough. She climbed on the Ninja and was away before the first shot rang out, with Viktor Anatoly's words hammering in her head.

Would she even recognize her own sister, if she was right in front of her?

She hoped the answer was yes. She feared it was no.

29

BURN

The police gave chase but never grew close, as Zero weaved north through local streets then fell back onto the 79 heading west.

She couldn't think. Everything was a jumble in her head. Occasionally Rex reported updates in her ear as Anatoly's team began the long, arduous process of physically locking down and erasing every server in the farm. It was one possible response to an encryption blackmail attempt: simply cut the lines, erase everything and reboot.

Millions in encrypted currency would be lost. All their data would be gone. The server farm's physical infrastructure would be saved, but at the expense of every transaction escrowed through the system, as well as every scrap of user data.

"Outer ports are closing," Rex reported. "They are blocking me. Attempting to find and export meaningful data."

Zero could hardly think about that now. Every event of the night vanished into insignificance next to the things Anatoly had said. It didn't matter that Rex didn't have nearly have enough time to scan the entirety of the server farm. He had algorithms to grab as much as he could before it was all deleted.

Right now, she didn't care.

She just saw those two dead Bratva members on the floor. Executed for firing at Girl Zero. Bratva was vast and powerful, and if vor were anything like made men in the movies, then you couldn't kill them without tremendous comeback. But Anatoly just had, seemingly on a whim, with no fear of the consequences.

It meant something. But what?

Her mind worked on the problem like a record player's needle stuck in a groove. The Real Boys had captured her alive once before, back when they'd been the Pinocchios. They'd carried her to a container ship off the Philadelphia coast, where they'd tried to livestream her rape and execution on an iron altar. Only Christopher Wren's intervention had saved her, then.

This felt very different.

It felt bigger. The Pinocchios had evolved into the Real Boys. Their relationship with Bratva had changed them. Joas Levi's words echoed in her head.

'They will surely industrialize your death too. You will make them trillions, and the exchanges will burn with your passing.'

What did that mean?

"Exit on your left," came Rex's dispassionate voice in her ear, and she pulled off into Skawina.

The coal factory's black plumes still belched into the sky, weighting the pre-dawn air with grit and coal smoke. She ran the Ninja down the churned clay road to the lot, where she let it drop to its side and ran inside.

The warehouse was empty but for the hot glow of Rex's computers. She fought with the tent's zip, almost ripping the canvas in her urgent rush to enter. Inside she tore off her helmet and started stripping her leathers, her armor, her blood-crusted stiletto blade, then dropped naked into the seat before the three-monitor array and plunged in, fingers hammering off the keys as she finally joined the battle for the server farm.

It was warm in Rex's embrace, as gentle heat spilled from his server rack. Zero tore into the data like a rabid animal, shredding through evidence of thousands of crimes in her search for Viktor Anatoly.

For Hope. For why he wanted her alive so badly.

But as the minutes passed without once looking away, it became agonizingly clear that she was too slow. Rex didn't have the processing capacity or the hard discs to stay ahead. Anatoly's people were cutting off and deleting servers too fast. Perhaps it was all for nothing.

Hours passed, and as the sun rose on a new day outside Zero fought in a delirium. There was a team of them out there now; she could sense them outmaneuvering her through the darknet's data highways. They were not only trying to suture the wound of the lost server farm, either; now they were hunting for her too.

Every move she made invited retribution. Every step could be tracked, if she wasn't careful, and she wasn't careful. She coded with abandon, but it wasn't enough. The Blue Fairy were stronger, like always. They were better, and with every second she felt Hope slipping away.

The frustration burned her up and she worked harder, losing more, until she was so far underwater she couldn't see the sky. She needed this so badly, but it wasn't there. Her fingers crashed on the keys and she felt empty, feeling exactly like the addict Gabriel had pegged her as.

She needed Viktor Anatoly. She needed him to die.

As another darknet server went down, erased, she flung her head back and screamed. She couldn't lose this. They'd harden all the server farms now. They'd be ready while she'd glean nothing. No location. No targets. No answers.

She was lost. She cast about but Rex was no help. He was a child still, nothing like the dogs of war she'd built over all these years, all compromised now.

There were only two people in all the world who could help her.

It required trust, but she'd already trusted Joas Levi and Maja Kominski and Gabriel too. She was in last-ditch territory and had no other choice. She typed in the number and hit the button to dial.

30

TRUST

It was 9 a.m., and this time the line picked up in less than a second.

"Clara Baxter?"

It was Hellion's voice again, that taut Bulgarian accent. It was an impressive guess; even with the best hacking skills in the world, there was no way Hellion could know this call was from Zero. She didn't care about that, though.

"You asked why I'm killing Real Boys." Zero went on, not bothering to give confirmation. "I'm ready to tell you, if you're still willing to help me."

Moments passed, accompanied by a blizzard of keystrokes coming down the line. No one could execute a hack faster than Hellion; she'd trained herself on real-time strategy video games, managing the resources and deployment of hundreds of individual units against other experts in worldwide tournaments. She'd dominated the adult class at the age of fourteen, before turning her prodigious 400 meaningful actions per minute to black-hat hacking.

Zero could manage perhaps half of that. It wasn't a matter of training, and nothing she could ever catch up with. It was raw human talent combined with a lifetime spent nurturing it.

"This time you are not calling on cell phone with dead man photographs," Hellion said calmly. She'd clearly executed another back trace, but Zero had hardly tried to secure the outgoing call. All Rex's ports were wide open. "This is invitation to me? I see you are now in battle with major server farm. This is darknet war, yes? What is happening, Clara Baxter?"

She took a breath then answered, barely thinking as the words spilled out. "You said you'd help me if I proved I wasn't a sadist. I'm not sure I can do that, because I am a sadist. I like killing them, Hellion. I live for killing Real Boys. I don't have anything else. No family, no friends, only a trail of dead Pinocchios. But there is one more reason; the Real Boys have someone I love. It's my sister. Her name was Hope. Is Hope." She sucked in another breath, unable to stop now the dam was open. "She was only five years old when my father sold her on the Blue Fairy exchanges, and I've been hunting for her ever since. The man I'm hunting now, Viktor Anatoly, he's the first Real Boy I ever met who knows about her. He says he knew my father. It's his servers I'm fighting. And I'm losing, Hellion. I can't fight him with this pocket AI and my home resources are compromised." She drew a sharp breath. "I need you to save the servers. There's got to be something on there I can use."

Long seconds passed, filled with clattering keys.

"So, it is not only vengeance?" Hellion asked. "You are addict and sadistic killing machine, of course, most naturally, but also you are more?"

"Yes," Zero answered. "I want my sister. That's it. That's who I am. Dead Pinocchios are my drug and she's the antidote. I need her. When I find her, I'll be better, I know it."

The pace of crashing keys accelerated, so loud and fast they became white noise. Four-hundred-plus strokes per second already, Zero guessed, surpassing world record territory. "Challenge accepted. This is sad story, Clara Baxter, and I enjoy sad stories. I will help you. Traumatic childhood is strong pity point in your favor. Perhaps only one time I will help, perhaps many times in future. I will toss coin, we will see. Now." She paused a moment. "Compensation for this help is simple. Do not enjoy killing Real Boys anymore. Kill them, yes, this is good. But do not enjoy. Is deal. Do you accept?"

Zero didn't have to honor that. She didn't know if she even could. "I'll try. It's a deal."

The storm of keystrokes continued, though Hellion spoke over them calmly. "Acceptable, but several further conditions. No more lies. No more manipulation. My friend Christopher Wren is off limits. Also his Foundation. Yes?"

Zero didn't care. In Tokyo she'd dragged Wren into her hunt by writing his name on the corpses of dead Real Boys. He was ex-CIA, a black-ops operative and head of his many thousand-strong Foundation; it made him a battering ram where Zero was a focused stiletto, capable of felling structures she couldn't. In Tokyo it had worked, but her tactics had clearly ticked his top hackers off.

"Yes, OK, I'll leave him alone."

"And Foundation? If you need help, will ask, not take, yes?"

"Yes, OK!"

"Good." Hellion sounded cheerful. "I am white-hat hacker now, doing good deeds for charity. We will find this bad man." Keys hammered for a moment. "Clara Baxter, I am concerned. You are naked. In warehouse. With simple AI called Rex. Is dog's name? This is most peculiar."

Zero didn't even bother to cover the built-in cameras in the monitors. "It's my process. Rex is just a puppy, but he's learning."

"Yes, I see. He is interesting. Components in Rex code,

they are unusual. What is this, replacement for human security oversight, taken from video game? Clever, perhaps. Should I feel concerned, human getting replaced by tech?"

"Feel whatever you want. Teach him, ignore him, just find Anatoly before they shut everything down."

"Yes. I will need help for this. B4cksl4cker!"

Seconds of flying keys passed, then a second voice came down the line; the heavy Armenian bass of B4cksl4cker, Hellion's hacking partner.

"Yes, I am listening. Hello Clara Baxter. I am not looking at naked camera feed. You caused much trouble for Christopher Wren. For Christopher Wren's most delightful girlfriend."

Zero couldn't help a wild laugh escape her lips; that they were both thinking about that at a time like this. "I won't do that again."

"We have signed verbal contract," Hellion said. "B4cksl4cker, please bring online botnet army."

A second passed. Where Hellion was infamous for her speed, B4cksl4cker was notorious for his ability to code AIs on the fly, using his vast 'botnet' of hacked personal and corporate computers as processing power to take down his enemies. "Whole botnet army? This is three million computers."

"I think all. Clara Baxter?"

She felt a rush of something pour through her system. Adrenaline maybe. Hope, perhaps. "Yes."

"Yes, B4cksl4cker. We are in war. You like war?"

"I like war," he responded. His keystrokes joined the white noise, these coming loud and authoritative alongside Hellion's endless storm. B4cksl4cker's slaved botnet was responsible for some of the biggest hacks in history. In recent years he'd used them to execute massive Distributed Denial Of Service, or D-DOS, attacks on the Belarusian and North

Korean governments, shutting them down with a flood of data requests just long enough to let him sneak in and steal millions in cryptocoins. "This will be short war. Who is enemy?"

"Mercileaa assassin?" Hellion prompted.

"It's a man named Viktor Anatoly," Zero said. "He's a captain in Bratva, also a top-tier Real Boy. They're working together."

"Together?" B4cksl4cker asked. "I hate both of these. Bratva killed my uncle."

"I remember," Hellion said.

Zero watched in real time as B4cksl4cker's botnet came online. In moments it began to hoover up vast swathes of data from the server farm indiscriminately, under the cover of a lightning-fast blitzkrieg assault by Hellion.

Zero stared in disbelief then flung herself into the battle, attempting to marshal Rex as a dog of war, flinging destructive code sets into the maelstrom.

"Who is interfering?" B4cksl4cker asked. "Botnet is taking friendly fire."

"This is Clara Baxter, B4cksl4cker. But she is naked and in high emotion level, not practical, not team player. Clara Baxter, please standby and do not help. Also bring dog named Rex to heel."

"Dog is puppy," said B4cksl4cker.

"Is cute. Interesting tricks. But not warrior dog. Clara Baxter, listen now? Put clothes on. Eat food. Camera shows you are wearing other men's blood. This is bad look. Also shaking, entering shock, perhaps hypoglycemia. You are diabetic? I am ordering food with much sugar, will arrive soon. Meet and eat. In clothes. Leave this battle to us."

"I can't-"

"Is not suggestion. Is order. B4cksl4cker and I are generals now. You are merciless assassin, yes, not soldier on battlefield. Special ops, prepare ground for army, but not open warfare. Do not try to dictate strategy to generals."

Zero opened her mouth then closed it.

"And clothes," B4cksl4cker said. "Hellion, do we notify Christopher Wren?"

"No," Zero said swiftly.

"Agreed," Hellion affirmed. "Christopher Wren is holidaymaking with girlfriend in Japan. Much needed rest. Perhaps later we will discuss notification. Now, we work."

They both fell silent apart from the static crash of keystrokes. The sound enveloped Zero just like the heat from Rex's servers. She stared at the screen as the tide of the digital battle shifted. Fresh holes punched through the server farm's sealed ports in ways Zero didn't even comprehend. Hellion and B4cksl4cker weren't just fighting the battle for the server farm anymore. They were expanding the battlefield and going wider.

Looking for more. Maybe executing on the threat she'd made to take the entire Bratva darknet, even stretching for the secret Real Boy shadow line.

It was entrancing to watch. The panic and chaos that had churned through her moments earlier were stilled as she tried to fathom how they were doing this. It wasn't just capacity or skill or AI, but a stunning fusion of all three. These two were data magicians. Zero felt like a gifted children's performer next to them.

"Clothes, Clara Baxter," B4cksl4cker ordered. "Food is almost there."

Zero blinked up from a trance. Thirty minutes had passed and it felt like she'd barely breathed. She stood up and looked around. Her cold, bloody leathers lay heaped on the floor, but she couldn't face putting them back on. The alternative was the clothing Gabriel had given her. His wife's jeans and blue sweater. At least they had no blood on them.

She pulled the jeans and the sweater on. It was pushing noon of the next day. A honk came from outside and she emerged through the tent into the gritty, cold air of another day, just in time to see the delivery driver pull up on a moped. He said something in Polish. Zero just grunted and took the package. Steam rose up as she opened the waxed card lid.

Pierogi; sweet and savory Polish filled dumplings boiled to delicious softness then pan-fried to golden crunchy goodness. The box looked to contain twelve in total, a real feast in several flavors, with sauerkraut and sausage meat, mushrooms and potatoes, and several sweet-smelling fruit pierogi topped with cream.

She didn't know if that was some kind of a joke or not. Over the last few months of hunting Perp 35 she'd acquired a taste for pierogi; Hellion must have dug through her fast food orders to find her favorites. Well, at least she'd eat well.

She carried the box back into the tent and settled down to crunch on the mouthwatering dumplings and watch the show.

31

SHOW

The shifting screens were mesmerizing, movements of power ebbing and flowing across the darknet, as visualized by a graphic Rex formulated in real time: thousands of tiny pixels shifting from blue to red from left to right as possession of different servers and nodes swapped.

Incursions came in and went out as spikes of red attacked and were rebuffed, chased by blue counterattacks, which were met by engulfing actions that variously failed or succeeded. Many times the battlefield expanded, with the existing squares reduced in size or conjoined as thousands more were added. At first every square represented clusters of thousands of computers, then tens of thousands, then hundreds of thousands.

Zero couldn't take her eyes away. The screen kept shifting and changing like three-dimensional chess, organically and entrancingly, at a scale she'd never before imagined possible.

This was a data war for a vast swathe of the darknet, and it kept on going until at some point Zero's adrenaline spike crashed and she slumped back in her chair, asleep.

When she woke it was to Hellion's voice.

"Clara Baxter, war is over, time to wake."

Zero blinked, rubbed her eyes and sat up on her chair. Daylight suffused the tent, shining in through the plastic view windows. The detritus of her middle-of-the-night pierogi lay around her, all finished, along with several crushed cans of coke. She peered at the screen until details resolved. At first she picked out the clock, saying it was nearly midday already.

She cursed.

"No need to curse," B4cksl4cker boomed through the speakers. "This is major victory. Very large part of local darknet now belongs to us."

"Not secret shadow line, though," Hellion added. "We could not find this. Connection points, perhaps, where current darknet feeds to shadow line. But these are severed. There is no way in."

Zero stood up. The trails of a nightmare pulled away like invisible roots; something dark and overbearing, trapped in a cell assaulted by dead pigs, while fires burned all around. She shook her head to clear it. There seemed to be so many things happening at once.

"So, what did you find?"

Hellion laughed. "Battle is just over. Looting can now begin. I have also upgraded your Rex. He is powerful now, backed with independent server array, stronger AI, many improvements. I like these ideas you use for him. He can be good bloodhound, find Viktor Anatoly himself, work as overwatch when your friends Hellion and B4cksl4cker are not available, perhaps sleeping."

"So there's no sign of Hope? What about the Blue Fairy exchanges? That's where they sell children. Could you find them?"

"We cannot see this yet," Hellion answered. "We expect many such transactions are on shadow line by now. Not open darknet. There is clear migration of Bratva data and services for some time. Most severe crimes, human trafficking, political manipulation, these are already shifted onto shadow line. It is carrying burden for much criminal activity. We cannot penetrate this digitally."

"Of course, this is bad," B4cksl4cker added. "Real Boys and Bratva together? Yes."

Zero said nothing for a moment, squinting against the light flooding in through the tent flaps. It seemed she hadn't bothered to close the warehouse doors.

"So what have you got?

"Working," Hellion said. "Truth is, Clara Baxter, much blood and treasure was expended last night. B4cksl4cker's three million botnet? It is gone. Used up. Our current physical location is safe, but this was close matter. Your location is also safe. Little else is safe. Bratva, Real Boys, they have deep pockets and learned much in war."

Zero struggled with that for a moment. "You're saying they almost hunted you down?"

"It was very close," B4cksl4cker said. "Now we have their darknet, and they have portions of Foundation and our past record. In war come casualties, Clara Baxter."

She thought about that; about Armitage, Korsakov and Anastasia and all the men she'd killed in the last few days and years. A lot of blood. A lot of treasure.

"You must have something. Even if you can't get to Anatoly or the exchanges because they're on the shadow line, what about top-tier Real Boys on the darknet? Big spenders, long-timers, men who might also use the exchanges? They could lead me to Hope."

"This is current search parameter. Of course, will take time, especially with diminished assets. In meantime, you should rest and-"

"I've rested enough. I want answers." Images of the previous night ran through her head, a picture lost in the fog that was coming back to her now. "Anatoly had his own people executed last night, Hellion. Two Bratva vor, killed on the blacktop in front of the server farm."

A few seconds passed and keys clattered. "This was Anatoly? We read report of gunfire, bloodstains in this area. We assumed it was you."

Zero shook her head. "That's just it. It wasn't me. These men came after me hard, with guns not hypodermic darts, and they were punished for it. Straight up executions."

Hellion was silent for a moment. "Yes. This is strange behavior. What is explanation?"

"They really want me alive. It's different from the last time. Back then they put me on an altar to sacrifice and-"

"This is fate Christopher Wren rescued you from."

"Yes, my white knight," Zero allowed. "The point is, the Real Boys have different goals now, and-"

"Point is you were reckless then also," Hellion pressed. "Charge in too fast, blind by anger. Just like you were reckless last night, taking on server farm alone. Reckless in Tokyo, reckless now. Stop being reckless, Clara Baxter. Rest!"

Zero bit back an immediate response. Long seconds passed as she swallowed her anger. Through the plastic window in the tent's canvas wall, she watched swirls of black smoke play against the pale blue sky. The fact was, Hellion wasn't wrong. She wasn't really right, either. In any case, Zero had never been any good at sitting around and waiting.

"I understand your concerns," she said, forcing her voice to be calm and reasonable. "But there is a ticking clock here. Like you said, the Real Boys are hunting us all now. Hope is on the line. I have to find Anatoly."

The sound of keys clattering ended. Zero suspected Hellion had muted the line and was speaking to B4cksl4cker directly. It was their wellbeing at risk now, too.

"Very well, Clara Baxter," Hellion came back. "We will take further chance and purchase boost to processing power through cloud services. If any sign of Viktor Anatoly is in this system, we will find him. Our only condition is rest, shower, change clothing and eat. Is this agreed?"

Zero stood up sharply. "Agreed. And be careful."

Hellion laughed. "None of this is careful. Now wash, merciless assassin. Enemies will smell you coming."

32

SOVIET STRING

Zero found a shower in the back of her warehouse; the spout was rusty, emerging through a chipped brick wall and coated in a thick layer of dust. There was no curtain and no walls, but Zero didn't care. Cold water jetted out in a freezing blast and she luxuriated in it.

Blood ran from her hair and down her body. Pinkish water puddled in dust on the concrete. She stayed there for long minutes, until her teeth chattered and her skin shivered, then stepped out into the muddy courtyard, where she let the sun dry her.

Black smoke churned ever upwards.

In ten minutes a delivery driver arrived. He gawped at her, standing there naked. She took the box and opened it. Not pierogi. This time it was an aromatic kielbasa dish; a long spiced sausage nestled in amongst caramelized sauerkraut, fried green beans and creamy polenta. The hearty scent rising off the food was intoxicating. She dug in with her plastic fork, finishing the meal in moments only.

It woke her up. It was delicious; the rich meaty taste of the kielbasa mingling with the tart sweetness of the sauerkraut, cut with the smooth polenta and crunchy greens.

"Clothes, Clara Baxter," came B4cksl4cker's voice from the computer as she stepped back into the tent.

She had her strike leathers to wear, or the jeans, t-shirt and sweater Gabriel had given her. One was coated in blood. The other still carried the perfume scent of another woman.

She pulled on the jeans and shirt. They felt right.

"These clothes are old," B4cksl4cker said. "Ripe."

Zero grunted, stripped the t-shirt and carried it back to the shower where she rinsed it thoroughly in freezing water. She wrung it gently then pulled it back on. The cold was bracing a second time.

"Not better," B4cksl4cker said when she returned. "Cold water has an effect on your-"

"Have you found Anatoly?" she countered.

"There is no Anatoly here," Hellion chimed in. "We believe he is absent completely from darknet. But there is much else. Go for walk, Clara Baxter. Get new clothes. This will take time."

"We haven't got time."

"So what do you suggest?"

There were lots of things Zero would like to suggest. Some of them involved swear words and varying parts of Hellion or B4cksl4cker's anatomy, but none of them would be productive. There was no better path to a lead than the entire Blue Fairy darknet, and she knew that, but it didn't help with the itchy, antsy feeling burning her up.

"Nothing, I guess. How long will a full scan take you?"

"How long is piece of Soviet string?"

"What?"

"Correct answer is same length as all other pieces of string. Clara Baxter, we will call when there are answers. Go."

Zero sat a moment longer, debating just diving into the data with her own algorithms and Rex at her side, but it seemed a bad idea. Hellion and B4cksl4cker were better at this, and like in the war, she would just get in the way.

"Call me the second you have something," she said, then pulled her phone and earpiece from their respective chargers, ordered a cab on the phone then pocketed them both. She took one blade, a triceps-holstered stiletto, then reconsidered and dropped it onto the pile of leathers.

"Look after the place while I'm gone, Rex," she said.

"Woof," Rex said.

She smiled. She hadn't programmed him to do that.

The Kawasaki Ninja remained tipped over in the courtyard, the fender half-sunk in claggy, drying mud. She walked past it to the approach road, where her cab was already waiting. A Toyota Prius. She grunted at the driver, an old guy who grunted back, then settled into the rear seat. Ed Sheeran was on the radio, singing about Bad Habits. Zero knew exactly what he was talking about.

The cab pulled away.

She rode it back to central Krakow, trying to think of nothing much. It wasn't a long ride, but still she replayed her conversation with Viktor Anatoly countless times. He'd talked about knowing her father, even about meeting her in person, and there was no way around it; that threw her.

It was certainly possible. The timeline wasn't so difficult. Zero was only twenty-three now. It had been a hectic seven years since she'd escaped, and a horrible nine years of captivity before that. Her life, neatly split into two. Into three, if you counted the first seven years of her life, when she'd been Mona Gebhart, and believed her mother and father had really loved her. When Hope had been there.

She refocused.

Anatoly had said he'd been a young man then. If he'd been the same age she was now, back when Zero was seven, that would make him thirty-nine now. Still a young man.

A stray thought of Gabriel dropped into her head. She reached back and found the girls' drawing still in her back pocket. She pulled it out and looked again at the picture. Gabriel. The two girls. Two discs that could be frisbees or the sun or hats caught in the wind. And Zero, standing between them.

NICE TO MET YU

So strange.

"Are you all right?" the driver asked.

Zero sniffed and refolded the paper. Suddenly she knew where she wanted to go, and said as much to the driver.

"That's not a tourist attraction," he answered.

She laughed at the repetition. "I'm not a tourist."

It only took a few minutes to arrive. The driver knew a few locations that would work. She thanked him and climbed out. The building before her was modern and nondescript: glass, chrome, wood. The lobby was cream and smelled faintly of pine sap. The woman behind the desk was able to sell her shorts and a t-shirt at a fair price, and rent her a pair of tight, thin-soled rubber boots, a chalk bag, finger tape, a harness and ropes.

She went into the changing room and came out feeling transformed. The phone was in her zip pocket, the earpiece in her ear, but already her focus was shifting. She walked between small group classes where children were practicing putting on harnesses and belaying ropes, then stopped at the 'ZOO'. It was an encircling three-wall climbing extravaganza of overhangs, incline slopes and crevasses, sprayed with a sandy gray rock texture.

She couldn't have asked for anything better.

Multiple routes crisscrossed the walls and continued up onto the ceiling, each marked out by monochromatic resin handholds bolted to the plywood and metal frame. By eye she could distinguish which routes were harder and which were easier; the darker colors graded toward higher difficulty. The black route looked extremely challenging.

She started on it from the off, boosting herself up and latching her first auto-belay point.

33

CLIMB

Time flew as Zero lost herself in the climb.

Ever since she'd left the Idaho farm at sixteen, she'd found relief in climbing. It had taken her years to discover the hobby, but on her first visit to the indoor wall in Boise she'd been a natural.

She had the hand and finger strength to brute-force climbing routes that others in her weight class could only achieve with technique and finesse. Even on her first passes at the beginner difficulty walls, just a nervous teen who'd barely spoken to other people all her life, she drew spectators.

Afterward, as she dropped to the mattresses and the small crowds dispersed, one of the climbing coaches had come over to her, a young woman with curly red hair and an easy smile. "You're really good. Where did you learn?"

Panic had struck and she'd left.

But she went back. The deep focus of climbing banished every other thought from her mind. When she was on the wall pushing herself to the limit, she couldn't think about Hope, or her dead parents, or the nightmares of the night before. She just climbed.

At times the woman with the red hair would watch her.

Lucy, her name was. Sometimes they'd share a few words; at first just Lucy giving her compliments, but later spreading into minor observations on form and how she could achieve the same results but with far less energy expenditure, if she just learned the correct technique.

Zero lapped it up. When she wasn't coding attack algorithms on the Blue Fairy or setting up catfishing groups to lure out Pinocchios, she gulped down WeStream videos on climbing technique, which she'd try out the next day: wall-slapping, three-finger pinching, toe pull rather than push, sitting starts, and so on.

Her technique skyrocketed. Soon she was lapping seasoned climbers on the overhang walls while they watched in dismay. It wasn't about victory for her, though. It was about the flow state she fell into on a challenging climb. If ever she'd grown addicted to a drug, it was that.

"You should come join my group," Lucy said one day. "We free climb. In a few weeks we're clubbing together to go to Big Sur. It'll be a hectic weekend."

Zero had mumbled a few words about checking her schedule. It was the kind of thing people said on TV, which she'd been watching with the same intense focus that she did everything since her escape. She knew it was casual, a throwaway comment.

Still, for the next three days she agonized over the offer like it was a gilt-edged invitation to the White House. There were so many basic life skills she hadn't mastered. Her small talk was abysmal and the thought of it filled her with dread. The person she'd exchanged the most words with in her entire life was either the instructor who taught her online programming class, learning C, C++, Python and the other coding languages her father had listed, or the receptionist at the climbing wall.

In the end though, with her cheeks burning and her heart

in her mouth, she approached Lucy for the first time and said sure, she'd like to come. If the offer was still open. If she didn't mind.

Lucy seemed surprised for a moment, then her face split in a gorgeous smile. "Of course. You'll be very welcome, Clara. Just get your parents to sign off, OK?"

Faking up her parent's permission was easy. Lucy barely looked twice at the signed paperwork.

Every day in the run-up to California she was terrified. She felt certain she was making a mistake, that trusting Lucy and her friends was going to get her captured or killed, but in the end none of those things happened. What happened instead was an amazing two days of climbing in a stunning natural environment like nothing she'd ever seen before. It turned out to be, without a doubt, the best weekend of Zero's young life.

For two days she didn't think once about Hope, or the past, or anything else. She did team-climbs in Slate's Spire, and free soloed a minor crag at Crab Town, and camped out with Lucy for hours on a wall platform fifty yards up Granite Creek, waiting for their route-setters to lay in their belay pegs, just watching the landscape of ocean, canyon and trees, talking about nothing much.

After that she was hooked. She faked up more permission slips and started traveling more widely to climb, at first with Lucy's group and then with others. She grew better at talking and handling herself around people. She made friends with a range of people from their teens to the mid-twenties. There were one or two boys who took an interest along the way, but nothing coercive, and she wasn't interested beyond a few stray kisses anyway. Still, their overtures felt very different from the things her father had done. Their kisses, while fumbling, were sweet. There was an urgency but also a generosity.

Always, the next day when they returned to the wall, everything of the night before was buried in focus. She loved that. For the first time in her life, she had something good to live for.

Now, hanging upside down off the ZOO's ceiling while a crowd of teenagers watched from below, all of that came flooding back. She reveled in the burn and strain in her fingers and forearms, in the tension carried up from her toe-tip holds through her calves, thighs and belly, making her whole body quiver like a bowstring.

In the last several months, she'd neglected climbing. Sometimes it happened, when she grew so focused and intense that there was room for nothing else. No release ever came, though, and she just grew more and more reckless until, inevitably, something bad happened.

Hellion was right about that. She needed this.

Sometime around 4 p.m. her phone rang and connected instantly, then Hellion's voice was in her ear.

"We have something, Clara Baxter."

"Anatoly?"

"Not Anatoly. But very good. Important Real Boy. Spider at center of Blue Fairy web."

34

JOHN PAUL II

Within three hours, Zero stood outside the John Paul II secure government hospital. It was a large, brutalist red brick structure on the east side of central Krakow, all sharp edges and clean lines lit by sweeping white lights. The entrance was no-nonsense and no frills, encircled by fences and gates.

She strode confidently into the narrow lobby, where a security guard eyed her at the metal detector gate. He said something in Polish and Zero just smiled.

"American," she said. "I'm here on a consult. Mikolaj Lewondowska, third floor."

The guard, a bull-necked man with a nose florid from alcoholism, brought up a tablet computer and tapped through. He took his time, but Zero wasn't worried. Hellion had inserted the consult request herself, building off an existing case that could probably use the extra attention.

"Card?" he said.

Zero held out her magnetic ID card to the scanner, hacked by B4cksl4cker and printed by a darknet ID mill. The gate beeped green.

"Bag and possessions."

He held out a small plastic crate and she set her cloth bag down. The guard opened it, where her purse, phone and a couple of packets of tissues lay amidst a general detritus of old receipts she'd fished out of a trash container.

"Pass through," he said.

The detector swept her clean. She boarded an elevator going up to the second floor. The hospital seemed quiet at the late hour. On the second floor she was faced with white corridors and a map, but she didn't need to stop because she'd memorized the route.

A right turn, a left, then she was closing on the secure wing of the hospital. There was a locked door with plate glass panels, beyond which she could see another security guard. She approached and held her card to the scanner; it beeped green and admitted her through. The security guard nodded in her direction. She continued on for three doors then turned in.

Not Mikolaj Lewondowska's room, though; that was just a cover story to gain access. This was the room of Inessa Sidorova, a female Real Boy and one of the worst in all of Europe.

Sidorova's room was glamorous and lush, unlike any hospital Zero had seen before, befitting her status as paramour to a range of millionaires and billionaires. A large, high-tech looking mechanized bed stood against the wall beside large windows. Krakow was growing dark outside, and the view of the classical skyline was only growing in grandeur, as the handful of tall downtown church towers lit up from below. Several tables fringed the walls, hosting a vast weight of flowers, balloons and cards that left the air hanging thick with perfume.

The light was dim. Zero strode over to the bed.

Once a beautiful socialite, Inessa now looked drained and withered. In her mid-forties, the heart attack had come on quite unexpectedly. The news had even made the inner pages of the Gazeta Wyborcza, such was her fame.

Back at the Skawina warehouse to make the transition, Hellion had shown her photographs of Inessa in her prime. They showed a woman defying aging through her thirties, always glamorously dressed in designer evening gowns on a range of red carpets at different premiere events: movies, classical concerts, museum openings, political fundraisers.

"Why would I target a woman?" Zero had asked, tucked inside Rex's glowing embrace as she reviewed the data. "They're most often followers in this kind of abuse."

"Not this one," Hellion said, "she is black widow at heart of Blue Fairy. Many of these men," more photographs flashed, showing dozens of men hanging off Sidorova's arm on red carpets, laughing beside her on private jets, yachts and in clubs, "are all identified Real Boys with little footprint, other than through Inessa Sidorova. She is daughter of petrochemical Russian oligarch Yuri Sidorov, sole trustee of her father's empire and worth millions. For early years she lived playgirl lifestyle, taking jets around world with football players, politicians, actors and bankers. From there into her thirties, she began using Blue Fairy services."

Zero grunted. She hated female Real Boys more than anything. "She accessed the exchanges?"

"Impossible to say. Exchange data has all migrated to shadow line. But she is everywhere. Knows everyone. If anyone can tell where Viktor Anatoly is, it is her."

Now Zero looked into Sidorova's worn face. A party girl without a purpose, who'd taken her bohemianism too far. The Gazeta had been forthright about her condition; the heart attack had severely weakened her, necessitating a medically induced coma while a full-heart transplant candidate was sought. It was tempting to imagine that her many crimes had soured her heart, but more likely it was the lifestyle of drugs, alcohol and overindulgence.

Zero felt a special surge of anger, looking down. She hadn't had a female Real Boy in her hands since her mother, but Inessa Sidorova wasn't just a follower who liked to watch, like her mother. She was an instigator, too. A corrupter of others.

That anger shaped into a cold, clinical stiletto blade. Zero knew exactly what to do with it.

There were numerous machines encircling Sidorova: one was a pulse monitor tied to the oximeter on her left index finger; one was a mechanical drip stand, feeding a steady flow of yellowish clear liquid into her right forearm intravenously.

Sidorova didn't look like she was sleeping easily. There was a tight set to her features even in unconsciousness. Zero knew all about the vivid terrors you could experience, even dosed to the gills with knockout drugs.

She pushed past a table of flowers to examine the drip feed. There was a clear plastic bag labeled with the name of the chemicals it contained. Pentobarbital. That was good. It was a short-acting barbiturate, which mean the moment Zero removed the drip feed into Sidorova's arm, she'd begin to surface from the coma.

Still, that could take hours.

She set her bag on the bed and plucked out both packets of tissues and ripped them open. Tucked within the tissues of each was a small syringe and four small medical-grade glass vials: each contained a single dose of a different wake up drug ordered via a darknet 'prescription': modafinil, dexamphetamine, methylphenidate and epinephrine.

Zero dismissed the epinephrine; she might have used that if they had Sidorova on a stronger sedative, but it was better to avoid. She didn't want the old girl surging up with an adrenaline spike which might also put the stake in her enfeebled heart. Better by far if she woke calm and a little sleepy still.

"Ready to fake her vitals, Rex?" Zero asked.

"Yes, Zero," Rex answered in her ear. "Taking over. Proceed."

"Good boy," she said, and gently pinched the fingertip pulse oximeter off Sidorova's finger. There was no interruption in the record of her pulse, and Zero let out a breath. She looked to the door but saw nothing. She had to be fast; security guards patrolled the floor regularly.

Next she turned the small red tappet on the pentobarbital line, instantly cutting the flow, and used the small syringe to suck up 50ml of modafinil; the best 'antidote' for the knockout drugs in Sidorova's system. She found the vein on her arm, gently pierced the skin and squeezed a small dose in.

The first effects showed in seconds. Sidorova's eyelids began to flutter, signaling she was rising out of slow-wave sleep. Her breathing pattern shifted as she pulled in deeper breaths. Then her eyes blinked open.

"Inessa Sidorova," Zero began, speaking low and softly. The last thing she wanted was to stress this woman so much that she entered cardiac arrest again. "My name is Julia and I'd like to ask you some questions, if I may. Can you understand what I'm saying?"

Sidorova blinked then said something in Polish, low and barely audible.

"That's good, Inessa. Now, can you answer me in English?"

A few seconds passed. "Yes," Sidorova answered weakly.

"That's good," Zero said, "really good. Now, I'm going to tell you something, and I want you to try to stay calm. I'm not a doctor. I'm a representative of an organization we both know well. A very important, secretive organization, Inessa. Do you know what I'm talking about?"

Sidorova gazed. Zero thought she was understanding. The sleepy haze was coming out of her eyes a little more.

"How long?" she asked, then screwed her eyes up, like she was in pain. "How long am I here?"

Zero didn't remember that detail and it didn't matter. "Just a few days, Inessa. Everything's OK. Your new heart is coming. In fact, we're poised to expedite that. I think you can imagine how we might do that."

Sidorova's brow worked slowly. Putting the pieces together. "How?"

Zero smiled, building out an imagined Blue Fairy response. For all she knew, it was true. "We have a donor. A young woman, a perfect genetic match. There'll be minimal rejection, few drugs you'll need to take. She is not exactly a volunteer, of course, but that won't present a problem."

Was that a faint smile ghosting Sidorova's frail face. "You took … your time."

Zero smiled too. "There's just one problem. The girl, she belongs to Viktor Anatoly. You know him?"

Sidorova stared for a long moment, then gave a slow nod.

"That's good, Inessa. Now, Viktor volunteered this girl. But in the last twenty-four hours, he's disappeared. We don't know where he is. We don't know the reason behind this, but we are concerned. You need that heart, Inessa. We need to safeguard our investment in both you and Viktor. Anything you can tell us about his whereabouts will help."

A long moment passed as Sidorova absorbed that. She gave the faintest nod, then smiled slightly and whispered something too faintly for Zero to hear.

She leaned in, holding her ear just over Sidorova's mouth.

"Say again, please, Inessa, I didn't catch that."

"I said," Sidorova wheezed, "hello, Mona."

Zero's heart sank. She pulled back. The smile on Sidorova's face spread.

"It's actually Zero," she said, the softness dropping from her tone.

"I don't … care. You'll always be … Mona … to me."

Zero stood stock still. This had always been a risk. Even through the pentobarbital fog, she might be recognized.

"If you know who I am, then you know what I'm willing to do. You can live, Inessa, or die. It's simple."

Sidorova jerked gently, then something like a wheeze emerged from her taut cheeks. Several weak coughs followed, and Zero realized what it was. She was laughing.

"Scratch that," Zero said, and surveyed her options. It would be an easy thing to start breaking Inessa Sidorova's bones, but that would most likely throw her into cardiac arrest. Instead she spoke while looking right at Sidorova's eyes.

"Hellion, I'm encountering resistance. Can you let me know who Sidorova loves?"

"Working," came the response.

Sidorova's laughter subsided. Zero didn't budge. It took almost a minute for an answer to come.

"She has many friends but few family. Mother and father both dead, no siblings, cousins but there is no record they see each other. Searching further." Seconds passed. "Wait… B4cksl4cker, what do you think of this?"

Seconds passed. They'd muted her again. She waited. Sidorova glared back defiantly. It reminded Zero of the way her mother had glared up from her seat, strapped in and forced to watch while her beloved husband was tortured to death.

Zero had felt nothing for her then but disgust. There'd been nothing left of sympathy in either of them; long burned by exposure to Lance Gebhart. If anything, Inessa was worse.

She was another Lance, but enfeebled already, days after Zero had put him on the rack.

Hellion's voice came back in.

"Is far from certain, but facial recognition search of local social media, as run through aging program and genetic facial features tracker, fine-tuned by socioeconomic status and correlated travel record, has turned up suggestion. Inessa Sidorova may have daughter."

Zero's lips quirked into a smile.

"They share facial bridge features, eye color, hair color, golden triangle of nose and eyes is similar. Connection is secret, but both were in Rome at same time, Paris, Vienna. This is quite coincidence. This girl is sixteen, rich with no clear source. Goes to best schools. Is good match for genetic link."

"What's her name?"

Hellion told her. Zero just repeated it.

"Maryam Toussaint."

Sidorova's eyes flared.

Bull's eye.

"She lives in Paris," Zero went on, repeating details as Hellion fed them to her. "She goes to the Ecumenical Sisters Grand École, she likes lacrosse and excels at mathematics. You've hidden her for years but funnel her money through…" Hellion's keys raced, "one of your AIDS charities. She's your daughter."

Sidorova tried to play it cool, but the frantic look in her eyes gave her away. "That's nonsense. I never heard of this girl."

"But I know you do. I will visit her, Inessa. I will do to her all the things you so enjoyed doing to me."

"You wouldn't," she croaked.

"I will," Zero said firmly. "I'm Girl Zero. And you're running out of time. Tell me where to find Anatoly before your little heart bursts, or I'm going for Maryam. Sweet, innocent Maryam. I'll put her on a rack, like I did with my father."

Inessa's eyes widened in terror. It didn't matter that Zero had no intention of ever visiting her daughter. She didn't punish the innocent. Inessa Sidorova didn't need to know that.

"No."

"Tell me where Viktor Anatoly is. Where the Blue Fairy exchanges are. Where my sister is, Hope?"

Sidorova's eyes warred, and tears sprang up then fled down her temples. "I only went once. To the exchange. Viktor, he took me. I was blindfolded, Mona. It was so vast. So many boys and girls." Her voice took on a strange, strained tone. "But I remember…"

She blinked then her eyes rolled back in her head. Zero swiftly put two fingers on her throat, but there was no pulse. She cursed, considering CPR, but the pressure of physical heart palpitations might just kill her outright. A crash cart was the same.

There was nothing else for it.

She took the little vial of adrenaline, filled the little syringe then plunged it directly between Sidorova's third and fourth ribs, into her heart, where she depressed the plunger.

With a jerk and a gasp Sidorova came back, every muscle taut and lifting her up in the covers, eyes flaring like she was about to burst from the inside.

"Last chance, Inessa," Zero pressed. "What did you remember about Viktor Anatoly?"

Sidorova blurted a few words in Polish or French, eyes roving before they caught on Zero, and she dropped into English.

"The stink!" she gasped. "Filth. Everywhere. So many. So strong. And all those girls."

"What did you see? I need landmarks, Inessa."

"A farm!" she blurted. "Pigs. I remember, ah, I remember…" Her face spasmed and the pulse in her throat under Zero's fingers entered a rapid fire race. Too fast, too many beats, and that could only lead to one thing.

"Give me a town name, Inessa. Any kind of name."

"I saw… I saw…"

Then she breathed her last. Her straining body relaxed into the bed like a cut bow string.

Zero sighed.

"Is she dead?" Hellion asked.

"She's dead," Zero confirmed, already scooping up her vials and turning the red tappet back on, allowing the pentobarbital to flow once more. She wiped down the single spot on Inessa's throat that she'd touched, wiped down the oximeter, then stood.

The room was quiet again, but for the rushing of blood in Zero's ears.

"We're looking for a farm," she said. "A pig farm. Just like my father's farm in Idaho."

"This is broad."

"I know. Now let's find it."

35

MUD

Zero sat perfectly still in the cab circling back to Skawina, lost in the past.

The Blue Fairy exchange was real. It existed on a farm; Viktor Anatoly's farm. Like the Idaho farm she'd grown up on. But here there were countless boys and girls. A vast structure to house them.

And pigs.

The stink, Sidorova had said.

Zero could almost smell it as the cab hurtled through the dark on highway 79. The same stink that had filled her childhood cell, pumped down via the ventilation fans. She could feel that stink like it was a physical thing, smothering her. Overwhelming her.

After breaking free from her cell, she'd let all the pigs die.

It wasn't personal or active. She'd just forgotten to feed them, caught up in one of the mad coding binges she'd plunged herself into in the weeks and months after her father died. There'd been so much to lose and not a moment to waste. She'd only noticed on a rare trip to the surface to resupply.

She'd felt nothing then, looking out over their matrix of

enclosures, now buzzing thickly with fat black flies. They were just one more piece of her father destroyed. She'd gone back below, making no effort to pick them up, bury them or dispose of them.

The darknet was the only path to Hope and the only thing that mattered, but it was a place filled with sickness, hurting her every bit as much as it helped, like sewing up a wound with steel wool. It taught her what she needed to know about hunting Pinocchios, while keeping her from pursuing anything like a normal life, until one night it had just been too much.

After nearly two years spent in her father's underground office, teaching herself to hack with the tools he'd left behind while the torture machine hammered and stretched his corpse day and night next door, she came to a dark revelation.

It wasn't enough punishment.

She needed more. She needed something and she didn't know what, so in a frenzy she'd splashed gasoline liberally over the farmhouse and the pig enclosures and the rotted pigs, then simply lit a spark and watched it burn into the night. The following morning she'd left. She was sixteen then, an adult by many laws, and rich with stolen funds from her father's accounts and her hacking activity.

For the first time she was out in the world. In between hacking and coding and climbing, she'd started up her earliest catfishing operations on the Internet, funding stings run by volunteers to smoke out Pinocchios. It had helped. Over the next four years, in-between training with stiletto blades and climbing and parkour, she'd set up dozens of such catfishing groups all across the country, pulling in hundreds of catfishers.

Most of her catfishers, like Armitage, were women who'd been touched by abuse in the past. They volunteered all the hours they had to spare, sometimes eighty-plus a week, laying out false trails of children on the Internet and darknet, using fake names and stolen photographs to lure out the sickest men.

Over the years, these catfishing teams developed hundreds of leads. Some of these perps were arrested. Some were arraigned. Some were even sent to jail. But many, the choice picks of the litter, were all referred to Zero, who went to visit them alone. It was with them that she refined her technique. The questions. The torture. They were her first experience of killing Pinocchios, outside of her own family.

Speaking to those sickly, greasy men in her torture racks, each compelled by their own warped logic and twisted drives, had taught her so much about the Pinocchio psychology. Why they did what they did. The excuses they invented. Some blamed childhood abuse, with themselves as victims unable to break the cycle. Some claimed to feel an unbearable attraction to children that they'd battled all their lives, only now surrendering.

Zero didn't care about their justifications. Once upon a time, she'd wondered why her father and mother had done what they did to her, until she came to a simple conclusion that answered the question once and for all. Zero didn't like broccoli. Some people did. Some people ate broccoli. Others didn't.

It was as simple as that.

To her, the excuses didn't matter, because each one of these men had made a choice, and it was the choice that made them monsters. Killing them was a service to the world. Their deathbed confessions under her knives did help her feel something, though. A strange connection to Hope, especially when she came to the third question.

But that connection never led anywhere. None of them had ever heard Hope's name, and their deaths, while satisfying, led her no closer to her sister. As she grew older, turning from nineteen into twenty, she'd grown frustrated and angry. She'd stretched herself thinner, desperate to break through the outer veneer of wannabe Pinocchios and find the Blue Fairy exchanges; find somebody who knew something she could use. She grew more and more reckless, until finally the Pinocchios staged a counter-sting against her in Detroit. They'd captured her, prepped her for sacrifice, and only Christopher Wren's intervention had kept her in the game.

It had also shaken loose a deeper understanding of the Pinocchios. There was an inner circle. The Blue Fairy exchanges existed.

After that, the real slaughter began. She cranked up her kill rate, burning through twenty-five more dead Real Boys in three years, spread beyond America's shores and all around the world. It helped, but it still wasn't what she needed.

She needed her little sister.

Everything came back to Hope.

Now she felt the old tide of chaotic frustration rising up in her, just like that day on her sixteenth birthday when she'd burned the Idaho farmhouse down.

Soon she was back in Skawina, on the outskirts of Krakow, and buzzing with delayed adrenaline. Somebody needed to die. The driver dropped her off at the approach road to her warehouse, with an excuse delivered in halting English about the terrible state of the churned clay road ahead.

The familiar tang of coal smoke wafted in the night air, blooming from the power station's stacks. Zero stepped out onto the mud and her foot sank in an inch. It was definitely worse than before, and threw instantly on the alert.

Had Anatoly found her?

As the cab drove away, Zero studied the wheel tracks cutting through the clay. They were thick and deep, leaving waterlogged troughs in the mud. It looked like multiple large trucks had passed this way, carrying something heavy.

She lifted her phone. "Rex, why no security alerts?"

"There are no security breaches," he answered after a few seconds.

"I'm looking at big wheel ruts. Trucks have come down to the warehouse. They must've passed right outside where you are. You didn't take that as a breach?"

A second passed. "There are no security breaches."

Zero clenched her fists. On some level she knew she should circle around, go collect some weapons and approach on stealth mode, but she was too pumped on rage to do that. If Anatoly was here, she would kill him with her bare hands.

She stalked straight down. The mud caked up as high as her knees within seconds. The smoke made her cough. She rounded the corner and saw that her courtyard was packed with trucks.

There were five of them. Three were max-sized eighteen-wheelers with full trailers hitched up, two were mid-sized box trucks.

She stared, and some of the anger lifted, replaced with confusion.

What on earth was this? She stalked closer. The first two trucks were branded with the names and logos of well-known companies, while the third had a triangular logo with the name 'Pyramid Eradication'.

At that her confusion turned into angry disbelief. She stamped a muddy path around the trucks and made a beeline direct for her warehouse. The roll shutter was open. The tent door to Rex was sealed, but from within she heard familiar voices. It wasn't possible. She ran the final few yards, unzipped the tent flap and ripped the canvas 'door' aside.

Two cheerful faces looked back at her.

One was about her age, a tan female with long black hair

knotted into tight, fat spikes atop her head. She had sweet, ruddy features; thick and full lips, wide-set black eyes and a pointy chin. She was dressed in a black workman's jumpsuit complete with black leather utility belt, slotted with various tools; one looked to be a soldering iron, another had to be a tangle of HDMI or ethernet cables, and a third was, yes, a Twinkie.

Sitting beside her was a huge man as big as a bear, in his late twenties perhaps, with a shaved head and a trimmed hipster beard. He wore a pair of brass glasses that looked like jeweler's loupes; miniature telescopes attached to a frame that clasped at the back of his head. He was dressed in a white t-shirt that showed off his muscularity, on top of baggy blue shorts and a pair of sandals.

Zero couldn't believe it.

Hellion and B4cksl4cker, in the flesh.

"What on earth is this?" she demanded.

Hellion cackled and stood, holding out her hand to shake. "Circus has come to town, Clara Baxter. Your lucky day!"

Zero just stared at it, even as B4cksl4cker rose and held his massive paw out too.

"No," Zero said. "We're not doing this. You said to be careful!"

"Careful is boring," B4cksl4cker said. In person his voice seemed even deeper. It was hard enough to take the size of him in visually, let alone his stone-grinding intonation. "Plus, we have brought you Attack Crate 2.0, just in time for best clue yet."

Zero felt like she was teetering on a cliff edge. "You've what? An Attack Crate?"

"Very large improvement from Attack Crate 1.0," Hellion said enthusiastically. "Contains many excellent weapons and technological advantages, as helped by special mechanical engineer in USA, my good friend. Her name is Alli. Also we thought it is nice to visit with you, merciless but lonely assassin Clara Baxter, have pierogi together."

She winked.

It was too much for Zero. She opened her mouth then closed it, then turned flat around and walked out of the tent.

"What did we say?" B4cksl4cker rumbled behind her.

She kept walking until she found her Kawasaki Ninja, tipped even deeper into the mud now, with twin eighteen-wheelers parked either side of it. She thought about hoisting it and taking off, but paused with her hands on the handlebars.

She turned.

They were standing right there behind her, watching in bemusement.

"Do you think she does not recognize us?" Hellion asked.

"We are easy to recognize," B4cksl4cker offered. "Also, convoy. Is not common."

"Perhaps this is mental breakdown? Mid-life crisis, perhaps? Old woman just died, but this is specialty of Clara Baxter, no?"

B4cksl4cker grunted assent, and that pissed Zero off. She let go of the Ninja and straightened up.

"Bullshit, mid-life crisis. We're the same age! If anything, I'm younger than you. And we just got the best lead we have yet."

Hellion's features wrinkled in confusion. "This is more reason we come. Work together. And same age, is she speaking to you, B4cksl4cker? It seems, she is looking at me."

"I am older than her, certainly," he said.

"Stop it!" Zero snapped, then started toward them, mud sludging underfoot. "That's enough nonsense. In fact I'm-" Zero's right leg stuck in the mud behind her. For a terrible moment she teetered, overbalanced with one arm out and raised to wag in Hellion's face. There was nothing she could do. Then she toppled.

The mud welcomed her in. She got both arms up but they hit and slid uselessly to the sides, dropping her chest-first into the sopping clay. Her face hit. For a moment all she saw was black and all she felt was the cold, yielding sludge compress around her cheeks and throat.

Then she was up again, spitting and casting about for something firm to hold onto. She settled on a handle of one of the trucks, then focused on the two hackers. They were watching her with perplexed expressions.

"Is this special trick of merciless assassin?" Hellion asked. "I have not seen this one before."

"It may be specialism," B4cksl4cker mused. "Drunken monkey fighting style. I have seen Jackie Chan do this."

Hellion turned to him. "Rush Hour?"

B4cksl4cker laughed. "Of course not Rush Hour. It is Shanghai Noon with Owen Wilson."

Hellion smirked. "Is certainly unusual. Clara Baxter, is this drunken monkey fighting style?"

Zero had already had more than enough. "Shut up, both of you. You shouldn't be here."

She stamped carefully out of the mud and past them into the warehouse.

"She is leaving mud trail," B4cksl4cker observed.

"Do not enter Rex's kennel like this," Hellion advised. "Much mud. We have made further upgrades, better integration, better brain, can even D-DOS attack government facility now, and-"

Zero spun. "You've tampered with my dog again?"

"Just improvements."

"I never asked you to do that!" she stormed. "The best thing you can do is go, right now. I already lost my operator.

This close to Anatoly, I'm not losing two more, even if they are total idiots."

She spun and stamped on.

"Are we her operators?" B4cksl4cker asked. "I thought she rejected this."

"Where are you going, Clara Baxter?" Hellion called.

"It's just Clara!" she shouted back without turning, rage pouring out of her in unexpected directions. "It doesn't have to be Clara Baxter every time. I made the name up anyway. You're Hellion. He's B4cksl4ckler. Just call me Clara!"

She passed Rex's tent, or 'kennel', and continued on into the shadows of the warehouse.

"I think she is angry about her name."

"Yes. From now on, do not address her this way, B4cksl4cker. She does not like it."

Zero's ears burned. Her fists tightened. She was angry but not sure why.

"Where are you going, Clara Baxter? Sorry, Clara?"

She didn't turn.

"She cannot hear."

"Is mud in ears. Shout louder."

B4cksl4cker did. "WHERE ARE YOU GOING, CLARA BAXTER? CLARA?"

At last she spun again, feeling on the edge of exploding. "It's not three names! It's not two names! Just one name. And in case you didn't notice, I fell in the mud, so now I'm going to shower it off. Is that clear? Then I'm going to go find Anatoly on his farm and kill the bastard. So can we stop with the running commentary now?"

There was silence for a moment. She reached the rusty showerhead emerging through the raw brick and looked up at it.

"Cold shower?" came Hellion's loud whisper, sounding distasteful. They'd followed her. They were watching her again, like this was some kind of show. "Followed by cold wash of clothing once more? Then wearing cold, wet clothing, again? Is this also Drunken Monkey style?"

Zero said nothing, just defiantly turned the faucet. The water that hit her was freezing. Worse than the mud.

"Perhaps this is remnant from awful childhood," B4cksl4cker offered. "I do not know."

"Just shut up!" Zero barked. "Stop making guesses like I'm some cultural anomaly. It's not difficult."

"Must make guess, Clara, because you do not talk," Hellion called back. "Only kill, kill, kill. Kill old woman in bed, hooray, what fun. But cold shower is not necessary. We have showers in convoy. Many showers, hot water, new clothes, good food. Hamburgers. Um. Pizza. Um. B4cksl4cker?"

"Uh, tater tots," he added, sounding a little flustered to be put on the spot. "Twinkies, very many of these. Also hamburgers!"

"I said hamburgers already."

"Hot dogs, then! With American mustard."

Zero spun to them, splashing water. "What about the farm? Please tell me you've run a search. That's where I'm going!"

Hellion shifted uncomfortably. "Yes. Farm. This is excellent clue, indeed, but Clara. There are many farms in Poland. Thousands. And is this farm even in Poland? Sidorova did not say. Could be anywhere."

Zero opened her mouth to protest, then closed it.

She hadn't thought about that. She was only in Krakow because of Perp 35, but he was just one prominent trap set by Anatoly. There could have been others. Bratva were handling her attempted arrest here.

The farm could be anywhere?

At that realization she felt her defenses failing. Already

this was too much. The cold water was a killer. The day was a killer. Rage and recklessness were pointless without any target at all. Hope wasn't coming tonight.

She turned and stared at them while cold water ran mud down her face. "If I get in your convoy, and have a hot shower, and change into fresh clothes, neither one of you is allowed to watch."

Hellion frowned. "Why would we watch this? We have never watched this."

Zero sighed. She turned the cold water off and stood there dripping. If you couldn't beat them, after all, you had to join them. "Well, lead the way then."

36

SPA

The shower was incredible. Zero luxuriated in the heat and water pressure, expecting at any moment for the water to run dry, but somehow it kept on coming. When she'd scrubbed herself three times and simply stood for twice that time again, she finally emerged into the spa-like changing room.

There were four mahogany lockers set into the wall of the trailer. The space was narrow, but it felt opulent. The air was fragrant with jasmine and Scandinavian pine. She noticed a sauna facility tucked into a corner, and marveled again at how the two hackers had chosen to spend their money and live their lives.

They were, after all, billionaires. Kitting out a convoy of trucks had to be considerably cheaper than custom-designing a superyacht or even buying up a penthouse. Perhaps a little luxury was deserved.

She couldn’t remember the last time she'd enjoyed a shower so much. The steam from it hung in the air, and she picked up one of two fluffy white towels and stepped over to the sinks, where a great array of moisturizing creams, scrubbing pastes and rehydrating body oils stood in racks.

In one of the full-size mirrors she caught a glimpse of herself and flinched. It was seven years since she'd escaped Idaho, but she still hadn't gotten over her distaste her own body, particularly the scars. Usually she wore loose clothes that covered them all. In some ways, she feared, it still belonged to the Pinocchios.

Now that thought made her angry.

She dropped the towel and stared at her body. She knew that, in silhouette or in the dark, it was attractive. It had curves, full breasts and hips, along with muscular arms and thighs with a lean stomach. In the light though, her scars were all that she saw.

Every one of these she remembered. Memories of pain and humiliation. She waited as the steam dispersed from the shower, running her fingers lightly over her ribs. Her father had enacted so many cruelties on her, and when he'd run out of ideas his Pinocchios had filled the breach with more. He'd followed their suggestions. Her mother had watched.

"Do it for Hope," he'd whispered. "Don't fight. Endure it so Hope never needs to come down here and join you."

She'd endured it.

Now the anger collapsed in a feeling of uselessness, just as it always did. She thought again of Gabriel, changing her clothes with the help of his daughters in his warm basement, and wondered if that made her angry too. Somehow, it didn't. She pictured him trying to look away as the new clothes went on, trying to be decent, but being drawn to her anyway. Somehow, she wanted that, like the kisses from boys on her climbing trips. She wanted his hands on her scars. It would be-

"Are you alive in there?" came Hellion's voice.

She grabbed a towel and swiftly wrapped it around herself, looking for the speaker and the camera. "If you're watching me now, Hellion, I will cut out your damn eyes."

Hellion laughed. "No cameras in spa. But come join us, Clara Baxter. Clara."

She hastily rubbed herself dry, while looking around for fresh clothes. "I'm fine. I'll go check in on Rex."

"Rex is here with us. He is good boy. Likes treats. Come."

Zero cursed and threw the towel on the ground. For a second she eyed the rack of beauty products, then strode in, picked three at random and smeared one on her face, one on her body, and emptied the third down the sink, waiting to see if Hellion protested.

She didn't. It wasn't proof, but it was something.

They'd laid out clothes for her, looked like some kind of high-tech strike suit all in black. She handled the pants then the top. They were thick and sturdy but flexible, perhaps some kind of new-weave para-aramid armor. She pulled them on and tried some movements. The maneuverability was actually world class. There were even custom-sewn slots for her blades, and an accompanying belt with slots that would work for her shuriken.

Not bad.

The outfit was completed with a pair of boots; they had ankle protection as well as built in blade holsters which strapped up around her calves like Roman sandals. Her blades lay alongside in a thick roll of black velvet, left clean and gleaming. She spent a few moments finding places for them in the loops, holsters and sheaths built into the suit.

They fit perfectly. They didn't impede her movement at all. Perhaps it was the best custom suit she'd ever had.

She popped the back door. The air outside was gritty with coal smoke and the sky was black. She eyed the mud below, then noticed a ladder-like metal walkway had been pulled out from beneath the trailer's baseboard and affixed to the next truck over.

Clever. She strode across this makeshift bridge and

knocked on the next trailer's rear door. In a moment the door opened and a wave of cold air poured out. Hellion stood there with a big silly grin, looking her up and down.

"Is good fit! Many knives, as I thought! Yes, Attack Crate is big win."

Then she spun and headed back into the trailer's interior. Zero's jaw dropped. She'd considered her mobile server farm in the van impressive; a supercomputer built out of two medium-height racks lining the walls, about a hundred times the capacity of Rex as she'd first built him.

This dwarfed that. If anything it felt like she was back in the Bratva server farm; a total of six rack columns in parallel stretched to the rear of the cab, each one crammed with servers that hummed and churned data.

"Oh my," Zero muttered.

"Is called Gargantua," Hellion called over her shoulder. "Number one top mobile computer in world. Come."

Zero followed, her eyes soaking in everything; everywhere were the absolute top-spec parts, the best optical data lines, the fastest drives. For the whole trailer, you were easily looking at ten million dollars. And that was just to buy the materials. To actually wire them all, and sync them to each other, then to have sufficient shock absorption in the tires and chassis the prevent their connections constantly coming unplugged, and to keep a mobile Internet signal live? She couldn't put a number on it.

"Is nice, yes?" Hellion asked.

As Zero advanced she felt like she was being absorbed into the intestines of a fantastic beast. Halfway along the trailer, the middle four racks gave way to a workspace with two facing workstations. Each had an array of six large screens and three keyboards set to different languages, along with a large trackpad, mouse and scroll wheel. The chairs in these stations were unique, and looked more like science-fiction hammocks than any ergonomic design she'd seen before.

"Is all our work," Hellion said proudly. "It is no Rex, but we are proud."

B4cksl4cker looked up from his station and flashed her a generous smile. "You are first outsider to see convoy. Even Christopher Wren has not seen this."

Zero didn't know what to say. They seemed sincere. "I'm honored."

"Yes," Hellion said seriously. "And you have not even seen Attack Crate yet. Is 2.0!" She beamed. "But first, debrief. There is much to say. Please, sit."

She pointed to the hammock thing in the one open station. Zero could see no clear point of entry.

"Uh, how?"

"Is simple." Hellion demonstrated, dropping in through the many straps, slotting her legs into massage tubes and resting her elbows on supportive platforms poised right above the keys.

"So this is how you do it," Zero murmured. Everything about this trailer, this lifestyle, was built around professional hacking.

"You try."

Hellion popped out. Zero dropped in. She tangled herself on a few of the support cables, had some trouble getting her thicker legs into the elevated massage tubes, but once she was in, she felt something close to transcendence.

"Wow."

"It is nice," Hellion said.

The seat fit like a glove. The constant low massage on her legs kept blood flowing. The forearm supports would help stave off carpal tunnel in the wrists; one of a hacker's greatest enemies. She already knew her next rig would be outfitted as close to this as she could get it.

"Nobody except Isabel ever sits in this chair," B4cksl4cker said, peering at her through a slot in the screens. "Is high honor. Perhaps she has crush on you."

"I do not! Is mutual appreciation."

Zero felt it. She looked up at Hellion, who was reddening slightly. "Isabel?"

"It's my name," she said, slightly sheepishly. "You can say Hellion or Isabel."

It put a lump in Zero's throat. It offered a path to something that she'd had few times in her life; friendship. "Clara Baxter's a fake name. My real name's Zero."

Hellion nodded. She looked so young when she wasn't being contrary. "We understand. Zero is enough. One-word name, like Beyoncé."

Zero smiled and looked back at the screens. They were displaying a range of shifting data. "Well. I'm here. What's the debrief?"

"Many items," B4cksl4cker said. "First is, we have narrowed down Anatoly's farm."

37

TARGET

"Narrowed to how many?" Zero asked, instantly tuning in.

"Still a very large number. There are many other leads, also. We have documents on hundreds of Real Boys, and millions in recovered cryptocoins."

That sounded like a good haul, but the only thing Zero cared about was the farm. "Narrowed to how many?" she repeated.

Hellion shifted her feet. "Unfortunately, this remains high number. Across Poland or Europe or world?"

Zero steeled herself. "Give me Poland."

"Number is precisely eight thousand, three hundred and twenty-six."

That was a blow. "Those are all pig farms?"

"Yes."

"With substantial buildings on the property? Enough to host the Blue Fairy exchanges?"

Hellion looked at her feet. "Yes. If we include many smallholdings, number is in tens of thousands."

Zero sighed. She should have known it wasn't enough to go on yet. "And the wider numbers for Europe will be in the hundreds of thousands, right?"

"Yes. Include the world, and it is approaching millions."

Those were big numbers.

"Is there anything further that can help narrow these results, Zero?" B4cksl4cker asked. "Any hint or detail?"

Zero racked her mind and something popped up.

"Yesterday I went to see a man called Joas Levi. He was a Bratva boss ten years ago, when the Pinocchios were starting their global creep. According to him they have a longstanding, well-developed relationship, executed at a high level of logistical sophistication, and they want me for more than just vengeance. There may be a way they can industrialize my death on a billion-dollar scale. Even trillion."

"Trillion, for livestream agonizing death of Clara Baxter, AKA Zero?" Hellion mused. "This would be very expensive pay-per-view event."

"Most expensive in history," B4cksl4cker said.

"But I would watch live," Hellion said with a wink.

"You would not watch live, Isabel."

"No, of course not live. But highlight reel, perhaps-"

"I don't know about the trillion figure," Zero interrupted. "Billions seems like a stretch, too; Levi must've been exaggerating. A livestream sacrifice is what they tried last time, but this is different. Definitely bigger. Worth killing their own people over."

"Different how?"

Zero considered. "I'm not sure, but if Anatoly's farm holds the Blue Fairy exchange, the physical heart of their child auction network, then it'll be a grand and longstanding investment." She thought back to the many times she'd crossed paths with the Pinocchios, in particular the bizarre temple-like layout of Pleasure Island, from when they'd captured her. "These men are all narcissists with a taste for grandeur. They may have evolved, but I think we're looking for something impressive in scale."

"OK," B4cksl4cker said, tapping keys. "I can cut smaller farms."

"But not by overall size," Zero said. "I'm thinking the fields don't matter. In fact, they're probably not that large. Focus on the scale of the buildings. Barns. Warehouses." She chewed her cheek. "Also recency. You can exclude anything that was rented, tenanted or built in the last, say, eight years. I think this farm goes back to the origin of the Real Boy-Bratva cooperation, ten years ago."

B4cksl4cker pecked his keys a little more enthusiastically. "Yes. On global scale, this brings us down to five hundred thousand farms. In Europe, one hundred and fifty thousand. In Poland, four thousand three hundred and seventeen."

There was silence for a moment.

"It is still a lot," Hellion said.

Something else occurred to Zero. "Legacy," she burst out.

"Bless you," said B4cksl4cker.

"I didn't sneeze. I'm talking about legacy. I told you about Anatoly's big plan to follow up on my father's wishes, right?"

B4cksl4cker looked at Hellion. "What?"

Zero sped on. "When I spoke to him outside the server farm, he was talking about legacy, about being true to my father's vision. I thought he was just trying to piss me off, but maybe it was a boast."

"Keeping pigs in Idaho is boast?"

Her mind cast back over the telephone conversation, seeing depths now where she hadn't before. If Bratva and the Real Boys had been working together for more than a decade, following a blueprint laid down by her father, then anything was possible.

"Maybe. It already sounds like he's modeling his farm on my father's, with the pigs. What if the rest of it mimics the

Idaho farm too? Then the one thing he'd need to complete it would be..."

She trailed off, hitting upon what seemed like the final step.

"What, Zero?"

"Me. Hope. Both of us in cells." She cursed. "I can't believe I didn't see it earlier. This is it. What if he's building his farm into some kind of museum to display us? Like some sick theme park for the Real Boys?"

"Theme park?"

Zero felt the revelation surging through her. The Pinocchios had done this kind of thing before. The last time they'd captured her, they'd taken her to Pleasure Island. That had been grand. Except this place wasn't going to be dedicated to her death. One death alone wouldn't bring in nearly enough money.

The final piece clicked into place. "Not a theme park - a zoo! He's already got Hope. Get me and that's the whole set. Real Boys will come see us there for as long as we live. It could be worth many millions of dollars."

A moment of silence passed.

"Zoo," Hellion mused. "Human zoo which is theme park. So, buildings should be like original farm? Fields also?"

"Exactly the same." Her thoughts traveled back over everything Anatoly had said, and only found more confirmation. "I think that's what he's been hinting at. He's replicated my father's farm as a prison for me, and a theme park for them!"

B4cksl4cker began typing. "Searching for photograph of Idaho farm. Checking land survey, satellite, aircraft belly-cams. And... yes, here is satellite photograph from within last six months."

He brought it up on Zero's screens too; the Idaho farm splashed across all six monitors. She'd never seen it from above before, but she recognized it easily: to the west the half-burned farmhouse, to the east the muddy splinters of the pig enclosures spreading in a large rectangle. To the south was the barn, to the north the gestation crates and farrowing cages.

Seeing all that thrust her back into the past; how her father used to talk about his intensive farming methods in the gaps between livestreaming for the Pinocchios.

"You have to dock their tails when they're born, Mona," he'd murmur, "or they bite them off and cause infections. You pull their teeth when they're babies so they don't cannibalize each other. You know what cannibalize means, don't you? Clip their ears, too, to save the energy it takes to grow them. The sows, that's the pregnant mothers, they go in a gestation crate. They don't like it, they can't really lie down, but it's best for them. Otherwise they roll over and crush the piglets. It all makes the meat cheaper."

Zero shook her head to clear her father's droning voice. She remembered hating him and hating the pigs and the farm with a visceral disgust, because of the stink and the cries and the suffering. All she'd ever wanted was to leave and take Hope with her, but now Anatoly had rebuilt it all.

If anything, as B4cksl4cker turned the photograph, mapping out the size, the structures, the access road and enclosures, she was reminded of Auschwitz: living creatures crushed into too-small spaces, forced to endure in their own filth, stress levels raised so high they lashed out at each other, fated to die and be mined for profit.

Industrialized death.

She felt sick, and only noticed Hellion bobbing on her feet impatiently after a few minutes. Zero watched for a moment while her mind spun, then realized. "Oh. I'm in your station. Do you want it back?"

"Yes, please," Hellion said politely. She sounded like a little kid.

Zero began to extricate herself. There were some tangles but she got it done without needing too much help. Hellion dropped into her slot smoothly and her hands began to fly.

Zero's jaw dropped.

Hellion's fingers were almost a blur; moving faster than anything Zero had seen before. All six screens immediately transformed. She recognized some kind of fresh matrix being formed up, and the bare bones of a new search algorithm being pulled together from component scraps of code.

"What are you doing?"

"Building search algorithm," Hellion answered without looking. "First step is identify target, could be many thousands of pig farms. Obtain photographs, then run search protocol comparing these farms to Idaho farm. Is not complex but may be difficult still. Algorithm will need to machine learn for several hours, to properly recognize features. Size is important?"

Zero blinked.

"What?"

"Size of farm. This farm is, hmm, four acres, B4cksl4cker?"

"Three point two five," he answered. "Not very large."

"I think so," Zero answered. "But I don't know for sure. Aim for around that size, but let's not rule too many places out yet."

Hellion's hands flew and the whole matrices of data danced at her command.

"Anything further?" B4cksl4cker asked. "I am now harvesting fresh crop of slaved computers for botnet. Starting with one million. We will have augmented search power."

Zero racked her mind. The farm. The pigs. Industrialized death dating back at least ten years. If Viktor Anatoly was really trying to replicate her father's work, to complete his legacy, what other features should he include?

"There was the dungeon. But that was underground, so nothing visible from the air except an air pipe or two. The farmhouse, barn, fences, gates, but you can see all that. They're all normal."

"Orientation? Idaho farm is east-west. Does this matter?"

"I don't know. Let's say not."

B4cksl4cker tapped away, inputting these parameters, then looked up. "I do not think this will be enough. Is there anything unique?"

"I can't think of anything else."

"Then we will attempt with this. Perhaps, by cross-reference to Real Boys we have data on, their travels and financial flows, something will emerge. Go."

Zero blinked. "Go where?"

Hellion grinned at her, already rising from her hammock. "Attack Crate 2.0. If attack on farm is imminent, you must have very best equipment. Follow me."

38

ATTACK CRATE 2.0

Hellion exited the trailer, walked along the suspended platform to the third full-size trailer, then down another metal 'bridge' to one of the box trucks. Though Zero was still marveling at the possible scale of Anatoly's vision, she couldn't help but marvel at the scale of this convoy too.

"Who does all this for you?" Zero asked as she followed. "Who drives the trucks, services them, sets all this up? Don't tell me the whole thing is run by AI."

"We have our own Foundation," Hellion answered. "Foundation inside Foundation. Mostly hackers who wish to be us. We train them."

"OK, so where are they? Crammed inside the third semi?"

Hellion laughed. "Of course not." She kneeled to unlatch the box truck's roll shutter. "This is not entire convoy, of course. There are more vehicles. Logistics. Resupply. Staff accommodation. Paramedic. Masseuse."

"Masseuse? How many trucks is this? And where are they?"

Hellion shrugged. "Many. Perhaps is ten, now. Maybe

eleven. They are circling. To stay together is very suspicious. We do not often cluster like this."

She hoisted and pulled the roll shutter up, revealing a dark interior with a large wooden crate in the middle, easily five feet on a side.

"That's bigger than I expected," Zero said.

Hellion beamed and hit a switch that lit up a central LED strip in the truck's ceiling, then unhooked a pry bar from the truck's inner wall. "Is because 2.0. Attack Crate 1.0 was half this size, contained clothing, weapons, medical equipment, small drones, also many technical innovations. This has much more. Have you heard of Body Snatcher?"

"What?"

"Ah, you will like it," Hellion said, and jabbed the metal bar into the crate's top seam and heaved, eliciting creaks. "Is clever mechanical device to turn normal car into self-driving car; controls brakes, steering, acceleration but not yet gear changes." She heaved harder and the crate's lid cracked open a sliver. "Very good in America, where most vehicles have automatic gears. Not so good in Europe, of course, with many manual drive. Still, Christopher Wren was very impressed."

Zero didn't care about what impressed Christopher Wren. "What else has it got?"

Hellion gave a final heave and the lid popped up with a bang. "Let us see." She unhooked a small folding ladder off the wall, unfolded it then climbed up to peek into the crate. "Guns?"

"I don't use guns."

"No guns? Christopher Wren often uses guns."

Zero sighed. "I'm not Wren. By the time I'd need guns, I've already lost. I'm an assassin, remember. I do things by stealth."

Hellion looked at her through narrow eyes. "No exception for Real Boys?"

"No. No exception. No guns."

The hacker shrugged. "Is your choice. Then tools for stealth. First one you are already wearing. Ghost suit."

Zero looked down at the black tactical gear. "Ghost suit?"

"Yes. It has many features. First feature, it has wireless detectors linked to Rex. Is imperfect, but should allow for instant recognition of CCTV coverage areas, allowing rapid hack by Rex, allowing for near instant 'ghosting' of your appearance."

Zero frowned. "What?"

"Yes. Suit can see cameras, hack them, and produce deep fake version of footage with you removed."

Zero was familiar with the technique, but not that capacity. "You're saying it can deep fake me in real-time, automatically?"

"Almost real time, automatic mode quite effective. Is not so difficult, actually." Hellion reached out and tapped Zero's arm. "Shape and contours of this suit are very familiar to Rex. He can cut you out of any image easily, with clean edges. You will be a ghost."

"Not bad," Zero said approvingly, turning her arms before her. "The military would pay plenty for this."

"They cannot afford it. Also there is modest thermal proofing built into the stab-proof fabric. It is not very bullet-proof, however, so be careful."

"Thermal and stab proof too?" Zero murmured. She'd had something like it before, but never as smooth and flexible. "What is it, neoprene mixed with Kevlar?"

"Carbon nanotubes," Zero answered. "Dense, strong, flexible. Extremely expensive. Multiple layers, actually. One layer is Vantablack. Do you know this?"

"Vantablack?"

"Means Vertically Aligned Nano Tube Arrays black. Blackest black there is, absorbs ninety-nine-point-nine percent of all light. Tough, also, in right conditions. Military grade, very hard to buy."

"Carbon nanotubes? I'd think so. It's got to be worth thousands."

"This suit is approximately thirty thousand dollars," Hellion said flatly. "Also contains full imaging system of cameras; ten five-millimeter sewn-in cameras give full three-sixty situational awareness. Rex will handle this and relay threat. Includes helmet also, made of hardened version of same fabric, with no loss of peripheral vision. So, yes, it is expensive. Try not to fall in mud with this."

Hellion smirked then rummaged in the crate some more, pulling out what looked like a round black ball perhaps one foot in diameter.

Zero was still marveling at the suit, but refocused as Hellion waved the ball in front of her. "OK, what's that?"

"Active decoy," Hellion said, pushed a recessed button then tossed the ball like a grenade. It landed in the mud with a splat, then there was a huge bang and the egg inexplicably burst into a large black shape. Zero flinched slightly, then just stared, picking out rough contours and shapes.

"Is that an inflatable human?"

"Yes! Joints have some articulation and can be positioned. Sitting, standing even, if pinned to ground, also lying and kneeling. Inflates with fast blast of air, similar to flashbang grenade. Contains super-conductive external thermal coating and tiny heating element; to infrared it looks like real human, making heat. Battery lasts for one hour. We are working on this. Can also be activated remotely via Bluetooth. Here."

Hellion tossed another ball to Zero. She caught it and turned it in her hands. It weighed barely a few pounds. The recessed button was clear enough. Beneath it was written a warning in capital letters.

DO NOT INFLATE INTERNALLY

"Internally like inside a vehicle?"

"Inside vehicle is not B4cksl4cker's main fear. He fears attempted inflation inside human body."

Zero made a face. "Did someone try to inflate one internally? How would you even get it inside a person?"

"B4cksl4cker is always very worried about many things," Hellion said. "But is true, main inflation device is detachable. Watch." She plucked another egg from the crate, dug her fingers in around the button and twisted. A much smaller orb came free, about the size of a golf ball, which she held up. "Here. Altered flashbang. Strange internal explosion fate has not happened yet, happily."

Zero found herself imagining what would happen if that small ball did inflate internally. It wasn't a pretty picture, and she quickly put a stop to the train of thought. "I guess that is happy."

"Is unlikely, I know." Hellion shrugged. "He is unlikely man sometimes, but very considerate. Now, one more item." She pulled out another black ball and held it up, slightly bigger than the last.

"Let me guess, it's an inflatable car?"

Hellion's brows furrowed. "Why would be inflatable car? No. Is drone."

She worked a switch flush on the ball's side and something clicked, then the top half opened like an automated Fabergé egg. Nestled inside within black molded foam was what looked to be a tiny black helicopter, no bigger than Hellion's palm.

"What the..." Zero murmured.

"Up, Rex," Hellion commanded, and the helicopter's tiny rotor blades, each no longer than a pen knife blade, began to whirr. It stole Zero's breath. Within a few seconds the tiny device rose up from the ball.

"This is same design as Black Hornet Nano," Hellion

said. "US military Unmanned Aerial Vehicle, or drone, developed for twenty million. We 'borrowed' one shipment. Shh, don't tell. Again, this can be controlled by Rex easily; one of upgrades we give him. Can launch and land freely, excellent for overwatch or forward reconnaissance inside buildings; can send ahead for eyes-on." She pointed at spots on the tiny Nano's frame. "Has three cameras, forward, down and forty-five degrees. Top speed is thirteen miles per hour, battery lasts twenty-five minutes. If possible, returns to egg and charges once more. Very quiet, as you can see. Climb this to fifty yards at night, nobody will know you are watching. Too small for radar." Hellion reached up and stroked the tiny Nano's belly. "Also very cute. Now, down Rex."

The Nano dropped neatly back into its egg. Hellion closed the shell over it.

Zero didn't know what to say.

"Attack Crate 2.0, very cool, yes?"

She just nodded. On one level she was stunned. On another she was already imagining how she would use these incredible new tools in a raid on Viktor Anatoly's farm. He didn't know what was going to hit him. They just had to find him first.

Then Hellion's expression shifted. Zero knew that look; she'd just heard something on her in-ear device.

"What is it?" she asked.

"We have just received message fed into darknet directly from shadow line," Hellion said. "The port is now closed, but there is photograph attached. I do not understand this message, seems opposite of true situation, but perhaps you will."

A shiver ran up Zero's spine. "Show me."

Hellion raised her phone. A message box popped on the screen. Zero read it, and the bottom fell out of her world.

DO YOU TRULY CARE ABOUT NO ONE, MONA?

I'M READY TO ACCEPT YOUR SURRENDER. WHERE SHALL I BEGIN?

The photograph showed a familiar setting, a kitchen table laid to five place settings. Gabriel sat at one, with a line of blood trailing from his nose. Zuzanna and Hanna sat across from him, white-faced and wide-eyed. One chair was empty. At the fifth sat a man Zero had never seen before, but instantly recognized, smiling a shark's grin at the camera.

Viktor Anatoly.

39

SURRENDER

A terrible cold filled Zero, as the photograph rang bells in her head that couldn't be un-rung. She was instantly back in Gabriel's basement, sleeping off another Rohypnol overdose with two little girls squeezed either side of her and their father on patrol above.

Had that felt like safety?

It was gone.

"How does he know them?" she said. Her voice sounded cold and alien, like it was coming from another person's throat.

"We do not know," Hellion said. "Who are they?"

She didn't really know. She didn't know their last name. She didn't even know their address, any more than the vague location their home occupied on the main road out to GOMA-49.

"Doesn't matter," she said, and rose to her feet. It wasn't a decision, more an automatic reaction.

"Where are you going?" Hellion asked.

Zero didn't answer, instead she dropped down to the mud and waded over to her Kawasaki Ninja. It felt like she was underwater again, gasping for breath.

"Strike now is highly inadvisable," Hellion called after her. "Zero, this message is clear effort to enrage you. It is working. Trap will be bigger this time. Better. Tell us who these people are. We will gain overwatch first."

"They're a family," Zero said, feeling distant even to herself. "I took shelter in their home. Near GOMA-49. Gabriel's the father, with two daughters. The wife died, she was Japanese."

"This is good data, we will find them with this," Hellion said, though it made no impact on Zero. "But strike now should not be attempted. You must wait."

"I don't need your permission," Zero said, closing on the Ninja. It remained tipped over, the fender half-sunk in claggy mud between two tall trailers. She squatted and hoisted it up and flung one leg over.

"At least take in-ear device," Hellion called, jumping nimbly after her along the metal 'bridges'. "Communication will be necessary."

Zero paused long enough to accept the small pea-sized device, slotting it into her ear, then she twisted the ignition and revved the throttle. Mud sprayed behind her as she tore away, bursting out of the courtyard in seconds.

"This is very poor course of action," came Hellion's voice in her ear, "but we will advise. Seeking this family now. Launching drone. Consider coming back and outfitting with Attack Crate 2.0, Zero."

"There's no time."

Every second that she wasted en route was a second Anatoly could be hurting Hanna of Zuzanna, and she couldn't live with that. Not after Armitage. Not after Hope. In minutes she had the Ninja up past a hundred, flying along highway 79 in the dark.

She'd been wrong when she'd said there was no one left to hurt. Anatoly had found them, and she couldn't think about anything else as she pushed the Ninja past its limits. Gabriel's words echoed back to her, about her being the second kind of junkie, one who saw no life beyond her addiction.

If Hanna or Zuzanna died tonight, she knew that prediction would come true. There could never be a life beyond killing Real Boys for her. Even finding Hope wouldn't end the hunger. Nothing would.

Hellion and B4cksl4cker continued talking in her ear, but she shut them out like she'd shut out the hammering of her father's machine in the next room, just focusing on how Anatoly could possibly have known about Gabriel and his daughters. There'd been no oversight any of the times she'd gone to their home. They clearly hadn't tracked her back from GOMA-49, or they would have taken her while she slept.

So how?

Then it hit her.

The yellow jacket Gabriel had given her, once belonging to his wife. She'd used it as a decoy in the forest near GOMA-49 and never gone back for it. In one pocket, along with whatever zlotys and euros that hadn't fit in her stolen wallet, was the card Gabriel had given her.

His name. His address.

Her heart plummeted.

Her recklessness, again. He'd only been trying to help her. Anatoly must have sent his men back to comb over the scene. If she'd been thinking clearly, she should have done that herself. Now that negligence had brought the full force of the Real Boys down on this kind man's head.

Twenty miles flew in what felt like seconds. Off the 79, she whipped past the hulk of GOMA-49, down the road where she'd crashed the Real Boys' SUV into a tree and killed her first four vor, then pulled onto a gravel track.

At once she saw them.

Bratva.

They were lining the gravel. First there were two Escalades, then more, flanked by grim-faced men with tattoos on their foreheads, cheeks, arms, with bulges at their waists where guns lurked just out of sight. They stood with their arms at their sides like an impassive parade crowd, watching her race by.

Ten, she saw. Twenty.

"This is trap you cannot escape, Clara Baxter!" came Hellion's voice, booming now through the hacked speaker of an SUV as she passed by. "Go back!"

She didn't turn back. Likewise, the vor made no move toward her. It was like the strange ceasefire at the server farm had extended through to today.

Hellion's voice continued ringing out from nearby vehicles, but Zero ignored her. She pulled the Ninja into Gabriel's driveway. The carefully raked gray sand of his wife's Japanese garden had been destroyed, rife with boot prints.

Bratva stood here too, lining her route. None made a move toward her. They just stared.

Zero dropped the bike onto its kickstand and raced forward to the door. At the last moment one immense vor stepped into her path. He had to be seven feet, a foot and change taller than Zero and easily two hundred pounds heavier, with a neck as thick as Zero's midriff and a face florid with steroid zits. She tried to dodge around him but there was no space.

"Weapons," he said, voice grinding low.

"I have your darknet by the balls," Zero hissed. "I'm here to see your boss. Stand aside."

The big man's expression didn't shift one iota. "Weapons, now."

Out from the road Hellion's voice rang in stereo from the speakers of multiple cars. Zero shut her out. Hellion couldn't help now. This wasn't a full-fledged war. This was work for an assassin on the ground.

An assassin without weapons. She reached down to her waist and started stripping blades; her stilettos in triceps and thigh holsters, her shuriken throwing knives in waist and ankle baldrics, they dropped into a heap at the big man's feet. When the last one fell, he stepped aside.

Zero entered the kitchen and stopped in her tracks. The table was set for five, with a tea pot in the middle and five cups, just like in the photograph. The blood had been wiped from Gabriel's face, but he still looked pale and worn. His two girls, Hanna and Zuzanna, were red-eyed.

"Clara," Hanna blurted as she came into view, but Zuzanna quickly stamped on her foot, squelching it. Gabriel's eyes flickered back and forth in disbelief between Zero and the other man seated at the table.

Viktor Anatoly.

He looked calm and in control; a handsome, dark-haired man in his early forties, dressed in a navy suit with a white shirt that was open at the throat, revealing the hint of a snake tattoo around his neck and a silver chain sporting a small cross. In the light of Gabriel's kitchen he seemed worse than she'd imagined.

Like a madman in perfect control. Like he could explode from sitting and drinking tea into hellish violence at any given moment.

Zero's heart pounded and her throat constricted. In some ways he reminded her of her father. Until she was seven years old he'd waited patiently for his vision to begin. He'd been a father. He'd started to dig the basement that would become her prison, and smiled throughout, and even let her help like it was all a game.

Then he'd just transformed.

"Leave them out of this," Zero said. Her voice sounded tight and reedy.

Viktor Anatoly smiled, revealing a shark's white teeth. When he spoke there was barely a hint of a Russian accent.

"We're only having tea here, Mona. There's nothing untoward. Won't you join us?"

She stared. In her ear Hellion was still braying warnings. Gabriel didn't even look at her now. He didn't look at Anatoly. He only had eyes for his daughters.

Zero could imagine how he was feeling. She'd felt that way every second of every minute of every day for years, variously challenging, begging and bargaining with her father.

"Please don't hurt Hope! Please don't do this to Hope!"

Gabriel had to be thinking the same thing; searching for some source of leverage in his mind that could guarantee his daughters' survival.

"I'm sorry, Gabriel," she said. "This is my fault. You're going to be OK."

Gabriel chanced a glance up at her, but there was nothing there. He didn't believe her. She didn't blame him. She was alone. Anatoly had come in force.

"Of course he'll be OK," Anatoly said warmly. He gave a great facsimile of being a normal, decent person, but the sinuous truth of what he really was shimmered underneath. "This is a discussion only. Come, Girl Zero. Sit with us."

Zero fixed her gaze on him. He seemed to luxuriate in her attention, like a snake warming its cold blood in the sun.

"Call me Clara."

He smiled magnanimously. "Clara. Please."

He gestured to the fifth chair. Just then Hanna looked up, saw Zero and released a whimper. Her eyes were wide and her cheeks were red with tear stains.

Zero knew in that moment that she'd go to the end of the

line right now. Lie, cheat, murder, turn traitor, even die, whatever it took to keep those girls safe. She'd failed with Hope, for years and years. She couldn't fail now.

She sat down.

"So talk."

40

SHOW OF FAITH

Zero stared at Anatoly. He gazed back at her.

"This is terrible situation," Hellion said in Zero's ear, a small voice that no one else could hear. "What is plan?"

She had no plan. There'd been no plan at any stage since she'd left Skawina, other than the same plan she'd lived by since taking her father down at sixteen years old. All the chips on the table, every time.

"Let the girls go to their rooms," she said.

Anatoly said nothing. Zero's mind raced ahead.

"I have your darknet," she pressed. "Should I put an auto-send timer on all that data? It's billions in crypto, along with thousands of loyal Real Boys. You want to keep this family sitting here under implicit threat, I'll start firing off chunks of evidence to different Interpol agencies every few minutes. They'll be all over you within the hour."

Anatoly waved a hand. "Escort the girls to their rooms."

Large men moved in from the sides.

"Let their father take them," Zero said sharply, and Anatoly held up a hand, halting the enclosing vor.

"Altogether, into the basement. There's no way out. They'll be safe down there."

Anatoly waved and the two vor shifted to a herding action. Zero tried to catch Gabriel's eye but he didn't look her way. He simply stood, pulling the girls up with him. Zuzanna stood numbly. Hanna followed. Together they filed to the basement and started down. Zero just hoped his shotgun was still there. It might not do much, but perhaps it could help.

The basement door slammed closed, leaving Zero alone with Anatoly.

She hated him so badly her skin itched. Every fiber in her body cried out for her to leap across the table and rip out his eyes.

But she didn't move.

"You want me alive," she said.

"Your surrender."

"And the darknet?"

"Naturally."

She leaned in. Time to deal. "In exchange for which you release Gabriel, Zuzanna and Hanna. You guarantee no harm will come to them, by your action or inaction, in perpetuity."

His eyes crinkled with something like pleasure. "Of course."

"It's not enough."

Anatoly said nothing for a long moment. He looked around the kitchen and she followed his gaze. It felt very different from the place it had once been. For scant moments over the last few days, she'd glimpsed this place as a warm, even safe place. A home. Now his presence defiled it.

"What would you like?"

This was her chance to learn something. Even if she couldn't act on it, perhaps Hellion and B4cksl4cker could.

"For the price of my slow and painful death? You do plan

to kill me, correct? Most likely on a livestream for all your sick little freak friends to watch. My father's legacy."

Anatoly didn't budge. "I'll ask again. What would you like?"

"Hope."

He smiled. "We've had this conversation."

"Along with a DNA test. When she passes it, you release her with the same promise. She will never be hurt by you, Bratva, the Real Boys or any affiliate, by action or inaction, ever again."

His eyes narrowed slightly. "That's a tall order."

"That's the price."

"For your life," he mused. "Interesting. If only all wars could be solved so simply."

"And the farm."

That seemed to tweak his interest. "You know about my farm?"

"I've heard rumors."

He smiled. "I'm impressed. What about it?"

"Shut it down."

"Impossible."

"Why?"

"You will see."

"What is it?"

His head tilted slightly. "So the rumors were not very complete."

"Tell me. A show of faith. You won't show me Hope. Show me something."

He surveyed her clinically. Again there was that sense of contained chaos, like he was keeping a demon in check. "Very well. Let's make a trade. Inform your Foundation assets, Hellion and B4cksl4cker, to release a tranche of data to us. I will tell you about the farm."

"He knows our names," Hellion said in her ear.

Zero said nothing.

"Failing that, I don't see what else there is to discuss here," Anatoly went on. "I've played your game, 'Clara'. I will release Hope. I will guarantee the man's life and his girls. I may even throw in your hackers, depending on how well you perform at the farm. But that is all."

She stared at him. He stared back at her. Behind the cool sense of violence he exuded, there was something slithering; a handle on his heart she might be able to grasp, if she could just figure out what it was.

"Release a tranche, Hellion," she ordered.

"This is second terrible idea, Clara Baxter," Hellion warned. "Is path where you will die. All of us will die. Is bad, bad plan!"

"I'm the general here," Zero said, speaking to Hellion but holding Anatoly's gaze. "I'm on the ground. You're up in the air. You don't know anything. So when I say release a tranche, perhaps one terabyte, I mean it. Do it."

Seconds passed. Keys flew. Anatoly gave her a look.

"Released," Hellion said.

"It's done," Zero said.

Anatoly nodded, and waited. None of his men approached. Zero figured he was wearing an in-ear device as well, taking messages from his own operator.

"We have it. Very well. You want to know what the farm is, Clara? It's many things. But most of all, it's a memory."

"Not enough."

"I expect not. But memory's a tricky thing, isn't it? When you see the farm, I'm sure everything will come flooding back. You and Hope, huddling in the fallout shelter in the midst of all those pigs, hand-in-hand and dreaming about the day you one day escaped Idaho."

Zero flinched; the words were a violation, like he was

reaching into her past and scooping out her most treasured memories. His smile only made it worse.

"You don't know anything about that," she said. "That was before my father built the dungeon. You weren't there then."

His smile widened. "Wasn't I?"

Zero said nothing for a long moment, fighting a battle inside as she stared into his eyes. There was that slither within them, like he knew her better than she knew herself. It was repellent. It made her feel sick.

But maybe it was the truth.

"You came before the dungeon."

Anatoly said nothing, and her stomach churned as her mind spun.

"You spied on us. No, not only that. A preview? Was that how my father sold Hope, inviting prospective 'buyers' to the farm? Was that the down-payment that financed the Blue Fairy? Did that come from you?"

He leaned closer, his breath fuming hot across the table. "You used to be such a good girl, Mona. I want to get back to that, with you as the foundation for all the wonders of the farm, our own Girl Zero." He smiled. "And to that end, I want you to know that, even now, my hands encircle your little sister's throat." He made a fist. "One order, and she suffers. More than ever. Worse than ever. I'll kill her, if I have to. And do you know why?"

Zero stared. Now she saw it all: why he wanted her alive; what the handle on his heart was. The pieces came together.

"My father's legacy," she whispered.

He smiled broadly. "Legacy. Justice. His wishes be done."

It was all there. Money. Power. With both Hope and Mona locked into his 'farm' like some kind of zoo, he'd have control of the Real Boys, which meant control over Bratva, which would instantly make him one of the most powerful men in the world.

"Now for your end of the deal," he said, and drew a dart gun.

Zero acted before he could fire, twisting her tongue and crunching down with her jaws. Both her remaining fake molars came loose and shattered, releasing the twin cyanide pills.

The gun was up and pointing at her chest, then Zero spat one pill out. It splattered to the table between them, onto a clean plate, speckled with blood and shards of ceramic tooth.

"What's that?" Anatoly asked.

"Cyanide." Zero rolled the remaining pill in her mouth until she held it between her front teeth. Already she could taste its bitter almond taste dissolving on her tongue.

Anatoly's jaw dropped. The gun wavered. He lurched to his feet but for the first time didn't seem to know what he was supposed to do. "It's not," he said softly.

"It is, now get out," Zero ordered, rolling the pill back into the pocket of her gums. "You, all your men, everyone. Get in your cars and go, or I bite down on this and your legacy disappears, unless you've got an antidote handy."

He teetered. She could read it in him. He was calculating. One shot, maybe, he thought. It might be enough. Perhaps he could prize the pill out of her mouth before she could swallow it.

Zero crunched the pill between her teeth. It became dust in her mouth and on her tongue, and she opened her mouth wide to show him, already feeling the poison seeping into her system.

Anatoly's eyes flared. "You're going to die."

"Go!" Zero shouted.

He hesitated a second longer then turned and ran. "Go!" he shouted at his men. The big man in the doorway didn't move fast enough so he shoved him harder. "Go, go, go!!"

Zero felt her tongue fizzling. She already felt noxious and

sick. Still she followed Anatoly with her tongue out, watching as they all fell into their vehicles and raced away.

Then she stumbled back. Already she felt consciousness escaping her. She slumped at the table and poured hot tea direct from the pot into her mouth, spitting out as much of the powder as she could. She did that again and again as the cars squealed away outside, and the sound of footsteps pounded up from below.

Hellion was talking in her ears but she didn't hear it. Her vision doubled and she felt woozy. It was worse than Rohypnol. Worse than opiates. This was the onset of the final trip, as the cyanide passed into her blood and started blocking the uptake of oxygen at a cellular level. Soon she'd pass into unconsciousness, followed by a heart attack, followed by death.

Somewhere nearby voices were calling out her name. Sirens were wailing. She slipped from the chair and hit the floor, then the black curtain fell and she was gone.

41

BLACK CURTAIN

Hope was singing again. 'When You Wish Upon a Star'. Her little voice was so high and sweet, barely audible.

Zero stood in her old cell with the door hanging open. She was terrified, but the terror didn't matter. She opened the door and ran. In the hall beyond her father lay in his torture machine; the mechanism hammering, his body deflated down to the bones, but there were camera lenses inset where his eyes should have been, red lights blinking.

Zero spun and saw her mother was the same; barely a ragged skeleton in her stained white gown, with shiny lenses peeking from her skull like insectile eyes.

She ran away, up the stairs and into the farmhouse.

The building was in a state of advanced decay; all the furniture was gone, leaving only charred sticks on soot-stained floorboards. The living room walls had been punched through by local kids in many places. There were old beer cans, cigarette butts and amateur graffiti tags on the walls. The air stank of urine and ash.

Up the stairs, the master bedroom was gone. Burned away, on that fateful night when she'd poured the gasoline and lit the match. Along the landing she ran, chasing the haunting sound of Hope's child's voice. The door to her room was closed. Zero burst through, and found herself-

For long moments she didn't know where. She wasn't in the house anymore. It was a dark, dank, narrow place; a floor littered with hay, a curving ceiling ruptured in places, revealing a bone-white sky above.

The singing had halted. Zero spun. Everywhere were ghosts of Hope, her little sister in a white gown, but none held still. Her golden hair, her warm little hand, her mischievous eyes.

Zero kicked through a door and emerged out into the open spread of the farm. All around were the pig enclosures, garlanded with the bones and leathery skins of so many dead pigs. She spun. Behind her was the fallout shelter, emerging through the flat earth of Idaho barely a couple of feet. Once there'd been a thin layer of dirt and turf over its low roof, but now the plains winds had blown most of that away, revealing the curved, corrugated iron roof structure, rusted through in patches.

They'd once called it the 'nose' of the farm, fated to forever smell the pigs. They'd hidden here at times from their father, dreaming of a future together.

"Hope!" she shouted, but no answer came. The farm was utterly silent. Zero ran back down into the shelter, but now the steps just led down and down until something yanked her into the light of consciousness.

She woke in a large room, on a hot bed, and pushed herself onto one elbow. It wasn't Gabriel's home. It looked like the suite of a hotel. Her arm shuddered under her weight. Her throat and head hurt. Light leaked in through blackout curtains, illuminating the small, sleeping bodies of Gabriel's daughters either side of her. Gabriel was on the other side of the king bed, fully dressed atop the covers.

A sob rose up in her throat and she swallowed it.

Safe.

She lay back down, running her hands up to her ear. There was no device. Her tongue probed the back row of her jaw, where two gaping chasms marked her missing teeth.

She remembered flashes of the last night: Gabriel pumping her chest and blowing air into her lungs; someone pushing a syringe into her arm; a ride in a truck that went on and on, and then this.

On some level she knew that Hellion and B4cksl4cker had rescued her. Their roving paramedic truck must have swooped in as the Bratva left. Anything else and she'd be dead or in custody, soon to die. On that same level, she also knew the hackers were now gone. She could feel it.

Reckless, Hellion had said, and she was right. Zero regretted it all. She regretted ever meeting Gabriel and his daughters. None of this was fair, and none of them deserved it.

This was her father's legacy.

This was Viktor Anatoly's plan; a theme park celebrating the Blue Fairy's victory over Girl Zero, with Zero herself on permanent display.

It was time to go. She pushed the covers back and worked her legs out. Every muscle ached. Her head boomed. But she had to get back. Find Anatoly, find the farm, find Hope and destroy her father's legacy once and for all.

"Where are you going?"

She turned to find Gabriel's eyes watching her.

"I'm sorry," she whispered. "I'm sorry any of this happened. I have to go."

He didn't say anything. Maybe there was anger in his eyes. She didn't blame him. She slid past Hanna and tried to walk, but her legs crumpled beneath her and she dropped to her knees on the deep pile carpet.

"You're sick, Clara," Gabriel said. "It's cyanide poisoning. You almost died."

She took a breath and tried to get up again. She made it to one foot then the other, but only managed two steps before she fell once more.

"Wait," he said.

She didn't turn. She couldn't face the anger or the pity in his eyes. It was better just to get away from that. She tried to walk again, but he came around to stand in front of her.

"Come on," he said, and took her by the elbow, guiding her to a breakfast bar with a cool granite top. The suite was large and luxurious, dimly lit by a single shaft of light. He helped her onto a stool then ran a glass of cold water and brought it over. Her hand trembled as she took tiny sips.

"You can't go anywhere like this."

She knew it.

"I'm not going to say it's OK," Gabriel went on. "It isn't. What happened yesterday has to be the worst experience of my life. Even worse than when I lost my wife, because I thought I was going to lose my girls, too. They're traumatized now. We all are. And it happened because of you."

She looked away.

"But you saved us. You took cyanide, and somehow we all survived! I don't understand how that worked, but it did." He stretched one hand across the bar to touch hers. "Now we're here. Your friends checked us in as a family on a skiing trip. Apparently you're an addict who had a relapse." A small smile crept briefly through. "We're rich and famous, so we wanted it kept quiet. This hotel specializes in that kind of thing." He gazed at her. "But what happens next, Clara? They said I shouldn't call the police, that it'll get us all killed. They also said we can't go back. So what do we do?"

She squeezed his hand. About this much, at least, she could be sure.

"I'm going to kill that man, Gabriel. Viktor Anatoly. All his men. They'll all be dead. Anyone who knows your name, they're going to die. I swear, I'll make it safe."

He watched her, then pulled his hands back. "I thought you might say that."

She said nothing, and the silence stretched, broken only by the sound of the girls shifting quietly in their sleep.

"Where are we?" Zero asked.

"In the High Tatras mountains, across the border to Slovakia. Two hundred and fifty miles from Krakow. It's beautiful out there, you know. The view last night was stunning."

"How long until I recover?"

"A few days, they said. Your friends had a paramedic. She gave you something, could be hydroxy or hydroxo-"

"Hydroxocobalamin," Zero said. Just like with Rohypnol, she knew all the chemical breakdowns. "It's a cyanide antidote."

"Then that."

"Also oxygen therapy," Zero added, remembering the mask on her face, and how she'd tried to fight them off, caught up in her nightmare of losing Hope. "You did CPR, too, didn't you?"

He shrugged. "A little. I've seen addicts overdose before, remember. I tried to call an ambulance, but your friend Hellion intercepted the line."

Zero smiled. Of course Hellion had intercepted it.

"You saved my life."

"I think it's fairly mutual at this point."

Zero didn't know what else to say. She sipped her water until it was finished then spoke. "I'll get another room. You're right that I need to recover. I'm good for nothing like this, and I'm done being reckless. I have to do this properly. And it's not good for you to be around me. Not good for your girls."

She took a slow breath. "Maybe you can pretend this is just a holiday. All of that back in the house, it wasn't really real. Kids are resilient, and their memories will adjust. You three go skiing. I'll stay in my room. Maybe a day or two, then I'll go finish the job. You won't hear from me until it's done."

She placed her palms on the worktop and pushed, slipping her feet off the stool's rungs to take her weight. This time her legs held.

Gabriel watched but said nothing. She walked slowly and carefully away, out through the door and into the lush hall, where a bank of elevators awaited her beside a window with the most beautiful view she'd ever seen in her life.

Mountains, snow and ice stretched for as far as she could see. The sky was a blazing white, pregnant with snow. Everything looked so perfect, like the landscape from a fairy tale.

The elevator pinged and she stepped inside.

42

FOOD

At reception Zero booked another room on another floor, asked for a rental laptop to be sent to her room along with five different items from the room-service menu, then headed back up.

Her new room was smaller, on the tenth floor. She opened the curtains and sat on the bed gazing out at the vast panorama. Everything hurt. She knew about cyanide poisoning from Auschwitz. It began with unconsciousness, progressed swiftly through fits and ended in death by heart attack.

All of that had happened to her, and she felt it all

A knock came at the door.

The laptop was generic. The food was waffles with bacon and maple syrup, a chicken club sandwich, eggs over easy with sausages, hash browns and barbecue beans, a chocolate milkshake and a tall cafetiere of hot coffee.

The laptop was bad but the food was not. She pulled the desk in front of the epic view and set the laptop to downloading SudVPN and the Tor browser, tucking into the food as it slowly loaded.

She felt famished. First she went for the milkshake; it was rich, frothy and heavy with double thick cream. It barely took the edge off her hunger. Next she went in on the pancakes, picking them up like burritos with the bacon and berries wrapped inside then dunking them in the syrup.

By the time she'd hoovered those up, the laptop was approaching operational. She ran a quick scan and turfed out a few spyware apps, then booted the anonymizing apps and put a call through to Hellion and B4cksl4cker.

It rang. She let it, going back in on the beans and sausages before they cooled down. The raging hole in her middle began to feel a little better. She went back and forth between the sausages and hash browns, then poured her first mug of coffee, loaded with cream and sugar. As the caffeine gave her a welcome kick, she started opening ports into Rex.

As far as she could see, he was intact. There seemed to be no spyware logged inside him, though there were a wide range of files on his hard drive. She clicked through as she went back and forth on the food and coffee; some of them were tranches of darknet data identifying Real Boys, while the rest comprised the full results of their hunt for Viktor Anatoly's farm.

There were thousands, still. Also, a recorded message. She hit play.

"Clara Baxter," came Hellion's voice instantly, rendered reedy through the speakers. She was back to two full names, which didn't bode well. "This behavior was reckless beyond our ability to accept. Both I and B4cksl4cker are very angry."

She paused to check the timestamp on the audio: 9 a.m. that morning, around two hours ago. Zero's heart climbed then sank again. If they'd sent her a message two hours ago, that suggested they were safe. So why weren't they answering her call?

She hit play.

"We are angry," Hellion went on, "and we also understand. But convoy is now compromised. We sent everything, Zero. More trucks than you know about. More people. Bratva saw this. Real Boys saw this. They are tracking us currently."

Zero's eyes widened. "What?"

"Yes," Hellion said, as if in response to Zero. "It is not worst outcome, perhaps, but bad. Convoy has split, as is designed. All heading away from Poland now. Ghosting and deepfakes will conceal us gradually. We will regroup. Will acquire new license plates, new trailers, new branding. But operationally, we will not be helpful for some time, and must focus on rebuilding security."

Zero chewed that over.

"You are protected, however. Your truck had ghost protocol protection. Stay in hotel until you recover. Of course, Gabriel and daughters are now known to Bratva. They are not safe and cannot go back. We know you will go back. Perhaps we will be ready to support remotely. But you are too dangerous to remain close to."

Again Zero's heart sank. She felt like she'd betrayed them and she didn't like it. She hadn't set out to befriend these two strange hackers, but in the last day or two she'd grown to like them.

"I'm sorry," she muttered.

Hellion carried on unaware. "Farm scans have been left with Rex. There are one hundred-twenty-six farms that meet your parameters within two hundred miles of Krakow. Many thousands around Europe and the world. It is too many. You need to narrow this, Zero. Recover. Rest. Perhaps we will speak soon."

The message ended.

Zero sat still, staring out at the expansive view of mountains, valleys, skies and snow. What had moments ago felt peaceful and calm now felt barren. She wanted to talk to Hellion and B4cksl4cker. But that wasn't going to happen, so she rolled up her sleeves and dug into the data.

43

FARMS

Zero started looking at farms.

According to Rex's calculations, they were all ninety-percent-plus matches to the Idaho farm; all that remained was to scan them by eye and see if something jumped out at her. On the tiny laptop screen she scrolled through them two-by-two, leaning in so close to pick out details that her eyes quickly began to burn and blur.

She wasn't even sure what she was looking for.

Pigs, she knew that much. Anatoly had doubled down on his farm being a replica. But all the farms were pig farms. They were all roughly the right shape and oriented the right way. They all had farmhouses, and barns of varying sizes, and fences and approach roads. Some had parking lots and additional buildings, while some didn't, but that told Zero nothing.

She pulled back from the screen with a sigh. Already three hours had passed and she was getting hungry again. There was a pain in her neck and shoulders from the hunched posture, so she stood up and stretched her arms and rolled her neck.

The movement was too fast and brought on a wave of

dizziness. She'd forgotten how drained she was, and sat back down to wait for the nausea to pass.

The key was to be methodical. Scientific. To focus intensely on one thing to the exclusion of all else. It was how she'd beaten her parents; planning and rehearsing and strengthening herself in ways they hadn't expected. It was how she'd gotten this far from an Idaho hole in the ground: learning her skills, building her network, hunting them down.

If she had a special skill, it was her ability to focus.

Already she'd looked at thousands of farms; she'd started with everything in Poland, then Europe, and now she was looking further afield. She turned back to the screen but couldn't bear peering into its feeble, low-contrast pixels any longer. An idea came to her and she picked up the room phone.

"Front desk, how can I help?"

"I'm looking to use a bigger screen with my rented laptop. Have you got a projector and screen I can rent?"

"One moment, let me check that, madam."

Madam. Huh. She waited.

"I'm afraid we don't have that service, but we do have the screening room."

"Screening room?"

"Yes. It's a private cinema. We host a film festival in September, but it goes unused most of the year, all except a few guest requests. If that would be useful, I could reserve the room for you."

Zero's mind took a big leap forward. "Can I book it for the whole of today?"

"All today? Well. I, let me check… Yes. That would be fine. I should say the rental fee is quite steep. I know-"

"Not a problem. Set it up for me, please. Also, I'll want a flipchart and some markers. Oh, and a double cheeseburger with fries and coleslaw."

"Yes indeed, madam, I'll pass this order onto the kitchen. The business center can provide the flipchart. Is there anything else?"

"Yes. Coffee."

"Very good."

"And chocolate cake. With fudge sauce. Do you have that?"

"Yes.

"Make it hot. With ice cream on the side. Vanilla."

"I will have these sent directly to the screening room. It's on the eleventh floor."

Zero felt like she was making progress. Only one floor away. It was like it was meant to be.

"Thank you."

She hung up and stood. The laptop's buzzy little screen flickered at her. She snapped it closed and started for the door.

The screening room had a ten-foot screen; a considerable improvement over the laptop. There were twenty seats and she took the two in the front row, controlling the laptop and therefore the projector via voice commands to Rex. On her right stood the flipchart with a full set of colored markers. On her left lay the cheeseburger, cake and coffee.

Again she dived in, beginning by having Rex cycle through all one-hundred-and-twenty-six farms on the right side of the screen, with the Idaho farm on the left. As they scrolled by, she hashed out notes on the flip chart's A1 paper and chomped on the burger or the cake.

The screen was far better than the laptop, picking out details with clarity while representing colors and shadows better. As she went, she narrowed the range of images. This was based on no particular criteria, just operating by feeling. Some felt more right than others. After one pass she went for another, going through the Krakow farms repeatedly until she was down to thirty.

She wasn't confident that Anatoly's farm was within them. It was just a technique to learn the farms. From there on, she slowed down. She had Rex zoom in on both the Idaho farm and each potential farm in turn, then scroll across the map steadily.

It took perhaps five minutes to study each map at that level of detail. Scouring every pixel. As she watched farm after farm, she found herself reliving old memories, both with Hope and alone. Strangely, the memories seemed to split themselves between the twin views.

As she looked at the Idaho farm, she remembered the days after she'd escaped: roaming the farm alone, feeding the pigs, burning down the farmhouse. As she looked at the farms on the right, she remembered the days with Hope that came before: toying with the pigs, running in the yard, and hiding in the fallout shelter.

It was late afternoon by the time she realized the one detail she'd overlooked when B4cksl4cker set the parameters.

The fallout shelter. The nose of the farm. Anatoly had mentioned it. She'd even dreamed of it.

Her heart began to race.

"Rex, center on the Idaho farm and zoom."

Rex responded at once, and the screen filled with the center of the pig enclosures; a rough grid with its once sharp lines blurred by the scattered splinters of fencing. There was no visual cue to pick out the shelter, though; just more uneven wreckage.

"Widen," she ordered, and Rex widened the view.

She still couldn't see it, but perhaps that wasn't a surprise. It was more than fifteen years since she'd hidden out there with Hope, and even then the shelter had been dilapidated, with holes in the roof allowing windblown dust to gradually fill in the gaps.

That brought on the next revelation. She was looking at the wrong map.

"Who took this Idaho map, Rex? How old is it?"

"It is a satellite capture from the Iota mapping project. It is seven months, three days, five hours and-"

"Got it."

That was the answer. The farm was a memory, Anatoly had said. It was a legacy. It made sense he'd want to match it to the golden days of the farm.

"Have we got an older map?" she called, approaching the screen so close that it almost enveloped her. "Fifteen years, twenty, maybe more."

"Searching," Rex replied. "I have a land survey photograph seventeen years ago."

"Bring it up."

The left side of the screen shifted. The farm was there, but sharper and neater than ever. With a gasp, Zero noticed a channel dug into the yard at the back of the farmhouse. Red clay gleamed within it, and there was a large yellow earthmover nearby, and even-

"Zoom in on the earth mover," Zero ordered, feeling fraught.

The image zoomed. The resolution wasn't high; this photograph was never intended to be used for these purposes, but still it showed enough.

Zero's heart skipped a beat.

A figure was standing beside the digger looking up. The photograph only caught the vague shadows of his features, but it was him. Disturbed at his work by a passing plane.

Her father, Lance Gebhart.

Her pulse raced and her breathing quickened. It was like he'd come back to life, in his prime. Her eyes darted to the channel, this gouge in the earth that would soon become the concrete-lined sole entrance and exit to his underground dungeon. And there in the channel was a blurry white shape that could only be a child in a muddy playsuit.

Mona Gebhart.

She stared. She had no childhood photographs, other than the videos shared still by Real Boys. Certainly nothing from those earlier days, before everything went bad. When her father was still pretending to be a father. When Hope was still there.

She scoured the rest of the red channel hungrily but could find no trace of Hope. It was a disappointment. Maybe she was inside the farmhouse with their mother.

A tear ran down Zero's cheek. She'd never understood the decision her father had made, when she'd stopped being his daughter and become something else.

She smeared the tear away. She wasn't here for family photographs.

"Center on the pig enclosures, Rex."

The screen shifted away to center on the enclosures. They were a perfect grid. Block after block, cell after cell, filled with pigs. It confused her and she took a step closer to the screen, looking for the natural break in the fences where the shelter had to be. The nose of the farm. She knew it had to be there.

"Analyze, Rex. Find me a break in the fencing."

The screen scrolled as he searched. Seconds later he answered. "There is none."

"There has to be. Look for a mound in the earth or the shadow it casts." She thought back, remembering how it had looked and felt inside the shelter. "It would be low, maybe fifteen feet long, five wide."

Rex ran the search again. Still, Zero couldn't see it, but that was impossible.

"There is none," he repeated.

She blinked. There had to be some mistake. The channel was there. The farmhouse was there. The shelter had to be there too. Perhaps her memory was tainted, somehow, though? Maybe her father had bulldozed the shelter at some point? Or had he actually built it himself in a later year?

"Have we got any older photographs?"

Rex searched. "1953."

Zero grunted. She knew the land wasn't even settled back then. It was also before the Cold War really got started, so there'd be no need for a fallout shelter. It was disorienting.

But it had been there. Even Anatoly had known about it, so he must have included it in his new farm, as well. Maybe the photographs had just caught it at the wrong angle.

"Rex, search all the other farms. Start with the thirty and scan the rest. We're looking for a mound or the shadow from a mound in the middle of the pig enclosures, big enough to break the line of the fences."

"Searching. This will take approximately five hours."

Zero laughed. "Fine. Lock screen. Call me if you have something."

"Understood," said Rex.

The screen faded to black. Zero looked around in the darkness and saw only the afterglow of that red clay channel. She remembered playing in it, 'helping' him to dig, just like she remembered the fallout shelter, which wasn't there.

It made no sense.

She hobbled out of the screening room. It was already 6 p.m. and she felt weary. Her eyes were watery from staring at screens for so long. She might not be able to sleep, but it would do her good to lie down in a dark room for a time.

44

SOUND

It felt like no sooner than her head hit the pillow that a sound woke her up.

She sat up swiftly, looking around the darkened room. The curtains were wide open, just as she'd left them, revealing the night view across the High Tatras mountains. The snow caps along mountain ridges and wedged into rocky valleys looked like sweeps of jagged cloud.

It was breathtaking.

She sat still, waiting for whatever sound had roused her to come again. She expected the laptop to chime as Rex announced his search was complete, but that wasn't the sound that came next.

It was a knock at the door.

She stood up. There was a slight head rush but less than before.

Who could be at the door? She walked over carefully, picked up a heavy vase on the way then opened it.

In the corridor outside stood Gabriel, Zuzanna and Hanna. For a second they all stared at each other, then the two girls leaped in and wrapped Zero up in a tight embrace, almost firmly enough to knock her over.

"We knew it!" Zuzanna shouted.

Hanna buried her head in Zero's thigh and snuggled.

Zero looked down, then at the vase in her hand, then at the flowers in Gabriel's hand and the sheepish look on his face.

"I see you're prepared," he said. "May I?"

He reached out. Numbly, she handed over the vase and he dropped the flowers in.

"I knew she was here!" Zuzanna cheered, then headbutted Zero in the belly.

"I'm sorry," Gabriel said quietly. "Really. I know it's a bad idea. I know we agreed we wouldn't. But you're all they've been talking about, all day."

Zero didn't know what to say. This was something totally unexpected. She was in hunter mode, but the kids grappling with her legs swiftly forced her back into the moment.

"I'll take them away, if you still think it's a bad idea. It's just, well…"

He trailed off.

Zero couldn't think. The world seemed to teeter between two extremes, absolute vengeance and absolute something else. Family? She didn't understand it, but despite her ability to focus, and her methodical plans, she'd always been impulsive.

The flowers were white roses, after all. Her favorite.

"Come in, then," she said. The words were out before she could stop them, surprising even her.

The girls cheered again, let go and ran into the room. Zuzanna started jumping on the sofa. Hanna leaped into the bed and rolled herself up in the covers. Zero stepped aside and Gabriel entered awkwardly.

"Are you feeling better?" he asked.

"Much," she said, and closed the door behind him, then turned the lights on.

"This place is so small!" Zuzanna called, from her vantage point perched on the back of the sofa.

Zero hadn't really looked around the room. It was small but tasteful; nothing like as grand as the penthouse suite. Hanna said something in Polish and Zuzanna translated cheerfully.

"She says she didn't know you were so poor!"

"Girls, please," Gabriel said and set across the room toward them. He looked harried and exhausted, and on some level Zero found that highly amusing.

"Of course I'm poor," she said, as Hanna came charging off the bed trailing a pillowcase as a headdress. "Don't you remember when you first found me? I didn't even have any clothes on, did I?"

Zuzanna laughed. Hanna looked confused, so Zuzanna explained it in Polish, then she laughed long and loud, so much in fact that Zero felt her cheeks reddening.

"We won't stay long, I promise," Gabriel said. "Just, I can't get them to sleep. They're crazy."

"They are," Zero observed, as Hanna pulled the pillowcase down over her head, laid on her belly on the floor then started wriggling like a worm.

"Catch her!" Zuzanna shouted. "Clara, help me. We are hungry eagles!"

"You don't have to do that," Gabriel said. "I'm sure they'll calm down in a few minutes."

They didn't. Hanna wormed around Zero's feet and Zuzanna dived on her, eliciting chortles and cries, intermittently tugging on her hand until something clicked over in her head. All four of them were fated to die, after all. They'd survived Viktor Anatoly together, but he wasn't done with any of them.

If anything, that threat bound her to these people tighter than any other bond she'd felt since Hope. That bond was there whether she wanted it to be or not, so why not try to enjoy it? Even find strength in it?

She fell in and started to play.

She was still drained, but as she chased Hanna, or tickled Zuzanna, or took her turn with the pillowcase pulled down over her shoulders worming around on the floor, she felt a new energy rising up. It was infectious, and soon Gabriel joined in, and after twenty minutes playing themselves breathless, swooping and cawing and worming, they all collapsed panting on the sofa together.

"You were there yesterday, weren't you Clara?" Zuzanna asked through red and puffing cheeks.

Zero looked at Gabriel. He shrugged.

"Papa says you weren't, but we know you were. You made the bad men go away. Then you got sick." Her hot hand found Zero's and squeezed.

"I was there," Zero agreed. "I know it seemed scary at the time. But you were always safe. I was always coming to help."

"I know that," Hanna said loudly, then dived on Zero's belly, pulled up her shirt and blew a big raspberry on her skin.

Zero laughed and pulled away and then they were all wrestling together. At some point Gabriel emerged from the scrum to order chocolate cake and ice cream. It came and they ate in gulping silence around the small coffee table. Already Hanna had molted a jacket, a sock, a small wool doll and an unexplained band-aid onto the floor. Zuzanna's shoes were hanging from a lamp and her leggings were tied around the stand, for some reason Zero didn't remember.

She felt worn out but full at the same time.

"Thank you for doing this," Gabriel whispered. "I know you're busy."

"I'm glad you're here," Zuzanna said. "I don't like those bad men."

"Me too!" shouted Hanna, then went back to sucking on her ice cream.

"We'll go soon," Gabriel assured her. "I know this is a distraction. We should-"

"You want to see a movie?" Zero asked.

She didn't know where the words came from. They just popped out.

"Movie?" asked Zuzanna, perking up instantly.

"There's a screen here, did you know that?" Zero found herself going on. "It's private, they only use it in the winter, but I've booked it for the whole day. We could go watch something there."

"And popcorn?" Hanna asked.

"Sure, why not?"

"And ice cream?"

"You're eating ice cream right now, Hanna," Gabriel chided.

"More ice cream!"

Zero smiled. The search for the farm was still happening in the background, and she needed to rest anyway.

"You're sure?" Gabriel asked.

"Let's go," Zero said, and stood up. "First one through the door gets to choose the popcorn flavor."

The girls fell over themselves to get to their feet and charge to the door. Zero looked down at Gabriel. He looked worn now, too.

"You too," she said, and held out her hand. He took it and she pulled him up.

45

SCREENING

It was 10 p.m., and the receptionist on the front desk wasn't sure about the protocol for screening a movie in the middle of the night, but Zero just winked and said it was going to be OK, they'd take both toffee popcorn and butter popcorn, along with caramel ice cream, and the movie could start as soon as possible.

"Yes, madam," he said, and she left him to get on with it.

The screening room was different with the girls in it. She unplugged the laptop and set it by the side while they capered along the seats and shouted about having the whole cinema to themselves.

"Now, if you break those chairs, you'll have to work here long enough to pay off your debt," she said in a solemn tone.

"No we won't!" Zuzanna insisted gleefully, running and laughing.

"I think they'll have you cleaning toilets and polishing the snow, twelve hours a day. Probably it's a week per broken chair."

"No it isn't," Hanna called gleefully, hanging off Zero's arm.

"It definitely is. At least that long. Ask your dad."

They turned to Gabriel.

"I'm afraid that's true," he said somberly. "Perhaps I should have mentioned that before you broke the lamp in our room, Hanna."

Hanna gasped.

"That's at least one week of polishing snow," Gabriel went on.

"No!" she bellowed, and went in to do another raspberry on Zero's belly, but Zero caught her just in time, flipped her and did a raspberry on her belly instead.

Just then the screen came alive. It was the credits pre-roll for an old movie.

"What are we watching?" Zuzanna demanded. "It looks old."

Zero smiled and took her seat. "You'll see."

Zuzanna sat beside her while Hanna jumped up into her lap. Gabriel was moving to sit beside Zuzanna when Hanna cried out. "Next to Clara, Daddy! Of course."

"Oh, of course," he mumbled, and sat down next to Zero. "What movie is it?"

"You can wait and see too."

The credit pre-roll ended, and the opening song began. An old man's sweet and reedy voice began to sing Hope's song: 'When you wish upon a star.'

"Ohh," Hanna said, already entranced.

"Pinocchio?" Gabriel whispered.

"Pinocchio," Zero answered, feeling the emotions surging already. This moment felt like seeing the red channel dug into the farm's clay. As a child she'd loved this movie so much. She'd begged her parents to buy her the dolls, and the bedcovers, and the wallpaper branded with it. She'd just adored Pinocchio himself. She adored his story of trying to become a Real Boy.

At seven years old her father had stolen all of that from

her and turned it into something hateful. She hadn't seen the movie since she was seven years old. She'd hated the thought of it, because of what they'd made it into.

Now, in this place with Gabriel and his girls around her, she felt like it was time to reclaim it. She'd loved this movie with Hope by her side long before the 'Pinocchios' were a real thing and the Blue Fairy became a watchword for terror. It belonged to her more.

As the music climbed, sung in Jiminy Cricket's sweet and lilting voice, she began to quietly cry.

"Clara," Gabriel whispered.

"It's OK," she said, and wrapped her arms around Hanna, and tucked into the popcorn. "I'm just tired."

The movie played, and it wrecked her. She cried throughout, when she wasn't laughing or holding her breath. Pinocchio's journey was beautiful, and every second of it was echoed by her memory of seeing it as a child, with Hope by her side.

She felt closer to her little sister than ever.

She watched on the edge of her seat as Pinocchio fought his way off Pleasure Island, and escaped the whale, and slipped through the fingers of the fox and the cat, until at the end he earned the thing he'd wished for most of all: to become a real boy.

That was a good thing. A beautiful, sweet, kind thing.

As the ending credits played, with Jiminy Cricket singing Hope's song once more, both of the girls were asleep. Zero lifted Hanna and Gabriel picked up Zuzanna, nodding like a rag doll. They took the elevator to the penthouse suite, which was now a mess. Bags, clothes, towels, sheets and dishes were everywhere.

Gabriel led the way to the girls' room, where he laid his murmuring daughter down on the bed, worked her shoes off and laid the covers gently over her. Zero laid Hanna down beside her, but the little girl clung on around her neck.

"It's time to sleep, sweetie," Zero whispered.

"I'm not sleepy," Hanna mumbled, barely able to open her eyes.

"I'll see you tomorrow, I promise."

Hanna squeezed Zero extra hard, gave her a kiss on the cheek which became a raspberry, then let go with a sly little chuckle.

Zero pulled away. She didn't know what to think. None of this felt real. Together with Gabriel she walked back over to the door. There they both stopped in an awkward, pregnant silence.

"Thank you for doing that," Gabriel said. "You don't know what it means."

Zero smiled. His shy smile was sweet. "I have some idea."

"They loved the movie."

"It's a classic."

Neither seemed to know what to say after that. Zero's thoughts went back to Rex and his search. Perhaps Hope was out there, on the farm now. Maybe Rex had found her. Maybe they'd be together again soon.

"I should go," she said.

"Yes," Gabriel agreed.

Another few seconds passed.

"I-" he began.

"Well-" Zero said at the same time. They both stopped and laughed.

"Thank you for the flowers," she said. "I'll go."

She turned, opened the door and stepped through.

Then Gabriel's hand caught hers. Her breath stopped in her throat and she turned. He was looking at her with an intensity she hadn't seen before. This wasn't anger, or disappointment, or even pity. This was something else entirely.

"Stay," he said.

So many thoughts flooded through her head in that moment. How she'd planned for none of this. How it wasn't smart, wasn't safe, but how she wanted it. That look in his eyes, and the warm touch of his skin, entranced her. The way he'd handed her tissues as she'd cried through Pinocchio. The way he'd saved her life.

She'd never done more than kiss a boy before. She'd never wanted to.

"OK," she said.

"OK," he repeated.

She stepped up against him. His arms were hot and trembling in her hands. He wrapped her up and they kissed. It started soft and uncertain, their lips meeting like timid birds, but grew warmer and firmer as the heat of hormones rushed through them both: chemicals for which there was only one known antidote.

Zero took him by the hand and led him deeper into the dark.

46

BLUE FAIRY

By morning, the bed was packed with bodies.

Hanna had somehow squeezed herself in between Zero and Gabriel. Zuzanna lay behind her. It was hot and cozy, like being held in the palm of a giant.

Zero looked at Hanna's head and Gabriel's sleeping face. There were faint rays of light creeping through the master suite curtains, illuminating the peaks and valleys of their noses, eyes and faces. She saw the clear resemblance, and perhaps also the ghost of their mother, forever memorialized in them.

"Are you awake?" Zuzanna whispered from behind.

"A little," she answered.

"Me too."

They lay in comfortable silence a while longer. Zero thought about what was going to happen today. First up was Rex. Hopefully he had narrowed the search to a single farm. After that, she would go plan her assault and go. Hellion and B4cksl4cker had left her bike outside the hotel. The Attack Crate was in her warehouse next to Rex. She would gear up and head to the farm.

"Are you leaving today?" Zuzanna whispered.

"Yes. I have to."

Zuzanna nodded against her back. "Because of the bad men. You have to go kill them?"

Zero shifted and turned. Hanna mumbled something but remained asleep. Zuzanna was looking at her with a very serious expression.

"What gave you that idea?"

"I'm not an idiot. I know who you are."

Zero smiled. "Who am I?"

"Girl Zero', that man called you. It sounds like a superhero. That means he's a supervillain. I know what was going to happen to us."

Zero wasn't sure what to say. She wanted to repeat the pretty lie that the girls were never in danger, but knew Zuzanna wouldn't believe it. To keep on insisting on the lie now would be cruel.

"Nothing bad is going to happen to you," she said instead. "You're safe here. I'll go and take care of the bad man and all his friends."

"Supervillain," Zuzanna corrected.

"Supervillain, OK."

"All of them?"

"I won't miss a single one. I'll get them all. Then you can go home. You can forget all of this."

Zuzanna blinked. "I don't want to forget. That's what happened in the movie."

"What do you mean?"

Zuzanna shuddered. "All the boys on Pleasure Island? They forgot who they were. They became donkeys. I don't want to be a donkey."

Zero shook her head and stroked Zuzanna's arm. "Honey, that's just a movie. It's not real."

"It is real," Zuzanna insisted. "I don't want to forget."

Zero said nothing for a time after that. She couldn't argue.

She'd held onto the memory of Hope with everything she had. If she'd forgotten that, despite all the pain the memory brought, who would she be today?

"OK," she said. "Don't forget. It was scary back then, I know. It's scary now, too. But it's not all bad. We're having a lovely time. Your daddy and your sister are here."

"And you're here."

"And I'm here. For now at least."

Zuzanna closed her eyes. For a little while Zero thought she must have fallen back asleep, and started to peel back the sheets to leave.

"Will we see you again?" Zuzanna asked sleepily.

"I hope so."

"Me too," Zuzanna mumbled, before nuzzling back into the covers. "He may call you Zero, but I know who you are, really."

A shiver ran down Zero's spine. "Who am I?"

"You're our Blue Fairy. You're magic."

Zero bit back a sob. Soon enough Zuzanna's breathing became deep and even again.

"I'll do my best," she whispered, then slowly slid out of the covers. The others didn't move. The clock on the wall said 5 a.m. She gathered her clothes and dressed, then went to the door.

"Wait," came Gabriel's voice.

He crossed the room in the near-dark and met her at the door.

"I have to go," she said.

"I know. Just." He paused and searched her eyes. "I know. That's all."

She smiled, then leaned in to kiss him on the lips. It broke her heart to see the sadness in his eyes when she pulled away.

"If you don't hear from me in a day, then you need to take precautions, Gabriel. I'll ask my friends, Hellion and

B4cksl4cker, to contact you. You may have to move; a new country, new identities. They can help with all that. I hope it doesn't come to that, and I'm sorry if it does."

He held her gaze. "I'll do what I have to for my girls. And I wouldn't change a thing."

"Don't say that."

"Why not? Since the moment I found you in the forest, what could I do differently? I'd be a different person; someone I wouldn't like very much. It's just…" he sighed. "I wish I could help more. You know? I'm not strong enough to protect you."

She nodded. Maybe she'd never met someone like that before. Perhaps Christopher Wren counted, but he was a very different kind of man.

"You helped more than you know," she said, then kissed him again. It was a little slower, a little fuller, and when she pulled back the chemicals were starting up again in the pit of her stomach. "I'll call. But if I don't…"

"I know. Good luck, Clara. I hope we'll see you again."

She touched his cheek and left the room without looking back.

47

FORTRESS

Her laptop was waiting where she'd left it in the screening room. She swept it up and returned to her room. The space seemed very empty. She sat at the desk by the vast panoramic view. It was snowing outside, thick white flakes tumbling across the landscape.

Like a fairytale.

She placed a quick room service order then opened the laptop and logged into Rex. It didn't take long to check the results of his search. The answer was conclusive.

Only one farm was a match to her new parameters.

She brought it up and zoomed in, flicking between that and the Idaho farm. Everything was the same. The east-west orientation. The farmhouse and the barn. Even the number of pig enclosures was an exact match. The one difference was the presence of a low mound in the middle, no more than fifteen feet long by five, disrupting the enclosure grid.

The fallout shelter. The nose of the farm, which didn't seem to exist in the Idaho photograph. Seeing it there felt strange, like watching Pinocchio again after all these years, and seeing so many new parallels to the world as she'd come to know it.

"Percentage match?" she asked Rex.

"Ninety-nine percent."

Zero sat and stared. It was one of the farms within a two hundred-mile radius of Krakow. Eighty miles to the east, near a town called Czarna. Viktor Anatoly was a local boy, after all. She scrolled across the farm, zooming in where she could, assessing lines of attack, even though she knew it all already. She'd grown up on this farm and burned it down once already, though this version was massively more secure.

The outer fences were higher, ringed by a 'moat' of empty space a hundred yards wide. Security lamps had circled it in an unbroken ring, likely paired with CCTV in a closed network she had no chance of hacking. Even the Vantablack strike suit, with its automatic ghosting protocol built in, couldn't get her across that huge moat of clear ground.

Add to that the vor. As a pakhan, Anatoly could have any number of Bratva thugs as a garrison. Ten. A hundred? Maybe more. She tried to guess at potential patrol routes, and guard stations, and barracks, but everything was possible. Between the pig enclosures was a labyrinth of walkways for them to patrol. There were guard towers at the farm's corners and a reinforced gate on the central east-west road.

The farm wasn't big. Less than four acres total. That would make total lockdown easy. In all likelihood, there was no way she could get within three hundred yards of the farm without being spotted.

On the map she marked the likely holding place for the Blue Fairy exchange. Inessa Sidorova had said it was vast. Underground was a possibility, but extremely expensive and therefore unlikely. Most likely the old cells under the farmhouse would be reserved for Mona and Hope alone, with the barn reserved for the exchanges.

Anatoly's zoo.

On the map she marked out potential fields of fire. A

single sniper atop the farmhouse could cover the entire farm. Another on the barn would double that. Add the guard towers, the patrols, the gate, and it seemed impossible.

A fortress.

Zero kept looking but found no route through. If she had time to plan, perhaps, she could bring in more forces and mount a full-scale assault: perhaps Foundation strike teams, even request Christopher Wren from his 'well-earned' vacation, maybe leverage some of those 'Body Snatcher' remote controlled vehicles Hellion had told her about.

It could take days. Weeks. She knew where the process would have to begin.

"Rex, anything from Hellion or B4cksl4cker?"

"Nothing." Rex paused. "But there is a message from Viktor Anatoly."

Zero blinked. "What?"

"It has just come in. I am sorry, Zero."

Her blood ran cold. "Why are you sorry? And how do you know it's him?"

"It contains the handshake signature of the Blue Fairy shadow line, received through an open port we did not know existed."

That was bad. "Into the darknet?"

"Yes. A pathway navigated by the release of that tranche of data."

She cursed and her pulse sped up. Hellion had told her not to do that, but she'd insisted. "Are we still secure?"

"Yes. They achieved one-time access only. The port is now sealed."

She let out a breath, but it was hardly a relief. Anatoly was still running rings around her. Encircling her.

"Bring it up."

A message with a photograph appeared on her screen. The photo showed an exact replica of the torture frame that she'd executed her father on, the one he'd built for her at sixteen years old and never been able to try out. A young woman lay strapped within it, naked and pale, her face and figure obscured from the low angle, but that long blond hair could only be…

Zero couldn't believe it. Her throat ran dry.

Was this proof of life on Hope?

Her eyes darted to the message.

'It's time to surrender, Mona. GOMA-49 within twelve hours, or this little piggy never comes home again.'

Zero couldn't think. She pored over the photograph while her heart boomed in her chest. There was nothing to go on but the woman's figure and hair, but was there something familiar about it?

"Rex," she managed, her lips tacky and dry. "Percentage analysis based on genetic markers and frame. Could that be my sister?"

Seconds ticked by.

"Yes," Rex answered. "There is a ninety percent possibility. She resembles you."

The world fell out under Zero.

Hope.

A photograph of Hope, locked in her father's frame.

A lifetime of suffering. A lifetime of humiliation. It was as if neither of them had ever escaped their father's grip

She stood up and stared out into the storm for long minutes, pushing those horrors away. Her father's legacy. Viktor Anatoly's dream. The food came and she forced herself to eat, cheese-drenched lasagna with boiled vegetables, feeling more afraid with every bite, counting every second as the minutes ticked down.

She didn't want to go back.

She wasn't afraid of dying. It was a long, long life in Viktor Anatoly's care that terrified her the most. Of having to see her sister's face as he dreamed up new torments for the pair of them, to keep the Real Boys coming back for more, like freaks in a carney show.

A successful strike on the farm was possible, she told herself. It had to be. With only twelve hours, there wasn't enough time to bring in additional forces, but maybe there was something she could do…

As the sun rose over the High Tatras mountains, and the snow kept piling up outside, she erased the laptop completely and left it on the desk. She pulled on her Vantablack strike suit and looked around the room a final time before striding out.

The Ninja was waiting for her outside.

48

D-DOS ATTACK

The ride north looked to be four hours, through the spiky Tatras mountains and back down to the lowlands of Poland. The skies were thunderous and black, dumping snow heavily. Zero gave commands to Rex throughout, beginning the groundwork for the breaking of the Czarna farm via a real-life D-DOS attack.

A D-DOS attack, or Distributed Denial of Service attack, occurred on the Internet when incoming information requests overwhelmed any given website's server capacity and forced it to fail. Infamously, it was one of B4cksl4cker's most favored tactics, using his three-million-plus computer botnet army to access any given web page at the exact same instant, starting a total cascade failure. Into that chaos he could insert a strip of code called a 'zombie agent', which would slip unobserved through the occupied cyber defenses. He'd hacked millions out of the national banks of North Korea and Belarus using the technique.

Zero's plan was to take that principle into the real world.

The first step in any D-DOS attack was to martial your army. For B4cksl4cker that was his three million computers. In the real world, Zero had a plan for how to build her own makeshift army, and it started with prepping the vast amount of data Hellion and B4cksl4cker had secured off the darknet.

In total, there were dozens of petabytes of data: chat logs, financial transactions, video streams, blockchain records and more. The hackers had already processed this vast amount into meaningful chunks, and Zero worked with Rex to scour those chunks for the exact data trails she was looking for: the trails of notable Polish persons.

There were far more than she'd expected. Corporate leaders, judges, politicians, entertainers, sports stars; many of them rich, wealthy and influential, and all of them compromised.

All of them Real Boys.

Once she had her core list of several hundred names backed by ample data, she had Rex channel a phone call to the reporter Maja Kominski at Gazeta Wyborcza.

"Kominski," she answered.

"This is Clara Baxter. Remember that I promised you an exclusive on my story, Maja?"

It took Kominski a few moments to register. "Clara. You're ready to go on record?"

"This is better than me going on record. Right now I'm making available to you a file filled with the names of hundreds of Real Boys, many tied up with Bratva, all of them Polish elites. It's in your personal intranet directory already, and includes everything you need to nail these men to the wall. You just need to start publishing immediately."

There was a long silence.

"You want me to do what?" Kominski asked eventually.

"Publish," Zero repeated. "I want this first batch of exposés out within precisely five hours, and each next batch on a slow trickle every ten minutes after."

Kominski said nothing for a few moments, keys rattling as she located, opened then started swiping through the vast tranche of data. "What is this? This is, I... This is a vast amount of material, Clara. I don't even know what I'm looking at. This is, uh-"

"Pulitzer-worthy?" Zero offered.

"If it's true? It's bigger than the Pulitzer. It's historic! Some of the names you've got listed here? These people are famous. Trusted. Respected. Where did you even get it all from? It's going to take days to wade through it all."

"Unacceptable," Zero pressed. "You put everybody in your office on this right now. I have faith you can vet the first batch by mid-afternoon. After that it'll be rolling deadlines for as long as it takes. Miss a deadline, however, and the data will self-encrypt and I'll send it on to Fakt or Super Express. Maybe they'll treat it with the urgency it deserves."

Kominski laughed nervously. "So, wait, are you blackmailing us? We have these hit jobs out faster, or we lose the data? And how would you even do that? I have a hard copy on my drive now."

"You have access, that's all. Try printing some of this out. Try emailing it to yourself and see what happens. I suppose you could take screenshots of every page, but my virus will just scramble those, too."

"Your what?"

"Virus. When you entered the Gazeta's intranet, I took total control of all its systems. Maja, I didn't want to do this. I could, technically, post all of my content directly and immediately through your online site, but I wouldn't do that. I made a promise to a friend I wasn't going to exploit people anymore. Plus, I want you to vet it and publish with your paper's seal of approval. I just want you to do it fast."

A few seconds passed. "So this is what, a kinder form of blackmail?"

"I like to think of it as a really tight deadline with a powerful incentive."

Another few seconds. "I can't decide this. I need to take it to the head editor. Would you come on the line and-"

"No. This is on you. Show them the material. If they're against it, I move down the line to the next big press, all within minutes. Goodbye, Maja. This is the scoop of the century, if you're able to pull it off. Give me the green light within ten minutes or we're done."

At nine minutes fifty-two seconds, Kominski came back with the green light. Shortly after that, Zero arrived back in Krakow, ready for the next step of her D-DOS attack.

Pulling back into the courtyard of the Skawina warehouse, the absence of trucks hit her like a gut punch. Even now Hellion and B4cksl4cker were running from the Real Boys, because of her. Still, they'd taken the time to push the Attack Crate 2.0 out of the van and into the mud, where the rain hammered off its wooden lid.

She set the Ninja onto its kickstand by her warehouse's roll shutter then headed inside. The reinforced plastic tent remained, humming and glowing with servers.

"Hello Rex," she called.

"Hello Clara," Rex answered, his voice ringing out through the warehouse. "Welcome back."

"We have work to do."

The zip opened. Zero dropped into her chair, reminded for a moment of Hellion's incredible hammock workstation. But there was no time for that. The hackers were on their own now, just like Zero, just like Viktor Anatoly, and there was no escape for any of them.

Less than eight hours remained, and there was so much still to do. She cracked her knuckles and her fingers fell on the keys. The darknet opened. Every fortress could be cracked; she knew that. Apply the right tool at the right place at the right time, and the walls would open.

For B4cksl4cker, the second step of a D-DOS attack was

simple; all he had to do was point his slaved botnet at a target and overwhelm it. It was the same for Zero, if a little more involved.

When Kominski started publishing, every Real Boy in Poland would feel the crosshairs on their backs as the world turned against them. Overnight they'd go from darling elites to the most hated people on the planet. They'd become desperate, reaching out for anything that could help them survive the storm of accountability coming their way.

Zero just had to channel that desperation toward her target of choice, and that process began by sending out thousands of emails, cell phone alerts and instant messages to all the Real Boys in the stolen darknet data.

It was a simple matter to 'spoof' each message, so it showed as coming from the email account, cell phone or web app of a 'trusted friend' in their Blue Fairy network.

She had them completely. Their crimes. Their complete social network. Everything she needed. And the message? She tailored it using Rex's smart algorithms to pick up the specific phrases and vocabulary used by each Boy's trusted friends, but following the same basic pattern every time, attached to a few screen grabs of the incriminating data she had on them:

'You need to get out of the country right now! News is about to break out of Gazeta Wyborcza about what we've done (see attached files). This is massive and implicates us all. We're ruined. There's only one safe place; the Blue Fairy exchange. Grab your family, your guns and your money and make a beeline. Viktor Anatoly is promising safe harbor and a route out of the country. Don't believe me? Try and cross the border yourself, or wait until Agencja Wywiadu comes knocking at your door. The exchange is located on a pig farm in Czarna, coordinates as follows, and is the only safe place for us now."

The Real Boys reacted to it immediately and in large numbers. It had to be the most effective phishing campaign Zero had ever conducted. At once Real Boys flooded Rex's various spoofed inboxes with questions, demands and expletives. Rex responded to each and every one in character, building a narrative designed to flush them all, whether earlier or later, out into the open and scurrying desperately to Czarna.

The one person she didn't send a message to was Viktor Anatoly. He would find out soon enough, when a tidal wave of refugee Boys turned up at his doorstep.

49

CZARNA

By the time Zero stepped back out of Rex's kennel, the brooding gray sky was turning black, as the faint glow of the sun through dark clouds was obscured by the fuming power station. It was raining still.

Two hours remained on Viktor Anatoly's deadline, and Gazeta Wyborcza had been publishing articles for three hours, with fresh rollouts every ten minutes. In that time Poland had blown up with the scandal of the century; an endless flood of revelations that kept on felling Boy after Boy from high places, as Kominski's team vetted, edited, proofed and published hundreds of pages of data.

The scandal was already spilling over into world media, taking top banner slots on the BBC, FOX, CNN and Al Jazeera.

These Boys were now hunted men. They had been martialed. The emails were out and the Boys were in the wind heading for Anatoly's farm. They had been directed. All that remained now was step three, insertion of a zombie agent…

Zero strode to the Attack Crate in the rain and levered off the lid. On top lay the Vantablack helmet that matched her strike suit, along with all of her blades. She swept up the helmet and slotted the blades into their concealed slots in her suit. Deeper inside the crate there was a sleek black backpack, which she filled with three of the active decoy balls and the one Nano UAV. The pack cinched snug to her back. She sealed up the crate and pulled the helmet down over her head.

At once her vision was overlaid with an abundance of wireframe data, via screens built into the helmet's visor as a Heads-Up-Display.

"Clear the screen Rex," she tried.

"Clearing," Rex replied immediately, and the HUD vacated. "Would you like any data overlay?"

"What have you got?" Zero asked, as she strode over to the Ninja.

"GPS navigation, satellite footage, clock and chat box are primary functions. Many additionals are possible, including Nano belly-cam, active decoy notifications, pulse readout, sonic detection field, proximity of all known friendly and foe positions, multilateral camera, status of ghosting protocol hack-"

"Let's just go with the primary functions for now, and keep them small," she said as she straddled the Ninja. "Make the clock a countdown."

Immediately several data feeds appeared in the periphery of her helmet's display. Navigation was a small map in the upper right corner, wired to GPS. One of the hacks she'd worked in the last few hours was to obtain satellite oversight of Anatoly's farm, and that feed appeared in the bottom right, showed a top-down view of the farm she'd been studying now for hours. The security lights were on, engulfing the fields and the pigs, highlighting the men patrolled the exterior. The countdown timer clicked down at the top left, already down to less than two hours. The chat box ran beneath it, and comprised a rapidly updating list of messages and data requests fired between Rex and the various correspondences she'd keyed into his algorithms.

The data was rich. She felt like she was back inside Hellion and B4cksl4cker's server truck.

The hack of the farm was ready.

She hit the Ninja's ignition and spun the throttle. The bike roared and she gave it its head, tearing out of the courtyard, up through the mud and hard onto the 79. Soon she was chewing up the miles. The chat box on the right continued to populate with all capital messages and exclamation marks from fleeing Real Boys. The satellite map below it tracked the first of an incoming flood of vehicles approaching Anatoly's farm from the west.

For the next hour it was just her and the highway, speeding east as the countdown timer ticked down.

Her whole life had been leading to this moment. She felt poised and fraught, just like when she'd walked down that passageway with her hand in her mother's, waiting for her chance to stab her father in the eye. Anatoly deserved no less. The exchanges were at stake. Her father's legacy. Hope.

Dread blurred with the anger. As the countdown breached the hour mark, she was far from the city and racing along dark country roads, interspersed by the lights of occasional villages.

"First vehicle arriving now," Rex said in her ear.

She focused on the satellite view of the farm in her HUD, where a truck was passing through the outer barrier of light and turning into the farm's central east-west road. She revved the Ninja faster as it the truck approached the outer gate, flanked by pig enclosures. She imagined the occupants of that vehicle only growing more panicked and afraid, with the stink of the farm filling up their cab like a living thing, getting into their lungs and driving them on harder.

At the first gate the truck halted and a line of vor stepped out from the guard station, leveling their rifles.

The hack was beginning.

Zero's final stretch to Czarna passed in what felt like seconds, as more and more Real Boy vehicles pulled in off the road and tried to access the farm. Soon they were backed up onto the road and passengers were kicking open their doors and spilling out into the mud, traipsing their finery through sopping pig filth in the hope of saving their skins.

With twenty-three minutes left on the countdown timer, Zero pulled off the road and into the forest, where she laid the Ninja down amidst a cluster of tall pines. Cold rain slashed through the darkness and crashed off the foliage. The sun was long down and the sky rumbled with nearing thunder. Lightning forked the heavens and Zero ran to the edge of the cluster, toward the farm's outer 'moat' of empty space, where she kneeled at the edge of the overlapping wall of light cast by the high-powered security lamps.

Twenty-one minutes. Ahead lay the farm. She picked out the farmhouse, where one light in her parents' old room was glowing blood-red. The great bulk of the barn stood like a dark ship moored amidst an ocean of pigs.

The presence of the pigs carried even through the thunder and rain: their constant restless shifting, and grunting, and the slapping of their flesh against muddy wallows; the stench of their waste, and their feed, and their bodies rising up like a swamp fever.

It felt like being back in Idaho. But she wasn't a scared little girl anymore, huddled in her cell. Now she was Zero, a one-word name on her own terms.

"How many more vehicles coming, Rex?" she asked.

The AI ran quick calculations. "Thirty-two have arrived so far. One hundred and two will arrive in the next thirty minutes. CCTV of the highway suggests," he paused a moment, "the densest locus of arrivals will be within ten minutes."

Right on time.

"Good boy."

"Others across Krakow and Poland are still taking to their vehicles. They will be coming for many hours, Zero."

"Good," she said, checking the satellite feed in the corner of her HUD. "Are you seeing what I'm seeing with security?"

A few seconds passed. "What are you seeing?"

"The vor are massing to handle the influx of vehicles. I count, uh, twenty-four on the main road and rising."

"Yes. There are twenty-seven men attempting to turn these vehicles around. The occupants are arguing back strongly."

Zero smiled. Of course they were. "Kill one or two of their engines with a remote hack, will you? Allow no escape."

"It would be my pleasure."

Zero dropped to her belly. Against the dirt, in the rain, with the Vantablack suit absorbing what little light spilled this far from the security lamps, she was functionally invisible.

How long would that last?

Seventeen minutes.

Sixteen.

Soon shouts and horns roared up from the spine road, as Rex remotely disabled several vehicles. Zero waited. She waited until tempers flared and one of the vor fired off a warning shot, which drove the shouting to new heights. Several vehicles tried to reverse out, but with the line jammed up by engine locks, there was nowhere to go.

Vehicles crashed into each other and bounced off into the enclosures.

"More than twenty vor are dealing with this issue, Zero. I believe there will be no better time."

"Agreed." Fifteen minutes remained. All she needed now

was to open a hole in the wall of light, just enough to allow an unseen insertion where snipers couldn't see her. From her backpack she extracted the UAV Nano egg and popped the lid.

"All yours, Rex," she said.

"I will remind you, this is a twenty-million-dollar piece of equipment," Rex said, not for the first time. "Not a rock for smashing lights, Zero."

"You sound like Hellion. It'll take out one of those lamps, won't it?"

"Yes. With sufficient speed."

"Get a run-up then."

The Nano's blades spun up, barely louder than a desktop fan and hardly audible through the rain, and took off back through the trees. In seconds it was out of sight.

"Ready," Rex said.

Fourteen minutes.

"Go," she said, and thrust into a rapid crawl across the open moat; the zombie agent in a massive D-DOS attack.

50

ZOMBIE AGENT

"Crashing light," Rex said in Zero's ear.

She'd already crawled fifty yards across the soaking grass 'moat' when the Nano UAV whizzed by overhead, homing in on the target security lamp. It found its mark and struck; the glass shattered, the Nano crumpled to the mud below, and the light went out.

Zero's section of the open expanse fell into near-total dark. She pushed herself up and ran, the Vantablack suit easily sucking up what stray light fell from the overlapping lamps. No sniper fire snapped in nearby, no vor came rushing to stop up the gap or replace the bulb; they had bigger problems.

Off to Zero's right the farm was engulfed in chaos and gunfire as the flood of Real Boys overwhelmed the defenses. A perfect D-DOS attack. More vehicles arrived every minute, and now some Boys were charging up the central road with weapons raised, while others were climbing straight into the enclosures, taking their chances with the pigs in their bid to reach the farmhouse.

Nothing was going to stop the Real Boys now. The world

was imploding at their backs, and this was the only way to safety.

Zero cleared the moat right around the time the thickest number of vehicles were coming in.

"Seventy percent of vor patrols have refocused on the D-DOS," Rex said.

Ahead she saw a clear route to the barn. There were still shadowy figures patrolling amongst the enclosures, but most had been sucked away to deal with the flood of rats.

It was the best she could hope for. Even if Anatoly suspected she was behind this attack, what could he do? She could be anywhere, disguised in any one of those Real Boy vehicles, hidden amongst their number at the heaving gate, clambering through the pig enclosures alongside. He had no choice but to stop them all.

She climbed over the fence and ran, staying low while horns honked and people shouted and guns fired, everything confused by the driving rain and drumroll of growing thunder. She weaved away from the entrance, heading west through the splashing mire of clay, mud and pig filth that lined the narrow walkways between the enclosures, beading on the barn.

From both sides came the panicky grunts of pigs, and she caught flashes of their thick pale bodies shifting in the dark beyond the fence, their frightened eyes gleaming in the security floodlights, their legs kicking up splashes and the stale stink of sewage.

"You are coming into visible range of a patrol, ten o'clock," Rex said in her ear.

"Understood." She raised her head slightly over the fence and saw them just ahead; two men tramping on a parallel walkway with their rifles raised, barely fifty yards away. These were not dart rifles but Heckler and Koch 433s, fully automatic assault rifles; hardly the standard tool for a farmer.

They were heading directly her way. She dropped back down and focused on the satellite map of the farm in the HUD's bottom right corner, but at that resolution she couldn't pick herself out.

"Will we intersect?"

"Yes, in fifteen seconds."

She cursed. "Reroute me, Rex."

"Working," he said. "I suggest you go back the way you came."

She turned and ran low, cornering a bend just as the patrol came into sight behind her.

"Which way now?" she hissed, dropping against a fence around the corner, feeling like Pac-Man in his maze, surrounded by ghosts.

"I am sorry, Zero, it seems there is no route through."

She almost laughed. "What?"

"There is no route. Three patrols are currently converging on your position. The nearest will see you in forty seconds. There is no-"

Zero was already moving. The pig enclosures were fenced with wooden posts and four horizontal rails; the gap between each rail was almost big enough to slide through, but not quite.

The math was simple. She couldn't go over the fence because they'd see her. The only way was through, but getting enough traction on the ground to kick through one of the sturdy rails was impossible. Instead she swiftly uncinched her backpack, pulled out one of the auto-inflating active decoy eggs, set it on the ground under the lowest rail and waited.

Five seconds. Ten.

Thunder rolled and she pushed the button.

"Ten seconds, Zero," Rex said.

The active decoy burst under cover of the thunder. A human shape exploded outward with all the pressure of a flashbang grenade, forceful enough to smash the rail upward. She flung herself through the gap and into the enclosure, driving the active decoy and the backpack ahead.

Instantly she was surrounded by great, lumbering, terrified bodies. She rolled amongst them, slithering through filth to the center as their hard trotters stamped and they squealed at the top of their lungs. The sound grew deafening and one of them went for her, ramming her hard in the back with its snout. Her carbon nanotube suit protected her, but she didn't want to take too many more hits like that; even without teeth, their stamping feet would soon shred her.

"Rex!" she shouted over the cacophony of thudding feet and squeals. "Where are they?"

"Four at the entrance you made," Rex replied smoothly, "Two at the south edge standing overwatch. The pigs are escaping, Zero."

Another laugh nearly escaped her. A pig stampede wasn't part of her D-DOS attack, but perhaps it was a good addition. One thought followed that, though; if her enclosure emptied of pigs she'd have no cover whatsoever.

Had she just locked herself in a killing cell?

She spun and scrambled through the rain-slashed mud toward the pen's south edge. A pig slammed her in the left shoulder and another fell across her knees, briefly pinning her in place as the others rounded on this intruder. One rammed her helmet, one nipped at her hand as she circled it to her triceps holster, then she was there at the fence.

Two figures stood on the other side, their backs to her and shouting to each other over the rain and the cacophony of the pigs. They were close enough, and with no pause she drove her eight-inch stiletto blade into the left knee of the first. The tip was pin-sharp but it thickened to a half-inch down the length, so it pierced first them rammed later, through skin, muscle, anterior-cruciate ligament, meniscus, patella.

The blade punched a hole clean through and she was already yanking it back before the man even begin to fall. The shout escaped his lips just as she stabbed his colleague in the right knee, making for a pair. The blade crunched and popped through his patella, then she yanked it back in and rolled away.

There was screaming everywhere now. The enclosure was already thinning as the pigs fled. Zero found the gap she'd torn through the fence, now abandoned as the remaining two patrols circled, and emerged.

All their backs were to her as they circled to their colleagues; one of the men on the floor was firing his HK433 wildly into the enclosure, unleashing a storm of pigs wailing. One vor was trying to stop him, one was on his knees trying to inspect the wounds, one joined him in firing blind into the dark, while the fourth simply peered into the enclosure's churned mud, looking for the unseen enemy.

Zero came up on them silently, a stiletto in each hand now. She planted double blows with one forward thrust, needling between the ribs and into the hearts of two men. They sighed like dying flowers and collapsed, leaving only the man at the rail and the man on his knees.

She spiked the kneeler with a downward slam into the hollow of his collarbone then followed swiftly with the man at the rail, only just now turning around. Her stiletto took him through the armpit and between the ribs, a perfect shot to collapse his heart's second ventricle.

He dropped on top of the man with a busted right knee, still trying to fire his HK even though the magazine was dry. The man with the busted left knee was on one foot and trying to hobble away, his weapon forgotten. Zero drew a three-inch shuriken blade and hurled it. It flashed like a star through the rain and buried itself in the back of his skull.

He fell.

That left one. She fell upon him, cracking him over the head with the grip of her right stiletto. His head slapped into mud and rocked back.

"Where's Anatoly?" she shouted.

He answered in dozy Russian.

"In English!"

He tried again, but it still wasn't in English, and this time she recognized some of the words from the last vor she'd interrogated.

"Ya ne znayo!"

I don't know.

She spiked his chest too. It took three minutes to drag all their bodies over the mud, into the enclosure and push them through the gap, but it should buy her some time.

"There are no current patrols in this area," Rex said in her ear. "You are clear to take the barn."

She straightened up and looked out. Down the walkway to the south a trio of pigs scampered by. Off to the east the influx of Real Boys continued. Incoming headlights stretched back down the road and figures continued to charge the gate and enclosures, desperate to find safety in Anatoly's embrace.

Zero spun to the barn. Overhead thunder crashed and lightning lit up the sky. Mud spilled slickly down her helmet in the driving rain, obscuring her vision; she pulled it off and tossed it into the enclosure after the bodies.

The rain felt good on her cheeks. The stilettos felt good in her fists. She stalked toward the farm's heart.

51

ZERO

The barn loomed ahead, far larger than the barn on the Idaho farm; three stories at least, and big enough to contain universes.

"There is a substantial gun battle developing at the east of the farm," Rex said in her ear. "Shall I call the police?"

"Not yet.

She closed the gap from the walkway to the barn on her belly. The main doors towered over her. To her right was the farmhouse, its red light glowing menacingly. To her left was darkness and shrieking pigs.

She pushed the door, but there was no movement. She looked closer and saw no hinges. Like a theme park, this entrance was just for show.

"Find me a door, Rex," she ordered.

"There is nothing visible on the barn's south side," he said. "The satellite cannot see the north or west. Perhaps if you had not destroyed our UAV Nano…"

Hellion had given him some of her sarcastic edge, it seemed.

"I'll check north."

She ran. At the corner of the barn a huge fork of lightning

cracked open the sky, chased immediately by a clash of thunder more total than GOMA-49's bass speakers. In the sudden brightness, Zero glimpsed a figure on his knees in the shadows of the barn, dart rifle raised.

The rifle discharged and a dart struck Zero's chest. She sidestepped at once but he tracked her, firing again. One dart slapped against her right thigh, another took her low in the belly, by which time she'd pulled and flung three shuriken into the dark.

Two clanked off his body armor but one struck him in the face; far from a fatal blow, snagging his cheek and rocking his head back. He fired the dart rifle blind and then Zero was there, covering the distance in seconds to plunge both stilettos into his throat. They crossed through his windpipe and she rapidly 'scissored' them like opposing levers, severing the flesh between the blades and near-decapitating him. He convulsed once and sagged back against the barn.

A radio crackled at his waist. Zero snatched it up and held it to her ear, barely able to make out a sound through the torrential downpour, and what little she heard was in Russian.

"Rex!" she barked.

"Translating," he said. "One moment. It seems they are on high alert, Zero. Minutes remain in the deadline. But they do not know you are here. They suspect, but do not know where."

"Yet," Zero said, and stood up, brushing down her body. The Vantablack suit had rebuffed the pneumatic hypodermic darts. She was lucky he hadn't hit her face or neck.

"They are calling in Bratva reinforcements," Rex went on, as she dropped back to running around the barn's north side. "Expected within twenty minutes."

"How many?"

"Impossible to tell. But I am recording mass movement

on inbound roads from three directions. Multiple vehicles. I would guess dozens, if not as many as a hundred."

Zero cursed and ran faster.

There were no entrances on the north side or the west, looking out over the pig enclosures and empty 'moat' into the black of the surrounding pine forests. As she cornered to the long south side, a figure tumbled over a nearby enclosure fence and came limping blindly in her direction. He was bedraggled and whimpering to himself, covered in mud and slipping wildly.

A Real Boy.

He clearly didn't see her and bounced once off the wall, close enough for her to get a good look at his face: a man in his fifties with thin gray hair, a delicately sculpted mustache and trident beard, now bloody and trailing flaps of skin where the pigs had gored him. She considered spiking him in the heart, but let him go, watching as he beaded on the red light in the farmhouse and lurched toward it.

Zero was about to run on when a gunshot cracked out and blood sprayed from the back of the man's head. He dropped dead in the mud some twenty yards from the farmhouse; just as she'd expected.

"Sniper in the farmhouse," she said.

"What shall I do?" Rex answered.

"I don't know," Zero said and kept running. In a minute she'd fully circled the barn and found exactly what she'd feared. No entrance. Perhaps it even made sense. As a child, she'd never been allowed into the barn. That was her father's domain. It was as an edifice only, not an actual place.

But he was in there. Zero could feel it in her bones. Anatoly. The children he used to stock the exchanges, the raw materials of her father's legacy. Hope.

"A new general order has just gone out on the radio," Rex said in her ear. "All intruders are to be shot on sight."

Moments after he said it, the farm exploded with gunfire. Muzzle flashes blasted like a fireworks display from countless different points around the enclosures, echoed by screams.

Her D-DOS attack was about to falter.

"They're running," Rex said. "The Real Boys are fleeing. Fifteen minutes until Bratva reinforcements arrive."

Zero gritted her teeth. The barn was blocked off, but there had to be access. Most likely there was a tunnel down from the farmhouse, which explained why they were guarding it so closely. With a sniper on alert, though, she was never going to get close. She needed her D-DOS mob to surge, not retreat, allowing her to slip in as a zombie agent a second time.

"Call the police," she ordered.

"Calling," Rex answered, "first response time estimated at six minutes. It will not be enough to fight the number of Bratva reinforcements."

Zero laughed and started running. It didn't need to be enough to take down the farm or battle Bratva. What she needed now, more than anything, was a way to drive her scalded rats to greater desperation.

Incoming sirens ought to do the job.

She climbed the nearest enclosure fence and balanced atop the uppermost rail. The poise of a decade spent climbing held her balance, and from five feet up she surveyed the battlefield.

Every vor highlighted himself with muzzle flashes. None were facing back toward the farmhouse. None of them knew the real threat lay within. The Real Boys would surge regardless when the sirens came, but every bit she could do to thin the Bratva ranks before that would help. She swiftly programmed a route in her head, man to man to man across the enclosure fences, then hit the execute button.

The wood underfoot was slick but her boots gripped it.

For five enclosures she ran straight then leaped. Three vor were charging a warren of fleeing Real Boys, HK433s firing into their backs, and Zero came down on them like a falling star. Two died as she landed, stilettos through the chest of one and the skull of another, while the third carried on running unaware, spraying his newfound enemies with bullets.

Five fast steps saw Zero reach him and thrust a blade into his back so firmly it jutted through his chest. He gasped then fell as his heart collapsed.

The gunfire halted. The Real Boys cowered against a fence in the flashing dark, penned and helpless and surrounded by a litter of their dead fellows, face down in the mud. Some of them tried to clamber into the enclosure beyond, but they were old and weak and unable. Others simply dropped to their knees with their hands out, entreating their new savior.

One of them shouted in Polish or Russian, barely audible over the terrible drumbeat of thunder.

"Dziękuję Ci!"

It sounded like thank you to her. The others joined in as Zero surveyed her next target. Lightning flashed down to illuminate her face, and that was when the cries shifted.

"Zero! To ona! Zero!"

'It's her,' she guessed. Girl Zero.

Zero smiled and stalked closer, twirling her stilettos, and their eyes widened to a new depth of terror. With renewed vigor they turned and poured themselves over the fence as one, tumbling in with the bucking, squealing, stamping pigs.

Zero climbed back to the fence and sighted in her next target. The cry of 'Zero' was spreading, and she intended to drive it on. There were two vor on patrol to her right, four just ahead and three to the left; amidst the chaos of scrabbling, shouting and gunfire none of them saw her coming. One by one she dropped into their midst and sowed her vengeance in their hearts.

She killed the two, then the four then the three, until the cry of her name rolled like thunder across the farm, chanted from Real Boy lips.

"Zero! Zero!"

Then the sirens joined the chorus.

52

THEME PARK

The sirens' call washed over the farm and changed everything.

The gunfire halted. The Real Boys fell still. There was even a lull in the crashing of thunder as all eyes cast to the road and all ears keened to hear.

The sirens grew louder. Blue lights flashed in the distance.

Then the cry went out. Perhaps it was Polish or Russian, Zero didn't know, but Rex swiftly translated.

"They're saying 'to the farmhouse'."

"How long until Bratva arrive?"

"Seven minutes."

Zero laughed. Soon the farm would really be a warzone. She holstered her stilettos then reached down, scooped up two handfuls of mud and drenched them down her head and face, slicking back her hair and disguising her features.

She wasn't Girl Zero anymore. Now she was just another fleeing Real Boy.

She hopped one enclosure fence and another, then she was on the central spine running along with dozens of Real Boys who looked just like her; mud-splattered and bloody, like refugees from trench warfare. Ahead lay the farmhouse, its red light gleaming like a lewd lighthouse. Sniper fire barked through the darkness, erupting a man's head to her right, bursting a chest to her left, but there was no stopping this final charge.

With the police at their back, the Real Boys had nowhere else to turn. This was it. Another had his face cratered and fell as the sniper's heavy caliber round boomed out, and another, then they were stamping up the steps and crashing into the front door like a zombie horde.

The wood splintered and smashed through under their mass, revealing the same elegant hallway Zero remembered, but stocked with vor. They picked off the first wave of Boys with sweeping HK433 fire, but the second wave pushed through and swamped them.

Zero came in on the third wave, bounding up the stairs she knew so well. Everything looked the same, smelled the same as it had when she was a child, the farmhouse before she'd burned it down. At the top of the stairs red light glowed from her parents' room to the right, but she ignored that and turned hard left, heart clamoring. Seven steps further lay her room on her right.

It was exactly as she'd remembered it, resurrected like a museum piece: the same Pinocchio wallpaper, and bedding, and books on the shelves. A theme park attraction, she thought, for Pinocchios to come view their dominant past.

There was no sign of Hope though, or Anatoly. Behind her Real Boys were screaming and more gunfire came. Three more steps took her to the door to Hope's room, and despite the chaotic clamor below and outside, she heard the high sound of her little sister singing her favorite song within.

The sweet notes of 'Wish upon a Star' almost floored her. A child's voice. It wasn't possible. Could it be?

She slammed into the door and it rocked inward, though

on the far side there was nothing. An empty room, stripped to pale plaster walls and raw wooden floorboards. Still the child-like singing continued from no clear source, flinging her back into the past, when she'd first escaped her parents and opened this door looking for her little sister, and found…

Nothing.

"Zero!" came Rex's voice in her ear.

She spun and a heavy caliber bullet fractured the doorframe. Two vor had emerged from her parent's master suite, each wielding long-barreled sniper rifles. There was no way past them, so she plunged into Hope's room, sprinted four steps then dived bodily at the sash window.

Her elbows struck first, curled protectively around her head, and shattered the thin glass. Her body followed out into the night air, giving her a fleeting panorama across the farm: bodies battled and wallowed in the mud below; sirens blared and blue lights sprayed at the east entrance; Real Boys charged while vor fired, then the ground rushed up.

Her left side cracked down off a fallen Boy, crunching his ribs and driving the air from her lungs, then she tumbled away over the mud. Her hip smacked off a fence post and she stopped flat on her back, looking up the barrel of a rifle.

There was a man at the end of it, not a vor but a Real Boy. It was over. One shot and she was done.

Then the rifle receded and an outstretched hand replaced it. He shouted something in Polish, clearly taking her for another Boy. She took his hand and he pulled her up. Her head spun from the fall and her lungs were too tight to allow in breath, but she gave him a nod. He smiled back then his head exploded.

Zero blinked away blood and looked to the farmhouse. The two vor were taking aim out of Hope's window. Another round hit the fencepost by her side, shattering wooden chips that clattered off her side.

She ran. A Boy ahead pitched backward as a slug caught him, a bullet pocked the mud directly in her path, then she was up the stairs and back into the farmhouse.

Bodies lay everywhere, blood splattered the white walls and mud coated the wooden floor while gunpowder smoke drifted thickly in the air. The two vor appeared at the top of the stairs but Zero was already ducking into the living room. There were two brown leather sofas and a vintage CRT TV and windows looking out on the madness outside, and there on the right was the hatch leading down.

Zero was ricocheted into the past. It was an exact replica. The trapdoor comprised a quarter of the floor and stood open on a hinge like the lid of a grand piano, supported by a thin metal prop. Gunfire chased behind her and her lungs finally eased up, allowing a merciful suck of air. Concrete stairs led down into the same underground channel, and for a second she hesitated.

The last time she'd gone down these same steps under duress, she hadn't come up for nine years. If there was no route to the barn here, she was effectively cornering herself. Maybe this was what Viktor Anatoly wanted. Maybe she'd never resurface.

But there was no choice.

She dropped onto the steps and started down, pulling the lid prop down after her. The trapdoor slammed shut, the clasp locked, and the sound from above immediately diminished.

The concrete channel stretched ahead of her, lit by industrial lights pegged to the walls. There was no thumping sound of the torture rack, of course, because this was the Real Boys' fantasy of a time before she'd wrought her revenge.

She ran down the channel she'd once helped dig and burst through the plywood-backed mirror at the end to see the tableau beyond, where she let out a gasp of disbelief.

Everything was just as she remembered it, as if no time

had passed since the worst days of her torment: the padded brown leather walls interspersed by floor-to-ceiling mirrors; the torture rack at the center ringed by cameras and lights; the shelves filled with equipment; and there at the side of the machine, unbelievably, stood two animatronic figures that had to be her parents.

For a moment Zero just stared. The likeness was uncanny. They both wore cream robes discolored by old bloodstains. Her father's face was identical to the one that had haunted her nightmares for a decade, the same bright eyes, the same rugged jaw studded with stubbly hairs. Her mother's brown hair hung down her back in a familiar plait, and she wore the same thong sandals.

As she watched, the figures moved and spoke. Her father held a hammer, her mother held a nail, and together they brought these together over the space where little Mona should have been lying, strapped into the machine.

"Do it for Hope," came her father's voice, playing through speakers that boomed around the room. It was her real father's voice, surely sampled from one of the countless videos he'd streamed.

"Hope loves you," followed her mother's real voice. "She's waiting."

The hammer hit the nail in slow motion and a clang rang through the space, then the figures pulled back to repeat the same movement again, endlessly, on repeat.

It was sick. It was pathetic.

Past the figures lay the narrow escape-proof channel to Zero's old cell. Even from here she could spot the Pinocchio wallpaper and the rucked Blue Fairy bedcovers. There was no sign of a route through, though, and that wasn't the direction for the barn, anyway.

A slam came from behind her as the vor wrenched the

trapdoor open. Their footsteps thudded down the concrete steps. Zero turned right and ran straight at a mirror in the center of the wall on the right, toward what should be her father's old office, and beyond it, the barn.

53

LOOKING GLASS

The mirror opened and Zero passed into the tunnel beyond. The office lay at the end and she turned as she emerged, taking in three steel filing cabinets on the left, a computer desk with three CRT screens on the right, and an end wall taped with various diagrams. There was a world map marked with international shipping lines, several design schematics for what looked like pig gestation crates, a map of the farm with various structures added, a wireframe drawing of a modified container ship that had been hollowed out in the center.

There was no further door leading through. Zero ran her eyes over the walls again. There had to be a way through, a secret door or-

Her eyes caught on the diagram of gestation crates. The design was unusual. Bigger than necessary for a pig. She'd spent years in her father's office, and while everything else was familiar to her, this wasn't.

She ripped the paper aside. Beneath it lay a recessed handle, which she seized, turned and pulled. A door-shaped section of the wall opened outward.

Then the vor were there; one grasped her shoulder and

spun her into a thumping gut punch while the second came in with a dermal jet.

The punch bowed her over and almost paralyzed her, but she managed to twist just enough to evade the jet, which hit and hissed pointlessly against the Vantablack suit's tough fabric. Another punch came into her temple, but she managed to roll the worst of it while shooting her stiletto blade into the puncher's groin.

He screamed and fell back, but another blow pummeled her head and a knee rose up into her face, then her left arm was twisted hard up her back and the dermal jet came in again. In one smooth movement she arced the stiletto up and over her left shoulder, plunging through the vor's eye and into his brain pan.

He fell away in silence, the blade lodged in his skull. Zero looked up at the one man left, now holding his crotch with both hands. She tried to straighten up but the punches had cracked something in her chest and she couldn't. The vor took his chance, releasing both hands from their grip and coming in like a bear, twin hammer blows that would flatten her to the ground.

Zero dropped to one knee, drew her second stiletto and plunged it sideways into his neck. His hammer strikes pulled in too late and gripped the handle.

"I wouldn't do that," Zero cautioned, but he pulled anyway, opening himself up like a turned faucet. Blood fountained out and he stared at the spray. Zero retrieved the blade from his hand and arced it overhand into the top of his head, like she was trying to split a cord of wood.

It slammed through bone and flipped his eyelids closed like a light switch.

Zero sucked in a breath, straightened up through the pain in her chest and side, and looked up at a camera in the corner of the office.

"Make an animatronic out of that."

No response came. She turned to the open door in the wall and hobbled through.

The channel was narrow like the others, concrete-lined, industrially lit and running due south toward the barn. There was a metal door some thirty yards ahead. Sharp stabbing pains greeted each step she took. Those punches had cracked ribs and possibly done internal damage.

"Your pulse rate is erratic," Rex said needlessly. She was in her body and could feel it.

As she closed the final distance to the door, it began to open. She sprinted the gap and dived, colliding with a young woman dressed all in white as she emerged. Zero's right shoulder hit her chest and pitched her backward into a metal spiral staircase. Zero dropped to her knees in the doorway at the foot of a narrow chamber just big enough to contain the staircase and an industrial elevator shaft.

The woman rose to her feet swiftly, but bowed her head and pressed her hands together before her like she was praying. Zero scanned her swiftly for weapons but saw none. Not a vor, then. Perhaps a victim?

"It's OK," Zero said, taking a small step closer. "I'm a friend."

The woman flinched but didn't look up. Zero reached across and lifted her chin. She had milky skin and pale eyes that tried to look anywhere but at Zero. This was just a girl, barely eighteen if that. There was a smudge on her left cheek that cleared up when Zero blinked; a tattooed number.

76

"Viktor Anatoly," Zero said, keeping one eye on the tunnel leading back and the stairs leading up. "Where is he?"

The girl flinched at the name but said nothing.

"Give it to us in Polish, Rex."

Her suit speakers kicked in and Rex spoke in smooth

Polish, his accent transforming. "Viktor Anatoly, gdzie on jest?"

The girl's eyes only danced around the walls and she shook her head slightly.

"Russian," Zero said.

"Viktor Anatoly, gde on?" he tried.

The girl just shook her head then pointed at her ears then her mouth and made a sound. It wasn't speech but perhaps something close, and Zero's stomach turned as she saw inside the girl's mouth.

There was no tongue.

She pulled back, momentarily stunned. She remembered what her father used to tell her about handling piglets on an industrial farm; you clipped their ears and docked their tails and pulled their teeth. With humans, maybe you just pulled out their tongues.

"Hide," Zero said, even though the girl probably wouldn't understand. There was nothing else she could do, so she patted her gently on the shoulder, made a hiding gesture and ran to the stairs.

Viktor Anatoly was going to pay for this.

54

BARN

Clara emerged up the spiral staircase into the barn's towering interior. This had to be the Blue Fairy exchanges. It looked like an all-white prison block. She was in the center of a central oblong pit encircled by three open stories of balconies and cells with barred doors.

She spun in search of vor but found none, only more young girls in white gowns. They all had number tattoos on their cheeks, and walked from cell to cell on each floor pushing trolleys and carrying trays.

Clara blinked. Feeding time?

"Bratva reinforcements are engaging the police," Rex said in her ear, but she didn't care about that.

On the ground floor around her were several ping-pong tables minus the rackets and balls, a basketball hoop was mounted to the wall beneath a large screen. To the side there was a set of ten skittles.

Clara's stomach turned.

'Enrichment', her father called it, in the raising of pigs. Lock every sow into a gestation crate that barely fit her body, then put bars between her and her piglets, then make her do the whole thing again and again, and even a pig went mad.

Even without teeth, it could still go on a rampage. It could break its own legs against the floor and cage walls, and as its cortisol stress levels rose, the effect could ripple through the entire herd.

Pregnant sows would lose more piglets in utero. Meat pigs would grow tough and gamey. Industrial pig farms, like her father's, had the science of enrichment down to a fine art.

Maybe it was just the same with humans.

Around the ground floor of the 'barn' were doors marked with various symbols. There was the symbol for toilets, and showers, and food, and others that she'd never seen before.

"Hope!" she shouted, and the word echoed flatly around the floors and railings. No answer came back. The numbered girls kept walking as if she wasn't there. "Hope, it's me, Mona, where are you?"

Still there was nothing.

Clara ran. A central staircase led upwards and she took the steps three at a time, conscious that Anatoly or the vor could be anywhere. On the second floor she found herself looking directly into cells, and her eyes widened.

Each cell was minuscule, barely big enough to fit a crib-sized bed, elevated above what looked to be a small desk, a toilet, a sink, a chair. The children inside these cells couldn't be older than eight years old. Some were asleep on their beds, some were sat at their desks and all wore a simple white smock.

Clara's mouth ran dry. This was the exchange. These were Bratva's raw materials.

There were a dozen cells on the wall ahead of her. Many more stretched down both of the barn's long sides and across the far end; maybe thirty per side, which made for almost a hundred per floor. If all three stacked floors were the same, that was three hundred children.

Where had they all come from?

One of the attendant girls walked past Clara, another older-looking teen, who continued on her rounds as if Clara wasn't there; a mud-soaked madwoman with wild eyes wielding twin blades.

"Hope!" she tried shouting again, but still no answer came. She went to the nearest cage and leaned in.

"Hey honey," she said. "What's your name?"

The child, a sweet little girl who looked no older than Hanna, just looked back at her quizzically but calmly. Maybe dosed? Clara scanned her small desk. She was working on a coloring book with a stock of five colored crayons worn down to the nub.

There was a baby's bottle on the desk too, filled with a white fluid. Perhaps milk laced with sedative. It would make sense; pigs were often dosed en masse, not only with antibiotics and growth hormone but also with sedatives as a part of their feeding program.

The only other thing on the desk was a photograph in a frame. It showed another little girl, tow-headed and blue-eyed, with a mischievous smile, like something straight out of Clara's memory.

Her heart skipped a beat. She pointed.

"Is that Hope?"

The little girl's eyes narrowed; the first kind of response she'd had yet.

"Hope," Clara pressed, "is that her? Is she here? Where is she?"

The little girl picked up the photograph, held it out then spoke.

"Little sister," she said.

Clara hadn't expected it and it knocked her back like a second gut punch. "What? I don't understand. What do you mean?"

"Little sister," the child repeated, then hugged the photograph tight to her chest, smiling. "Hope."

Clara reeled backward. The clinically white barn spun around her. An attendant passed by pushing a trolley stacked with small white towels and plastic boxes containing single portions of rice. Cell were all around.

She went to the next. In this there was a little boy lying on his bed staring at the ceiling, where a simplistic light show was taking place, cast by a beam built into the wall. Like a baby's hanging mobile. On his desk was another coloring book, half-filled-in, and a baby's bottle, and the same photograph.

Hope.

Clara ran on, from cell to cell, past attendants who continued at their duties, and in each cell she found the same thing. A book, a bottle and a photograph of Hope, exactly as she remembered her. Her little sister. Not theirs.

What was this?

She grabbed one of the attendants.

"Who is that little girl?" She pointed at the photograph in the nearest cell. "Where is she?"

The attendant just smiled back at her, patted Clara's face gently and tried to go back to her cart.

Clara let her go.

The barn spiraled. White was everywhere. Little children everywhere. She ran up the stairs to the third floor, where she found something far worse.

55

LEGACY

The cells were no longer cells. There were no bars here, only a wide-open space attended by a dozen of the young women with their trolleys and trays, moving in pairs down walkways like vor in the enclosures outside.

Except they weren't walking around pigs, but cribs.

Zero walked closer and looked down, eyes welling with tears. In each crib lay a single, perfect baby in a white onesie. Each had a tiny human-shaped doll beside them, with straw-colored hair and blue eyes, just like Hope. Each had a bottle of the same milky liquid.

Zero looked up, eyes swimming. Here one of the young women was nursing an infant. Here another was having a nappy change.

There was no crying. No whimpering. How many cribs? Another hundred, or more. A newborn's ward, in the midst of this hell. Tears spilled down Zero's cheeks.

Where were the mothers?

On the third floor she found them. In tiny cells scarcely bigger than a pig's gestation crate, where they lay flat on their backs watching lights play on the ceiling, barely able to move. Their bellies all swelled up. Zero was gasping now. All the mothers were young. No more than teenagers.

"Hope!" she called, but barely made a sound. Here too, attendants moved around, feeding the mothers from a bottle, wiping a hot brow here or there.

Finally Zero understood her father's true legacy, and the vision Viktor Anatoly was fighting for.

The farm wasn't just the site for the Blue Fairy exchange, where children were bought and sold at auction. It was also the source of those children. Here they were reared like pigs. Here they were bred in an endless, ever-expanding cycle.

It was a Bratva breeding program to supply 'raw materials' for the Real Boy demand.

Sickness swallowed Zero up, as the pieces finally fell into place.

This was the next step in their evolution. Just like the Real Boys had evolved from the Pinocchios, and the shadow line had evolved from the darknet, this was an evolution of what her father had started in his dungeon all those years ago.

Zero staggered back against the railing. She imagined the cycle going around and around, producing more and more children every year. Breeding like pigs. Kept like pigs. Groomed and grown and sent out to service the Real Boy world, for who knew how many millions of dollars.

Trillions.

More barns.

More farms.

She almost gagged at the scale of it, jaw dropping open. This was worse than anything she'd seen the Real Boys do before. This was industrial-level, and there was nothing to say. Only disgust. Then she remembered what Joas Levi had said, and glimpsed the final piece.

'You will make them trillions, and the exchanges will burn with your passing.'

Except he was wrong, because Anatoly didn't want her dead. He wanted her alive. Girl Zero, the foundation of the Blue Fairy. The one who'd gotten away. This was their revenge, for the way she'd brought her father down.

They weren't going to kill her.

Maybe this had always been his dream, she realized. Maybe this had always been his goal for Girl Zero.

They were going to breed her.

She saw the punishment stretching on and on, watching as they used her to pump out babies again and again, and turn those babies into breeders, so she had to watch the same thing being done to her daughters, and her granddaughters, and would the demand ever ebb?

Every Real Boy despised her more than any other person alive. Every Real Boy would pay a fortune to enact his little bit of vengeance on her and her progeny. It would drive an entire industry. He'd already hinted at it earlier, she just hadn't understood what it meant.

"Legacy," she whispered.

"Legacy," came Viktor Anatoly's voice.

Her head shot up, seeking him out. She scanned the cells of mothers in their gestation crates, and looked down to the floor below with the babies and the children below that, but saw no sign of him.

She started to run, the sickness pumping into adrenaline which fueled a bonfire of growing rage.

He had to die for this.

She circled each of the three floors in minutes then dropped back to the ground floor where she started ripping open doors. Toilets. Showers. A room with a birthing frame, forceps hanging from the wall. A room with a projector screen. A room with a gurney and cabinets filled with syringes and vials of drugs. The stairwell in the bottom of the pit remained empty, and her sense of dislocation only grew.

There was no Viktor Anatoly. There was no Hope except the little girl in the photographs, who should be twenty-one years old now. Every child's little sister. She tried to make sense of that but couldn't get there; it felt like her mind was trying to pull itself into parts. Was that the sound of Hope singing in the air now, echoing again up through the stairwell? She couldn't tell. Nothing made sense.

Then she heard it.

"Mona!"

She froze.

It wasn't a little girl's voice. It was a young woman's. She spun but still saw nothing.

"Hope?"

"Mona, it's me! Help me, please."

Zero swirled. The three tiers of prison cells spiraled. "Where are you? Hope!"

Then the screen at the head of the hall, above the basketball hoop, flickered to life. It showed a beautiful young woman all dressed in white, standing against an old redbrick background. A man stood behind her, holding a knife to her throat.

Viktor Anatoly.

"These were not the terms of your surrender, Mona," he said, his voice transmitting through unseen speakers.

"Is that Hope?" she shouted back.

"There are new terms, now," he answered, his shark's eyes beaded directly on her. "You come alone. You give yourself over. I will let Hope go."

Zero couldn't think. Nothing made sense now.

"And all these boys and girls? Are they Hope's children?"

He just stared. "In a sense. Come now, Mona, or you will never see your sister again. All I want is you."

She understood that. She was beginning to understand it

all, all her three questions had been answered, and there was nothing else to say. "Where are you?"

He smiled. "I think you know, Mona."

She did. Only one place on the farm had that kind of exposed brickwork. The 'nose' of the farm, a mound pushed up through the stench of the pigs, ever straining for fresh air.

"The fallout shelter."

"Yes. There's a tunnel in the north wall. And come quickly. The police are almost here."

He squeezed Hope's throat and she cried out, then the feed died.

Zero's chest heaved.

This was it.

She ran.

56

HOPE

Zero ran along the north wall like she was in a dream, trying door after door with inexplicable symbols, until at last one opened on a stairwell leading down.

She plunged in. Rex spoke in her ear but she didn't listen. A long concrete chute ran ahead with a glow of red light some two hundred yards off. She ignored the pain in her chest and sprinted under the farm, under the pigs, heading to the shelter where she'd once curled up with Hope dreaming of a better life.

Maybe now she would save her. Maybe now she could sleep again at night.

The red light drew closer. The sound of the battle above grew louder with every step; shouts, gunfire, thunder and screams. Then she was there.

The shelter was long and narrow, with the chipped red brick wall that she remembered, and the raw concrete floor strewn with molding black straw, and the stench of the pigs and the rusted corrugated iron roof, but something was wrong.

She didn't understand it and couldn't put her finger on it and it didn't matter, because dead ahead was Viktor Anatoly holding the woman who could be her little sister, Hope, with a knife to her throat.

"Stop there, Mona," he commanded, and she did.

He may have been Viktor Anatoly, but all she saw was her father. He had the same burning excitement in his eyes, the same thrill in his voice. Hope in his arms looked like all her nightmares. Those eyes, that hair, that quivering lip. A line of blood trickled down her throat where the knife pressed in.

"Hope," she whispered.

"Mona," Hope answered, and it almost brought Zero to her knees.

"Let her go. I'm here."

"So drop the blades," Anatoly ordered.

She dropped the bloody stilettos and they clattered to the floor.

"On your knees," he said, and she did that too, dropping to the hard concrete. The pain up through her bones felt good. It felt deserved, for taking so long to reach this point.

"Let her go."

"Look to your right."

She did.

There was another tunnel leading away into darkness. An escape route. Beside it lay a silver device she recognized, framed of surgical-grade steel and already loaded with a four-milliliter vial: a dermal jet, capable of pushing drugs across the skin and directly into the bloodstream.

She shook her head. Already she could see the future stretching out. A lifetime like her childhood, but worse; reduced to a sow in Anatoly's gestation crates, producing child after child, only for them to be sold one after another.

"No."

"Pick it up."

"Let her go!"

He just pressed the blade deeper. Hope cried out and a second trail of blood joined the first down her throat.

"Mona, please!"

"Pick it up," Anatoly repeated, and she could have sworn it was her father's voice. So familiar. So hated. Always to be obeyed.

She reached out and collected the jet.

"I recommend against this course of action, Zero," Rex said in her ear.

"Put it against your neck."

"You have to let her go," she whispered.

"I will. I promise you, Mona. She will be free. Now put it against your neck."

Hope's eyes swelled with tears. It had been so long. Too long. Zero's vision blurred.

"I'm sorry, Hope," she whispered, and pressed the jet to the soft skin under her jaw.

"Now press it."

"Zero!" called Rex.

There was no choice.

She pressed the trigger. The jet hissed as liquid Rohypnol pushed through her skin and directly into her bloodstream, hitting her brain like she'd been dunked underwater.

The world went vague and echoey, and she remembered how her mother had once whispered stories in her ear, about how Mona and Hope had always snuck into this shelter together, huddling close and holding tiny hot hands together, dreaming of the day they escaped the farm.

The Rohypnol had her. She sank and rose on tides of memory while her father stood there, triumphant. Hope was so close she could reach out and touch her. She tried to frame words but the weight of water was too heavy.

"You never learn, Mona," Anatoly said, then dragged the blade across Hope's throat.

57

SISTER

Zero tried to scream but her lips barely shifted, the faintest sound emerging.

"Stop that," Anatoly said, as blood sprayed from Hope's throat and she fell. "That wasn't your sister."

Zero was drowning and the drug pushed her deeper. She couldn't move. It took everything she had to stay upright on her knees.

"Wha-?" she managed.

Anatoly sank to his knees before her, and now her hands were in his, and he squeezed them like he cared, and looked into her eyes like the father who'd once loved her.

"You still don't understand, do you? I already said you'd never recognize Hope, and you didn't. That was just some girl I trained to say 'Mona'."

Zero struggled to follow him, the words barely tracking to the movements of his lips.

"Wh- wh…"

"Why? Because Hope's too valuable, Mona. She's always been the handle on your heart. All I have to do is tweak her, and you jump. I wouldn't keep her here."

"Wh- wh…"

"Where is she?" he smiled. "You're like a broken record. She's safe. You will see her, I promise. We'll do that DNA test. Now stand up."

She didn't stand. The water was weighing her down, but it wasn't just that. There was something else, though she didn't know what. Something important that didn't make sense, and-

His fist lashed across her face. She barely felt it, but the shelter rocked left to right. He pulled her back and did it again, and this time the world spun right to left. She saw the dead 'Hope'. She saw the tunnel leading away, and the dermal jet where she'd dropped it, and knew that all was lost.

She'd done this.

She'd been reckless.

This was what she deserved, and not even the Jiminy Cricket voice of Rex in her ear could undo it. Gabriel was hiding in the Tatras mountains. Her hacker friends were fleeing for their lives.

Nobody was coming to save her, just like it had always been.

And then she understood. The revelation crashed over her and shifted everything.

"Fa…" she mumbled.

He leaned in. "What's that?"

"Fake."

He laughed, then he punched her in the nose, but it couldn't stop the truth from coming.

She was back in the screening theater in the Tatras Mountains, comparing the Idaho farm to the target farms and failing to find the fallout shelter. She was back in the farmhouse, where her room was full but Hope's room was empty, only the lilting sound of her child's voice singing a song. She was back in the barn, where every child had a picture of Hope, their little sister.

The handle on their hearts.

She tasted blood in her mouth and it helped. "Fake," she said again, stronger this time.

Anger made Anatoly's eyes shine. "Of course it's fake, it's all fake, now get up or I'll carry you."

She didn't care. It didn't matter, because she was back in the torture chamber with her father in the rack, watching the look of confusion on his face when she'd asked about Hope, and how he'd laughed then said they'd sold her.

Sold her little sister. Sold her to the Blue Fairy exchanges.

But not one of thirty-five dead Real Boys had ever heard her name. She was nowhere in the darknet. There'd been no room for her in the farmhouse. There'd been no fallout shelter on the actual farm. There'd been no photograph of her in the whole house.

The truth came like a stiletto blade through her heart, setting her free.

"Hope … is … fake," she whispered.

At that, Viktor Anatoly flinched. He didn't say anything, just stared at her, and that was all the confirmation she needed, because now she remembered; now every memory of Hope felt greasy and unreal, because they hadn't ever happened. She remembered her mother whispering in her ear all the stories she'd invented, just to make her do as they said.

To make her obey.

'If you don't do this, we'll hurt Hope.'

She remembered how she'd always defied them. She'd fought with everything she had, even through the drugs, even through the pain, until Hope.

Hope. It was in the name. Someone to protect. A reason to comply. Every memory she had of Hope, they'd invented. Huddling together in a fallout shelter that didn't exist, their little hot hands in each other's.

How else had Viktor Anatoly known that memory? Her

father had shared the lie. That was his true legacy: how to control children through love.

Tears streamed down her face.

There was no Hope.

"It doesn't matter," Anatoly said finally, shaking her roughly by the chin. "The others all believe. Your children will believe. That's what matters."

He rolled her over his shoulder, stood up and started to run.

58

EGG

Zero rocked against his back. Rex spoke in her ear. There was no hope.

But there was. There always was. She'd escaped the Idaho farm. She'd escape this.

"Rexxx," Zero hissed, pushing all her energy into air and sound. "Fire … egg."

Anatoly didn't hear.

"You want me to fire the eggs, Zero?" Rex asked.

"Act…ive … dec…"

"Remote firing active decoy," Rex said. "Brace yourself, Zero."

Maybe five seconds passed, and she did the opposite of brace herself, letting every muscle go limp, because the best way to survive an explosive impact was like a ragdoll. The Rohypnol should help with that.

Viktor Anatoly ran.

Her backpack exploded.

Contained within the backpack, there was nowhere for the incredible force of the active decoy to go but hard into Zero's back. The blast buried itself across her strike suit's carbon nanotube weave, carrying through into Viktor Anatoly; her chest slammed into his back and the force flung them both forward.

Together they came down hard; he hit the ground face first, too slow to bring his hands up to protect him, and the bulk of Zero's weight landed off-center, on the crux point of his shoulder, which dislocated the ball and socket joint with a pop.

He shrieked.

Adrenaline flooded Zero's system, and she focused it into motion. Her left arm found Anatoly's face, her index finger and thumb found his eyes, and drove inward.

He lashed out instantly, kicking and trying to roll away, but it was no use. Zero's powerful grip locked hard; the same grip that had yanked out her mother's tongue and held her to rock face overhangs across the country. He screamed and shrieked, sending out wild and blind blows that glanced off the strike suit, while she moved her right arm.

The backpack had shredded with the blast, but the final egg was still there. Her fingers found the button, dug in, twisted and pulled.

"Open … your … mouth," she whispered in Anatoly's ear.

He screamed, and that was good enough. With her last ounce of strength Zero pushed the button and shoved the ball into Anatoly's mouth. The scream was buried. She pulled both hands away and rolled to the side.

Do not inflate internally.

The explosion came hard and wet, as Viktor Anatoly's face blew apart. Zero's ears rang and she felt the blast on the side of her head. Blood and fragments rained down for a few seconds, then his body was largely still but for twitching feet. She opened her eyes.

His jaw was gone. His throat was opened up. His nose and cheekbones were blasted outward in bony shards.

She'd warned him she'd tear his face off.

"Bratva are coming," Rex called in her ear. "Police also. Zero."

It might as well have been heard through a thick layer of earth and pigs, like the song Hope had once sung to her, but never had, because Hope had never been real. She was a fantasy, like all of this. A means of control. A handle on her heart, and that was enough.

She sank deeper. She had nothing left. In the end, her father's legacy had won.

59

SHELTER

Rex called something in her ear, but she was so tired. The world detached itself from her, and her from it. Buried alive in the fake fallout shelter, and it was OK.

She'd failed so many times. She'd believed so many lies. For sixteen years she'd lived to save a girl who had never existed.

Darkness called and warmed her. It was right. She could just lie here forever. Bratva might find her. Real Boys. Corrupt police. It was fine.

She'd failed.

Then through the darkness, she heard something. It was singing. She couldn't tell where it was coming from. Her little sister's voice?

Yes.

It was Hope, singing 'Wish upon a Star', just like she always had. It was a memory only, implanted by her parents to control her, but in the darkness of that lonely hole, it felt more real than it ever had.

The words carried through her like the voice of the heavens, like Hope was real, and in that moment, none of it mattered. Maybe Hope had never existed, but that didn't mean she wasn't right here now. She was. They'd used her to compel such terrible acts, but she'd also kept Zero alive. The Real Boys thought she was their tool, but she was something else, also.

She was Zero's secret weapon. Her reason to be, and you couldn't just destroy that with a few words.

The song grew stronger. Zero couldn't tell if it was coming through the earpiece or if someone was really singing it. She was back in those first minutes after lashing her father and mother to their torture frames, switching on the machine and running back up the stairs into a farmhouse she hadn't seen in nine years.

Everything was exactly as she remembered it. The smells were the same, the grain of the wood under her fingers as she ran up the stairs, and the song was everywhere now, filling her up. She charged past her parents' room and her room and came to Hope's door one final time.

Always she'd been disappointed. Always there'd been nothing. Now she just touched the door and it vanished, and on the other side-

Hope.

Her little sister, just as she'd always imagined her. Tow-headed, mischief-minded, preserved by time and memory; never harmed, never sold, never hurt.

"Zero," she said, holding out her hand, "come sing with me."

Zero took her hand. Together they sang the same song, about wishes and love and hope, until her eyes opened in the fallout shelter again.

Lights flashed. She could barely move. Rex was shouting somewhere, and guns were firing, and she reached for the pack. It lay on the other side of the cratered body of Viktor

Anatoly. Not a man anymore. Not a Boy. Not even a puppet, barely twitching on his strings.

She found the pack and her fingers wormed slowly down through the pockets, down to where she'd stowed a batch of vials from the medical room in the barn, and found broken shards and stinging liquid.

Not enough. All broken.

All except one. Liquid flumazenil, the antidote to Rohypnol. It wouldn't be aerosolized into her blood, it wouldn't be fast or thorough, but perhaps it would be enough. Achingly slowly, focusing all her effort on holding the vial and ferrying it to her lips, it drew near. Her lips felt its chill. She slipped her jaw open, dropped the vial in and clamped her teeth down.

The thin glass shattered. Liquid spilled into her throat and she swallowed.

Gradually Hope's hand in hers fell away. The song died down too, replaced by the roar of combat above. Bit by bit Zero came back to herself as the flumazenil temporarily drove away the Rohypnol.

She rose to unsteady feet. She looked around, but there was nothing for her here. There never had been, because it had never been real.

"Goodbye, Hope," she whispered, and staggered forward. Everything hurt. Nothing responded properly, but the memory of Hope's song carried her on. The tunnel led into darkness and she took it, walking like a ghost from some forgotten past beneath the gunfire, sirens, grenade blasts and screams above. She kept on until the tunnel ended in a ladder, then climbed up to a cover which she pushed aside and emerged into the dark and wet of the forest.

To her right was wild sound and motion; muzzle flashes and flashing blue lights and the farmhouse itself burning high into the sky. She turned the other way. It was hard to see, but

Rex guided her constantly. She left the farm behind and walked and walked until she fell.

"Just a little further," Rex coaxed, but she didn't have it and couldn't do it. In the shelter of a tall pine encircled by thick ferns, she laid her head down on the loam, thinking maybe she could just sink away and nobody would find her ever again.

A hesitant voice came from nearby.

"Zero. Is that you?"

She opened her eyes.

"Zero?"

She couldn't make out the voice at first, nor the face that followed it, hovering above her. Someone she knew but didn't really know. Someone who shouldn't be there but was.

"Maja?" she asked.

The young journalist stepped up and took her tacky hand. She pulled Zero up, and walked with her, and guided her into the backseat of a car.

"Rex," she mumbled, as Maja strapped her in, as the flumazenil's blocking effects elapsed.

"My first priority is to protect you, Zero," he answered, in the seconds before she passed out. "Hellion and B4cksl4cker's orders, whether you like it or not."

She laughed, then she sank. There'd be no coming up from this sleep for some time, she knew that. As the door slammed and Maja started the engine, she imagined Rex in his kennel, and her hacker friends even now roaming Europe in their convoy, keeping her safe at a distance. It felt good not to be so alone.

Then the dark curtain came down.

60

THREE DAYS LATER

Zero rode her Kawasaki Ninja out past GOMA-49.

For three days she'd recovered in Maja Kominski's home. Kominski herself applied bandages to the scrapes and bruises she'd picked up along the way. The main injury she'd taken though was in her head: the loss of her little sister. But to her surprise, there'd been no nightmares. Instead she'd dreamed of Hope and the life she might have had. Each morning she woke feeling a little lighter. To lose a sister she'd never had wasn't so bad. If anything, it was a relief.

Hope had never suffered the way she'd feared. Hope had never felt abandoned. Hope could never be used to control her again, and those were good things.

There were other children, though. There always were.

Maja kept her apprised of the news as it developed. Zero couldn't bear to watch the television coverage, which meant no TV, because the Czarna bust was global news that dominated every channel. Three hundred and twenty-four non-verbal children had been scooped out of Viktor Anatoly's Blue Fairy exchange. Hundreds of Real Boys had been arrested, and a substantial wing of Bratva brought down.

There were always more, though.

"Are you sure you don't want to go on the record?" Maja asked, as they said their goodbyes in the forest where she'd left the Ninja, close to the edge of the police tape marking an active investigation.

"When I am I'll come to you."

The young journalist smiled. "And you'll tell me about Hope, too?"

Zero frowned.

"You said her name in your sleep. Many times. You sounded happy."

Now Zero smiled. "Maybe, then. Maybe I'll tell you about Hope, one day."

"I look forward to it."

She climbed on the Ninja and rode away.

Krakow was beautiful, really. For half a day she walked around Rynek Glówny and the Main Market Square. She read the placards and followed a tourist map. Apparently it was the oldest medieval square in Europe, which impressed her. She checked out the Cloth Hall, and St. Mary's Basilica, and even walked around Planty Park. No inline skaters bothered her this time. From there it was a short walk across the Vistula River to Oskar Schindler's Enamel Factory.

At the front gates, she debated not going in. The last week had carried so much weight, she didn't think she could handle any more. But it was a beautiful, sunny day, and she felt like something was owed.

It turned out to be a beautiful, uplifting experience. Schindler and the people around him had saved more than a thousand lives by risking their own. It was sobering and inspiring.

There were good people. Zero hadn't wept at Auschwitz, but she wept on the tour. The guide put a hand on her shoulder and gave her a small smile.

"It's OK," he said.

It was.

In the early afternoon she got back on the Ninja and drove west. They should be home by now. She pulled up to the house with the high windows and the Japanese garden in the front. Neat lines had been raked into the gray sand again. The little red gate stood upright.

Gabriel and his daughters were back. They were safe. Everyone who'd ever known about their connection to her was dead.

"Are you sure about this?" Rex asked in her ear.

Zero set the Ninja onto its kickstand.

"I'm sure," she said, "going offline, Rex. Stay out of trouble."

She removed the earpiece.

Nothing had to last forever.

She felt different, that was true. Her hunt was less urgent, in one way, but in another it was more urgent than ever. Now she knew just how far the Real Boys would take their disease. The shadow line was still out there. With Viktor Anatoly gone, there'd be a power vacuum, and that meant violence.

Worse yet, she'd heard nothing from Hellion and B4cksl4cker. They weren't responding to her calls or messages. Maybe they were angry at her still. Maybe it was something worse.

She'd find out.

Today though, she had a date. She walked up the path to Gabriel's home and knocked on the door. This was the first time she'd come here without unconsciousness playing a role. The thought made her smile.

This time he was expecting her. The girls were expecting her. She couldn't wait to see their faces.

THE NEXT GIRL ZERO THRILLER

ZERO DAY

They're coming for revenge. So is she.

Russia's Bratva. Japan's Yakuza. China's Triads. South-America's cartels. They all want revenge against Girl Zero. She feels the same way.

Let the carnage commence.

PREORDER NOW ON AMAZON

www.shotgunbooks.com

PREVIOUS GIRL ZERO THRILLERS

NEVER FORGIVE

Want to hear all about Zero's escapades with Chris Wren under Tokyo?

Tokyo, Japan. A city in uproar. Five people are dead - their bodies carved with a simple message:

FOR CHRISTOPHER WREN

Ex-CIA agent Wren doesn't know the dead. He doesn't know the killer. But it doesn't matter.

A dark new world is rising. His family is no longer safe. Japan may hold the solution, and Wren will dig it out, whatever it takes.

Some crimes can never be forgiven. Some crimes can only be avenged.

AVAILABLE IN EBOOK & PAPERBACK

PREVIOUS GIRL ZERO THRILLERS

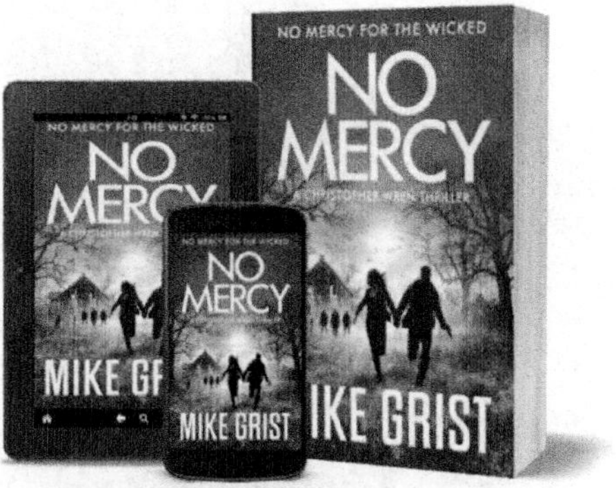

NO MERCY

Want to hear about the time Chris Wren rescued Zero from the Blue Fairy?

Ex-CIA agent Chris Wren has hunted the Blue Fairy for months - a hacker group stalking innocents on the dark Internet. Including his kids.

Now a Blue Fairy army is kidnapping and killing in the real world, and a mass hacking attack threatens to cripple the USA.

Only Wren and his brilliant lieutenant Sally Rogers stand ready to enforce true justice:

No mercy for the wicked.

AVAILABLE IN EBOOK & PAPERBACK

www.shotgunbooks.com

THE NEXT CHRIS WREN WITH GIRL 0

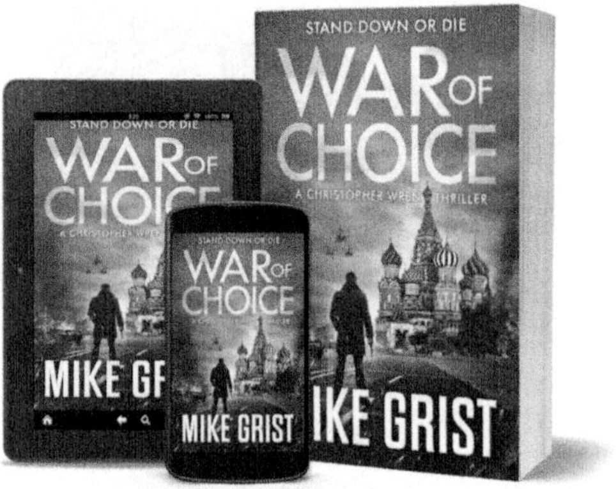

WAR OF CHOICE

The next Chris Wren adventure, featuring Girl Zero!

CIA legend Chris Wren is finally out of 'the life', and happier than ever - then his brilliant hackers Hellion and B4cksl4cker are violently taken.

A message follows: Stand down or they die. But Wren never took well to direction.

Now the race is on to find them, with the help of merciless assassin Clara Baxter, before a devastating cyberattack clears the way for something far worse. Millions could die. America could fall…

Not on Wren's watch.

This means war.

AVAILABLE IN EBOOK, PAPERBACK & AUDIO

www.shotgunbooks.com

START THE CHRIS WREN THRILLERS

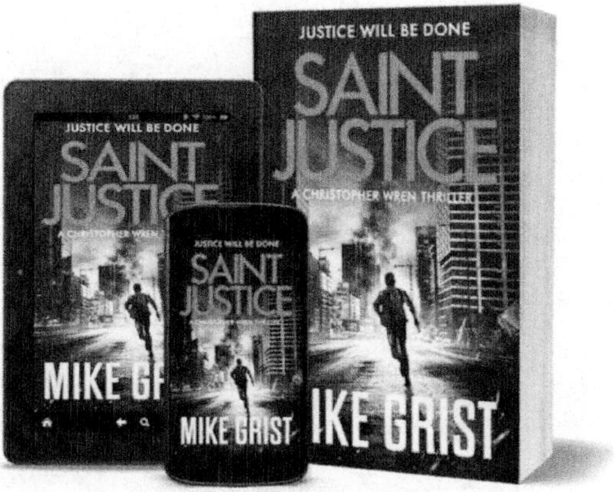

SAINT JUSTICE

They stole his truck. Big mistake.

CIA legend Chris Wren pulls over on a Utah highway after three weeks on the road. An arbitrary decision he's about to regret.

A biker gang attacks Wren, leaves him for dead and steals his truck. Now he's going to get it back.

From a secret warehouse in the desert. Ringed with fences. Filled with human cages.

As the body count mounts and a shocking national conspiracy unravels, one thing is for certain.

Justice will be done.

AVAILABLE IN EBOOK, PAPERBACK & AUDIO

www.shotgunbooks.com

HAVE YOU READ EVERY GIRL 0 THRILLER?

HAVE YOU READ EVERY CHRIS WREN THRILLER?

Saint Justice

They stole his truck. Big mistake.

No Mercy

Hackers came for his kids. There can be no mercy.

Make Them Pay

The latest reality TV show: execute the rich.

False Flag

They framed him for murder. He'll kill to clear his name.

Firestorm

Wren's father is back. The storm is coming.

Enemy of the People

Lies are drowning America. Can the country survive?

Backlash

He just wanted to go home. They got in the way...

Never Forgive

His home in ashes. Vengeance never forgives.

War of Choice

They came for his team. This time it's war.

Learn more at www.shotgunbooks.com

HAVE YOU READ THE LAST MAYOR THRILLERS?

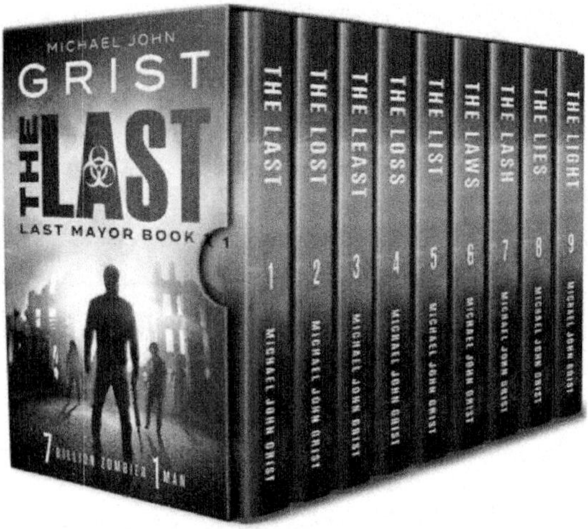

The Last Mayor series - Books 1-9

When the zombie apocalypse devastates the world overnight,

Amo is the last man left alive.

Or is he?

Learn more at www.shotgunbooks.com

JOIN THE FOUNDATION!

Join the Mike Grist newsletter and be first to hear when the next Girl 0 or Chris Wren thriller is coming.

www.subscribepage.com/christopher-wren

ACKNOWLEDGEMENTS

Sincere thanks to Julian White, Barb Stoner and Sue Martin.

- Mike

Printed in Great Britain
by Amazon

13619060R00200